Big Sky Homecoming

LINDA FORD

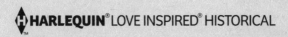
HARLEQUIN® LOVE INSPIRED® HISTORICAL

If you purchased this book without a cover you should be aware that this book is stolen property. It was reported as "unsold and destroyed" to the publisher, and neither the author nor the publisher has received any payment for this "stripped book."

Recycling programs
for this product may
not exist in your area.

LOVE INSPIRED BOOKS

ISBN-13: 978-0-373-28298-2

Big Sky Homecoming

Copyright © 2015 by Linda Ford

All rights reserved. Except for use in any review, the reproduction or utilization of this work in whole or in part in any form by any electronic, mechanical or other means, now known or hereinafter invented, including xerography, photocopying and recording, or in any information storage or retrieval system, is forbidden without the written permission of the editorial office, Love Inspired Books, 233 Broadway, New York, NY 10279 U.S.A.

This is a work of fiction. Names, characters, places and incidents are either the product of the author's imagination or are used fictitiously, and any resemblance to actual persons, living or dead, business establishments, events or locales is entirely coincidental.

This edition published by arrangement with Love Inspired Books.

® and TM are trademarks of Love Inspired Books, used under license. Trademarks indicated with ® are registered in the United States Patent and Trademark Office, the Canadian Intellectual Property Office and in other countries.

www.Harlequin.com

Printed in U.S.A.

"You've got a nasty gash on your forehead."

"I can feel it clear to my toes." Duke watched emotions flit across Rose's face as she leaned closer to look at his head. First, concern, and then worry. Worry? Rose Bell worried about Duke Caldwell? It didn't seem possible.

Her gaze returned to his and he caught a flash of something else he almost believed to be tenderness. For him? Hardly. The Bells were known for helping the sick and injured. That was all it was.

A tiny grin tugged at her lips and amusement filled her eyes. "Your handsome face will be forever marred."

"I can live with that."

"You're fortunate to be alive." Her eyes snapped in anger. "Why are you riding a wild horse around the country? Don't you know you might have been killed?"

"Seems you should be happy about that. You haven't exactly thrown out the welcome mat to me."

Her expression slowly hardened, grew impassive.

He missed being able to read her emotions.

She sat back and pulled her hands to her lap. "That doesn't mean I want to see you dead."

"Good to know."

Linda Ford lives on a ranch in Alberta, Canada, near enough to the Rocky Mountains that she can enjoy them on a daily basis. She and her husband raised fourteen children—four homemade, ten adopted. She currently shares her home and life with her husband, a grown son, a live-in paraplegic client and a continual (and welcome) stream of kids, kids-in-law, grandkids, and assorted friends and relatives.

Books by Linda Ford

Love Inspired Historical

Montana Marriages

Big Sky Cowboy
Big Sky Daddy
Big Sky Homecoming

Cowboys of Eden Valley

The Cowboy's Surprise Bride
The Cowboy's Unexpected Family
The Cowboy's Convenient Proposal
Claiming the Cowboy's Heart
Winning Over the Wrangler
Falling for the Rancher Father

Visit the Author Profile page at Harlequin.com for more titles

I will praise thee;
for I am fearfully and wonderfully made.
—*Psalms* 139:14

To mothers everywhere who bind the family together around the kitchen table with their meals, their treats, their advice and their love.
May your children arise and call you blessed for you turn houses into homes. God bless.

Chapter One

Rose Bell pushed back a scream of frustration. Even so, she spoke with more anger than sorrow. "The poor creatures. Pa, let me off here. You take Ma to the house and I'll take care of these animals." The sheep had been turned out of their pen and one of the older ewes was mired in a snowbank next to the shed. The others milled around, uncertain as to whether they should enjoy their freedom or panic because there were no fences to keep them safe.

At least they wouldn't drown in the river today. It was frozen over. That was a mercy.

She hopped down before the wagon stopped moving and raced toward the ewe. "Come on, girl." She pulled and tugged and cooed but the sheep had been there long enough her wool had frozen to the snow, anchoring her firmly.

"Can I help?"

With a startled squeak she turned around to stare at

Douglas Caldwell, the golden-haired son and heir of the Caldwell family.

Everyone else called him by his nickname, "Duke," but she couldn't bring herself to. It sounded friendly and neighborly and the Caldwells were anything but that. Pa had bought this bit of land eight years ago and turned it into a productive farm. But it happened to encroach on the boundaries of the Caldwell Ranch. They learned later that the filing clerk had made a mistake. Despite that, the land belonged to the Bells—clear and legal.

To this day Mr. Caldwell refused to accept the facts. He had tried every means he could think of to get them to leave. He'd offered money. He'd talked; at first kindly then threateningly. When none of that worked he'd had his cowboys harass the Bells and their animals. The garden had been trampled a number of times. Caldwell cows had eaten or destroyed portions of the oat crop. Just a few months ago, one of the lambs had drowned when the animals had mysteriously escaped their pasture and found their way to the river. But the worst thing they'd done to date was stampede the cows through the yard as the Bells harvested the garden. Pa had been injured. He still had sore ribs. She knew by the way he moved and the number of naps he took that he felt poorly.

The cowboys always managed to make their activities look like accidents, so the sheriff couldn't do anything.

It was on the tip of Rose's tongue to tell young Mr. Caldwell she didn't need his help but he'd already dismounted and come to her side. "It's going to take a good pull to get her out of that."

"I know."

He grinned down at her. "Hello, Rose. How have you been?"

She pushed her hair back under her knit hat.

His gaze followed the movement of her hands. She half expected him to say something about her red hair as he'd done when they were in early grades at school. Instead his blue eyes darkened and he swallowed hard.

As if he liked what he saw.

She pressed her lips tight. The cold must be affecting her brain. Except she wasn't cold. She'd worked up plenty of heat struggling with the ewe.

Surely she only imagined his look. She stole a glance at him. He still looked at what little of her hair showed from beneath her hat. He still had a bemused look about him.

Remembering his question, she said, "I've been just fine, Mr. Caldwell. Did Philadelphia survive your visit?"

He'd been gone a year, visiting his grandparents, and had returned a couple of weeks ago. In time to spend Christmas with his family.

"Philadelphia won't even notice I've left."

Odd way to put it. She hadn't given it much mind but if she had, she would have expected him to sound regretful at having to leave the city. No, she hadn't given it much mind, she silently mocked herself. Only thought of it maybe once or twice a day. She'd half expected to see him every time she went to town and every Sunday at church and even when she was out riding. That's what happened when two people grew up in the same community. You got accustomed to seeing each other even if you weren't on friendly terms.

The young man who seemed to be his new sidekick hurried over to the ewe and fell to his knees at her side. "You poor thing." He wrapped his arms around her neck.

"Billy, this is our neighbor, Rose Bell." Duke spoke softly, which brought Rose's attention back to him so fast her neck creaked. She preferred to think of Duke as brash. Hearing him speak so gently, so tenderly—

Good grief, she was losing her mind.

"Rose, this is Billy Taylor."

Billy got to his feet. "Hi, Rose. Pretty name. Just like your hair." Billy stared at her hair.

Rose resisted an urge to push it more tightly under her hat. She felt again Duke's study and forced herself to look directly at the young man he'd introduced. "Nice meeting you, Billy."

Billy's grin was wide and eager. He pressed a hand to his mouth and looked embarrassed.

It was hard to gauge his age but she guessed him to be in his early twenties. He didn't seem the kind of companion she'd expect Duke to pick. But then, what sort did she expect?

She couldn't rightly say. She'd done her best to avoid Duke all her life—partly because he teased her about her red hair but even more because he was a Caldwell. It had proved difficult to ignore him. They'd attended the same school. He was only a year older so they'd often ended up working together on some project. They'd gone to the same church. They'd even gone to the same gatherings where he'd often managed to become her partner at games.

Mostly, she assured herself, to annoy her and to tease her about her red hair.

Duke stepped into the deep snow beside the ewe.

"What do you think, Billy? How are we going to get her out of this?" The ewe bleated at his arrival.

"You won't hurt her, will ya?" Billy's face wrinkled with concern. She realized he had the mind of a child, which confused her even more.

"Not if I can help it." Duke tried to lift the edges of the ewe's fleece. "She's froze in." He stood to his knees in snow, tipped his hat back and scratched his forehead. "I don't know anything about sheep. Can we pull her out?" He turned to Rose.

She realized she'd been staring at him and jerked her attention back to the sheep. What was wrong with her? She sucked in a steadying breath. The same thing that had been wrong with her the year before he'd left. She'd struggled with reconciling the teasing boy he'd been with the handsome young man he had turned into. He was even more handsome now. His blue eyes drilled into her thoughts and sent them skittering back and forth like the sheep around her. Some running, glad to be free, but then stopping, uncertain what they wanted to do with that freedom.

Now she was thinking like a stupid sheep. She closed the door to such foolishness. She, Rose Bell, age eighteen, was a levelheaded, practical sort of person. One who dealt calmly with challenges.

She moved closer to the ewe, which brought her closer to Duke. She stumbled in the deep snow and he caught her by the arm.

"Steady there." His voice deepened.

Her cheeks burned and she knew they would be almost as red as her hair. He dropped her arm. A warm spot remained where it had been. She forced her attention to the bleating sheep. "She wouldn't feel it if we pulled her wool free from the ice. Though she'll likely be frightened."

Billy tipped his head down to meet the ewe's eyes. "We're going to help you so don't be scared. Okay?" He patted her head.

Just as Lilly would do.

Rose missed her twin sister so much. And her older sister, Cora, too. Not that she didn't see them almost every Sunday. She even visited Lilly most Saturdays, as well. But Cora had married Wyatt in the fall and Lilly had married Caleb in December. Rose, alone, remained at home. Likely she'd stay with her ma and pa until they passed.

She was happy for her sisters in their newly wedded state but she didn't figure she'd ever marry. Too many people cared about the background of the Bell sisters— or rather, their lack of background.

Ma and Pa Bell had found the three of them on the prairie when Cora was five and the twins only three. The girls could remember their papa riding away in a wagon with a promise to return, but two days and a night later, he had not. The Bells had taken the girls home and when no birth parents could be located, they'd adopted them. Not everyone approved. Not everyone thought the girls belonged in the community.

When she was about eight, Rose was in the store with her sisters and Ma. She had wandered down the aisles, fascinated by the display of the many colors of embroidery threads. Two women were in there, as well, and one had said to the other, "I wonder what the Bells have gotten themselves into. Taking in orphans like those girls. Who knows what sort of family they came from? I tell you, there's something wrong with people who would abandon their children, and goodness knows how those traits are passed down to their offspring. Mark my words, you'll see that mental weakness come to light soon enough."

Then a teacher in school had made a point of calling the girls "adopted" at every opportunity. As if it marked them in a special—but not good—way.

All of that she could have overlooked if it hadn't been for her unhappy experience with George Olsen. She'd thought him kind; a gentleman who'd eagerly accompanied her on walks about town.

But his mother had put an end to that. "We know nothing of their background. It's important to think about that when you court a girl. You never know what kind of family you are getting involved with in Rose's case. What kind of bloodlines does she carry? No, it's better that you know what you're getting into." Mrs. Olsen had been unaware that Rose had seen and heard every word.

Rose had turned and fled. Her sisters and parents had persuaded her to tell them why she'd been so upset. Ma had hugged her and assured her the only background she needed was to know she was loved. "You are my sweet Red Rose. A young woman with determination in her veins. Rose, my dear, you will someday thank God for giving you your strong nature."

After that, Rose had forsaken any idea of finding a beau. But she had not thanked God for her strong nature. Or her red hair.

Cora and Lilly had found men who were willing to overlook their lack of background.

Rose did not expect to be so fortunate.

Especially with someone the likes of Duke Caldwell…

She pressed her hand to her forehead. Where did such foolish thoughts come from?

Duke watched her with steady eyes filled with concern. "We can't leave her here."

He'd mistaken her despair for concern for the sheep, not concern for her own security. She knew where caring about a man would lead. Especially a Caldwell.

Not that she cared about Duke. Not in the least. Never had. Never would.

She started to pull the wool from the snow, strand by strand.

Billy murmured comfort to the sheep and Duke worked by Rose's side, following her example. His hands were sure and gentle. He seemed not a bit put out to be helping a sheep even though he was a cattleman and they hated sheep. How many times had she overheard remarks in town? "Woolies destroy the grass. They eat it to the roots. It never grows back."

She could have told the cowboys they were wrong, but knew there was no point. People believed what they chose to believe.

But Duke acted as though the ewe was no different than a cow or a horse. Or maybe he didn't care what others thought of sheep.

It must be sweet to be so sure of oneself.

"This is Lilly's first ewe. She calls her Mammy. Mammy will come when Lilly calls her." She couldn't stop talking. "But she won't come when I call her. You wouldn't think it would make a difference, would you?"

"I hear Lilly is married now."

"And Cora, too. Cora and Wyatt and his brother, Lonny, are on Jack Henry's ranch. You remember Jack Henry?"

"Yup." He continued loosening wool and she continued her endless chatter.

"Lilly married Caleb. He has a little son, Teddy. They're in town for now, though Caleb says he'll be getting his own ranch come spring. Right now they want to be in town so Teddy can go to school. He couldn't walk for a while."

"That so?"

"It is." And as suddenly as the burst of words had come, they ended. She couldn't think of a thing to say.

They had Mammy's wool loosened on one side and together they moved to the other.

A couple of minutes later Duke straightened and stuck his hands on his hips.

She grinned to herself and ducked her head. His stance should look powerful but with snow up to his knees it only looked as if he might lose his balance.

"What next?" he asked.

She waded out of the snowbank and turned to call, "Mammy, come, Mammy."

Mammy bleated but made no effort to move.

Rose jammed her hands into fists. "Why will you come when Lilly calls you and refuse to come when I do?"

Billy hugged the sheep around her neck. "It's okay. She's not mad at you." He backed up. "Come on, Mammy. You don't want to stay here. The snow is cold." As he backed toward Rose, Mammy followed.

"Good job. How did you do that?" Rose asked Billy, so pleased to see Mammy out of the snowbank she could have hugged the young man.

Duke chuckled. "Billy gets along well with animals."

Billy beamed at Duke's praise, then turned to Rose. "Where do you want her?"

She led him to the sheep pen and Mammy followed, bleating happily to be back inside.

Rose turned to contemplate the other animals. "Now, if only they would come as easily." Then realizing it sounded as though she meant to ask them to help, she smiled at Billy. "Thanks for your help." She turned to Duke. Her breath stuck halfway up her throat at his wide smile and flashing eyes. Must he look so handsome? So happy? So appealing?

"Thanks for your help, as well." She managed to squeak the words out.

"Thank me when we're done." He held her gaze a moment, then turned toward the other milling sheep. "Billy, do you suppose you could call them in?"

"I'll try... Come, sheepie. Come."

A couple trotted toward him but the rest acted as though they couldn't hear.

"Stupid sheep," Rose muttered as she marched around the furthest one—the headstrong ram—hoping to head it in the right direction. Of course it ran the opposite way.

Duke ran around the animal, waving his arms. "Shoo. Shoo."

The sheep skidded to a halt and looked around for a way of escape.

"Shoo. I said shoo." He jerked his hands toward the sheep.

The sheep baaed and lowered his head. Should she warn him about how the ram reacted to being chased?

But before she could, Duke jumped toward the ram. She stared at the way the animal backed up, still bleating his protest. He turned tail and trotted toward the pen, never once losing his voice.

Duke hurried after the ram. "Shoo. Shoo."

A cowboy on foot chasing a sheep! Who would have thought she'd ever see the day? When she told Lilly, they would get a good laugh out of it.

Grub, their flop-eared, useless but well-loved dog, loped toward the sheep. Until now he'd been supervising Ma and Pa unloading the wagon, hoping for a handout.

He ran straight into the midst of the sheep, scattering them every which way.

Duke's eyes grew wide. "Stop. Shoo. Shoo." He waved his arms madly at the sheep.

Rose started to giggle.

Duke pulled to a halt at her side. "Share the joke."

She shook her head, not because she didn't want to but because she wondered if he might be offended.

He nudged her with his elbow. "No fair. I like a good joke."

"Very well." She fluttered her hands toward the sheep who'd decided to ignore Grub and follow the ram. "Shoo. Shoo." She tossed her head like an annoyed sheep. "Baa. Baa."

No doubt seeing in her actions how silly he looked, he grinned at her and then a chuckle rumbled from him. They held each other's gaze as they laughed.

"They're all in," Billy called.

Rose pulled the gate closed and secured it firmly, as she did each and every time.

"How did they get the gate open?" Duke asked.

"Not by themselves, you can be sure." She slowly came about to face him. "And I think you know it. This is another of the Caldwell tricks."

He crossed his arms over his chest. His expression grew fierce. "I have no idea what you mean."

"Oh, come on. Since we moved here, the Caldwell cowboys have harassed us endlessly." The injustice of it burned a hot path through her thoughts. "Cows stampeded over the garden. Sheep turned out." She waved at the tracks through the snow. "This fall a lamb drowned."

Billy gasped.

"And my pa was injured when cows were run through the yard this fall."

"I had nothing to do with it," Duke averred.

"You're a Caldwell." She faced him squarely, her eyes burning with her raw feelings.

He studied her for a moment. Shock gave way to indifference. "Come on, Billy. It's time to go."

Without another word, they returned to their horses.

"Thanks for your help," she said, reluctant to end the afternoon on such a sour note. For a few minutes they had worked together and laughed together.

Too bad it couldn't be like that more often. But the land feud put them at enmity. That fact burned up her throat.

"Tell your father that the Bells aren't leaving."

"Rose is a pretty lady," Billy said.

"She sure is." In the year he'd been away, she had blossomed from child to woman. Not that she'd ever been ugly. He'd known her most of his life, attended the same school and the same church. But ever since he'd turned eleven years old they'd been separated by a wide chasm.

His father had never, nor would he ever, accept the mistake that had allowed the Bells to start a farm jutting into the boundaries of the Caldwell Ranch. Father resented the Bells taking advantage of the clerical error. The honorable thing to do, he'd insisted throughout the years, would be to stick to the spirit of the law rather than the letter of it. Worse still was the fact that the intruders were sodbusters who broke the land and put up fences. But the worst of all was that the Bells refused to budge despite every offer to buy them out and numerous attempts to drive them from the land. The whole disagreement had grown over the years until it had become a feud that made no sense.

"I like her," Billy continued.

"Me, too." He always had, though he hadn't been able to express it properly when they were kids so he'd teased her. She'd gotten all prickly but beneath the prickly thorns was a beautiful Rose. He'd always known it but it had never been more evident than today.

He sat back in his saddle, reliving every moment of the afternoon. Rose, her face flushed from her exertion. Rose, her green eyes flashing as she laughed at him chasing the sheep. He grinned. He didn't normally chase things on foot, but it had been worth it for those few moments of shared laughter.

His pleasure was cut short. She held him at least partially responsible for the feud simply because he was a Caldwell.

This feud should have ended years ago. His father had no call to try to drive the Bells from their land. It had to stop before someone got seriously injured. He'd noticed Mr. Bell limping the few times he'd seen him in town. He'd put it down to age. His teeth clenched. Instead, Rose held the Caldwells responsible. He knew Father would say it was an accident. Not the Caldwells' fault in the least.

But Duke knew Rose was likely correct—Caldwell cowboys had done it. And next time it might not end so well.

He rode up to the ranch house and dismounted.

"Billy, can you take care of the horses?"

Billy grinned as he took the reins of both animals. "I'll brush 'em really good, Boss."

Duke chuckled. Normally he wouldn't have been so eager to take care of the animals, except all the cowboys were away, so no one would tease him. He'd met Billy in Philadelphia and, when he realized the young man had no family, had brought him back with him. Billy hadn't started calling him "boss" until they'd arrived at the ranch and Billy had realized Duke's family owned the place.

Still chuckling, Duke entered through the kitchen door. Mrs. Humphrey slipped cookies from a baking sheet onto a cooling rack.

"Mmm. Cookies. Smells good." He snagged up two as he passed and bit into one. "Hot."

Mrs. Humphrey shook a towel at him. "They just came out of the oven. What did you expect?"

"I sure did miss your cooking while I was away." He crossed toward the sitting-room door.

"Glad to have you back, Duke," she called.

"Not half as glad as I am to be back." He'd enjoyed meeting his grandparents, aunts and uncles and cousins in Philadelphia but every day he'd missed Montana.

He stepped into the sitting room and stared at the traveling bags lined up. Mother laid a coat across a nearby chair.

"You going away?"

"Governor Toole has sent your father an invitation

to attend some meetings. Your father thinks he might be asked to work on a committee."

"I need to speak to him before he goes."

"You'll find him in the office."

Duke crossed the room and stepped into his father's office. Father gathered papers together and slipped them into a satchel.

"Can we talk?" Duke waited, hoping his father would give him his undivided attention. He didn't.

"By all means. I'm leaving you in charge while I'm gone."

Duke's chest swelled with anticipation. Since his return, he'd wanted to take on more responsibility.

"Not that there'll be anything requiring attention. Ebner has things under control."

The foreman. Duke's chest deflated. Would his father ever see him as capable? It was ironic. Father—the one person who should value him as a Caldwell—didn't, while others couldn't overlook it.

He'd experienced it many times over his life. Like the time when Duke was fourteen and a man befriended him. Duke soon learned it was only so he could approach "Mr. Caldwell" for a favor.

Then there was Jane Johnson, a gal he'd courted for a very short time before his trip to Philadelphia. She'd expected gifts and tokens, and when he'd failed to bring them she'd claimed surely a Caldwell could afford to win her affections that way. He wasn't interested in her anymore.

In Philadelphia, being a Caldwell had brought the ladies flocking to his side. He'd thought they were truly interested in him. Especially Enid Elliot. She'd hung on his every word. Made him feel ten feet tall. They'd even discussed marriage. He'd been about to offer his hand when he'd overheard her talking to her friends.

"He's a Caldwell. His name and money are worth overlooking the fact I find him a bit loutish. All he talks about is his horse and his ranch." She'd made a dismissive noise. "I have no intention of living out west. He'll soon come to see my point of view."

He'd come to his senses rather quickly after that and the offer of marriage had never been made. In hindsight, he considered himself fortunate to have discovered the truth beforehand, but it hurt to know her attention had been for such a selfish reason.

To Enid, being a Caldwell meant she could benefit from his name.

To Rose, being a Caldwell meant he was her opponent.

He wished he could just be Duke and have someone care about him for his sake alone.

He sucked in a long breath and focused on what he meant to say to his father. "I'll manage everything." He sank into a chair in front of the big mahogany desk. How often had he tiptoed into this room when Father was away and sat in Father's chair, taken up pen and paper and pretended he was in charge? He'd planned the things he'd wanted to do, the changes he'd like to make. He'd implement a new breeding program with imported bulls. He'd put up hay for the winter—

Now was not the time for dreaming. "Father, could you sit down a moment?"

His father gave him a distracted look, then sat. "I don't have long. We're planning to leave first thing in the morning."

That would give Father plenty of time to listen to

Duke's request and to act on it. "Father, I happened to ride by the Bells on my way home and found their sheep had been let out of the pen."

"They should have better fences."

Father and son studied each other, measuring, assessing. Duke would not blink, would not show any sign of weakness in front of this powerful man who considered his word to be law.

"Their fences and gates are perfectly adequate and I think you know it. Someone opened the gate and let the sheep out. Just like someone purposely drove the cattle over their property and did a number of other destructive things. Father, the land is theirs. We have no right to harass them. It's wrong." Knowing his father meant to go to Helena to see the governor, Duke saw how he could use that to his advantage.

"Governor Toole would not view it as appropriate. Don't you think it's time to end this?"

Father tented his fingertips and looked thoughtful.

Duke pressed his point. "Inform the cowboys to end their harassment before you go, then you can go to Helena knowing you've done the honorable thing."

"Son, I think you'd make a good politician."

Duke would be happy being a good neighbor.

Father pushed back from the desk and got to his feet. "You have a point. I'll deal with this before I leave."

Duke got up, too, and offered his hand to Father. They shook.

The feud was over.

He'd tell Rose himself.

He'd fine-tuned his plans last night and rose Sunday morning eager to start the day. He knew the Bells didn't work on Sunday, so that afternoon would be a perfect opportunity to pay them a visit.

His parents left early for Helena as he and Billy prepared for church. They rode their horses into town, many greeting him as he swung down and strode toward the church steps.

The Bells were already seated in their customary place. He studied the new husbands some. They looked like nice enough fellows.

The Caldwells always sat on the left side of the church, two pews from the front. But today he chose a spot across from the Bells, in a back a row where he could watch Rose without appearing to.

She wore her rich red hair braided and wound around her head in a fetching way. Strands of it had escaped to hang down in little curls that brushed her neck.

His hands curled with an urge to lean across the aisle, capture a strand and let it drift through his fingers.

She turned and caught him staring. Her eyes widened.

He jerked his attention to the front and pretended he hadn't been looking at her.

But as soon as she turned forward again, his gaze returned to her. Why had he never before noticed her slender neck and her high cheekbones?

Pastor Rawley stepped up to the pulpit and called them to worship.

It took every ounce of Duke's self-control to concentrate on the service. As soon as it ended, he stood and waited for Rose to acknowledge him.

The two Sundays he'd attended since his return he'd been with his parents and they'd always avoided the Bells. Duke had no intention of doing so today.

Lilly approached first, introducing her husband, Caleb, and the little boy, Teddy. Then Cora introduced her husband, Wyatt, and his brother Lonnie. Mrs. Bell welcomed him home.

Mr. Bell, moving slowly as if in pain, shook his hand and greeted him pleasantly enough.

Only Rose passed by him without a greeting. She met his eyes steadily, pink blushing her cheeks as if she saw him through the eyes of a woman and not the eyes of an adversary. He hugged the knowledge to him.

Wouldn't she be pleased when he told her that the Bells need no longer fear being hurt or having their property damaged by the Caldwells?

Other worshippers stopped to greet him.

Pastor Rawley spoke to him and asked about his parents.

Slowly he made his way down the aisle and reached the yard in time to see the Bells leave in three wagons. It appeared the whole family gathered together after church.

He considered riding over later, so eager was he to see Rose's response to his announcement. But no, he'd delay until the next day when he could see her alone.

The rest of Sunday passed slowly, though Billy enjoyed it. They rode into the hills, where Duke showed the other man some of his favorite places—a grove of trees where he'd camped out several times, the buffalo wallow where he'd found several buffalo bones, the pond where he used to swim.

It was good to be home. It would be even better when Rose knew the feud was over and done with. How would she show her gratitude? He realized he stared into space, lost in dreams of possibilities, and forced his attention back to the here and now…

Finally, Monday arrived. He decided to wait until early afternoon, when she'd have her chores done.

"Billy, how about we go pay Rose and her family a visit?"

"Oh, I'd like that."

"Let's go saddle up."

Billy rushed ahead of him. The young man loved animals and the horses responded to his entrance into the barn with welcoming nickers.

A few minutes later they rode across the prairie toward the Bell place. Duke took in a deep breath, full of fresh air the likes of which he had not breathed the whole time he was in Philadelphia. He pulled his horse to a halt so he could drink in the surroundings. The mountains were draped in white. The pine and spruce were almost black in the distance. Nearer at hand, the snow-dusted hills rolled to the river where the willow and poplar had shed their leaves and stood like quiet skeletons waiting the renewal of spring.

His gaze returned to the mountains. "You never saw anything like that back in the city, did you, Billy?"

"No." Billy stared at the mountains. "Can we go there someday?" His words were round with awe.

"We sure can. But maybe we'll wait until spring."

"Okay. Are we almost to where Rose lives?"

Duke chuckled. "Are you anxious to see her?"

Billy ducked his head. "She's pretty and nice."

"How can you tell she's nice?"

"I could tell by her voice when she talked to me."

"I suppose you could." The young man likely had more experience than most with hearing different tones in voices. As Duke well knew, people often mocked him. A kind voice would be refreshingly different.

"We're almost there." They crested a hill and looked down on the Bell farm. There was a new barn since he'd seen the place last year. The fruit trees had grown some and, if he wasn't mistaken, there were more of them.

Pigs grunted in one pen, sheep milled about in another. He smiled as he recalled helping Rose chase them in. She'd made him laugh. He liked that.

Three milk cows chewed their cuds in another pen and a horse drowsed in the afternoon sun. It jerked awake and neighed at their approach.

"This is where Rose and her sisters lived with their ma and pa," he told Billy. "I guess only Rose lives with her parents now."

"How many sisters she got?"

"Two. You met them yesterday. Both of them are married and moved to their own places."

"Aww. So Rose is all alone."

"She's still got her ma and pa." He'd never considered that she might feel alone with her sisters gone. "She and Lilly are twins."

"I never knowed any twins before. It makes her extra special." He hesitated a moment. "I guess she misses Lilly."

"I suppose so."

"She'll be glad you've come to visit."

"We'll see." They continued toward the buildings.

Rose stepped from the barn and shielded her eyes to watch them approach.

As they passed the pigpen, his horse, King, snorted and sidestepped. "Settle down."

He rode up to Rose and she looked at King as he

pranced nervously. "Your horse looks like it belongs on a closed racetrack, not out on the prairie."

"He's a great horse." Though a little high-spirited. Duke gripped the reins firmly. "I can handle him." He waited for her to invite him to step down but when she didn't, he swung off his horse and landed in front of her.

"Rose, I have good news for you."

Her eyebrows rose.

"The feud is over. You won't be bothered again."

Her look went on and on, unblinking, steady and full of doubts.

"Believe me. It's over."

She nodded once, quickly, as if she meant only to acknowledge his words, not agree with them. "I'll believe it when I see the evidence."

Chapter Two

Rose sighed as Grub, their not-so-fine watchdog, suddenly realized there was company and let out a woof. Johnny-come-lately, as Caleb described him.

At the doggie intrusion Duke's horse reared and backed away, dragging Duke after him. "Whoa, there. Settle down." Duke spoke firmly but the animal's nostrils flared and he had his hands full controlling him.

Rose watched, amused and at the same time annoyed because he chose to ride a horse that was so headstrong.

Billy led his horse forward and caught her attention to him. He laughed as the floppy-eared dog trotted up, tripping over himself on the way. "What's your doggie's name?" He reached down to pat Grub and earned himself undying devotion.

She'd been so distracted by Duke's presence the other day that she'd neglected to inform Billy. "Grub."

Billy rubbed behind Grub's ears. "You're a good dog, ain't ya? I can tell." He straightened and sighed. "I wish I had a dog."

Three cats wandered from the barn, curious as to the disturbance.

Billy cooed and scooped one up in his arms. "I wish I had a cat, too."

"You're welcome to play with ours anytime." She'd suggest he take one of them home with him but she had no idea if the Caldwells would take kindly to the idea. She wouldn't let a cat go where she couldn't be sure it would be treated properly.

Billy studied Rose, his brown eyes wide. "You're a nice person."

She smiled. "Thank you." It was nice to be appreciated. "How'd you get to be friends with Duke?" It puzzled her no end that Duke would pick Billy for a sidekick. She'd expect a Caldwell to choose someone big and brawny. Perhaps Billy had done the choosing.

Billy's chest puffed out. "He saved me from drowning."

Rose stared. "He did?" She squinted at Duke a few feet away, his horse now reasonably calm.

Billy hung his head. "I jumped in deep water." He gulped. "On purpose."

His comments didn't make sense, unless— "Can you swim?"

"No, I can't."

"Then why did you jump in?"

Billy hung his head and kicked at a lump on the ground until it dislodged and skittered away. "I wanted to die," he whispered. "People always call me bad names."

"Oh, Billy." She squeezed his shoulder. "I'm sorry people say unkind things and I'm glad you're okay."

Billy's eyes were awash with joy. "Me, too, 'cause now I get to meet you, and Duke is my best friend."

Duke led his horse back to them and Rose studied

him out of the corner of her eye. He'd saved Billy's life, which made him a good man. So could she believe him when he said the feud was over? But no matter what, he was still a Caldwell. If she didn't remain cautious and alert as to the goings-on of the Caldwell cowboys, some-one might get hurt. Worse than last time. She wasn't about to let down her guard.

Duke stood in front of her, his eyes watchful, as if he expected something from her.

Perhaps he expected her to greet his announcement with unbridled joy. She studied him, his strong fea-tures and his blue, blue eyes that seemed to see clear through her.

He smiled and his eyes danced with crystal light. "Have you decided you like what you see?"

Heat rushed up her neck and she jerked away to stare toward the river, hoping he wouldn't see her cheeks col-oring. Never would she admit she thought him hand-some and considered the blue in his eyes as vivid as any sunny Montana day.

She shook her head. "I'm trying to decide if you truly believe the feud has ended or if you have some partic-ular reason why you want me to believe it." For years the Bells had hoped and prayed for this dispute to stop. She couldn't believe it could end so easily—simply with his say-so. The doubts twisted through her thoughts.

"What do you hope to gain by saying it's over?" she asked him. Would he make such a claim if he simply wanted to spend time with her?

Why would he?

All he had to do was ask. Would she agree if he did? Her head said no. He was a Caldwell and, as such, not to be trusted on the Bell farm. In fact—her eyes narrowed—

it seemed likely he was looking for a weakness, an opportunity to drive them off.

But her heart pushed forward a protest. There was something about Duke that drew her like a moth to a flame. She'd always been attracted by his power, his energy, his happy spirit. Now, seeing Billy's devotion, she was drawn even closer.

Moths got burned if they got too close to the flames, she reminded herself.

"Maybe I just want us to be friends and neighbors." His voice carried a harsh note, as if her doubts offended him.

"We've been neighbors for eight years," she pointed out. "But the Caldwells have never wanted to be friends."

"Not all the Caldwells." He spoke softly, but there was no mistaking the firmness in his words.

They considered each other, neither blinking. The air between them shifted and shimmered like a summer mirage. It seemed full of possibility.

With a great deal of effort she pulled her gaze away and stared into the distance. For the life of her she couldn't explain what was happening between them. Nor could she pull a single word from her confused brain.

After a minute Duke turned with a muffled sound. "We better go." He swung up into his saddle.

"Can I come and visit you again?" Billy asked.

Her voice returned, though somewhat croaky. "You're welcome anytime, Billy."

He cheered as if he'd won a goal as he trotted away on his horse.

She continued toward the house, which had been

her initial intention before Duke and Billy had ridden into the yard.

He'd said the feud was over.

She hoped it was so, but she meant to wait and see. In the meantime she'd keep her emotions firmly under control.

She stepped inside to the welcome warmth, hung her coat on the nearest hook and turned to face her parents.

Pa was curled up on the cot across the room. She watched the covers rise and fall rhythmically. Her own breathing eased with relief.

"He's fine," Ma said. "I wish you'd stop worrying."

But he hadn't been fine since he'd caught a cold shortly after Lilly's wedding. Ma figured his ribs had been hurt when the cows ran over him, which made it hard for him to cough and clear his lungs. Plumb wore him out, it did.

Rose crossed to the cupboard where Ma prepared vegetables to add to the pot of meat stewing on the stove. She draped her arm across Ma's shoulders. "I'll never stop worrying about both of you. After all, you're all I've got."

Ma patted Rose's arm. "You've got Cora and Wyatt and Lilly and Caleb and a host of friends and neighbors."

Rose gave a laugh, half teasing, half serious. "And yet here you are, stuck with me."

"Not stuck, my dear. Blessed." The look Ma gave her was so full of love that Rose had to blink back a sting of tears.

"Speaking of neighbors…" Ma continued. "Wasn't that young Caldwell I saw you with?"

"It was."

"His parents will no doubt be pleased to have him back."

"Not so pleased they didn't take the first train to Helena."

Ma nodded. "I suppose they're anxious to take part in some of the celebrations of Montana achieving statehood. Perhaps Mr. Caldwell will become a politician."

Rose stared at her mother. "Would that mean he would live in Helena?" Her brain raced. Would he leave Duke in charge? Would that truly mean the feud was over? She could barely contain the hope bubbling inside her.

"Why, I don't know. I suppose it would depend on the sort of position he fills." Ma turned her attention back to the simmering pot. "But who knows? It's pure speculation on my part."

"It does seem the sort of thing Mr. Caldwell would do." He could rule an even bigger portion of the world. Maybe thinking of it made him realize how small and petty a feud with the Bells was. If only it could be so.

"Who was the young man with Duke?"

"Billy Taylor. A sweet young man who seems a little simpleminded. He says Douglas saved his life." She repeated Billy's story.

"What did they want?"

"Just being neighborly." She didn't see any point in repeating Duke's proclamation that the feud was over. Not until she could be sure.

Pa stirred at that moment and sat up. "Smells good in here."

Ma hurried to fill the kettle. "I'll make you some tea."

Pa rose and stretched.

Rose took note of the fact his arms barely rose above shoulder height and that he clenched his teeth as if holding back a groan.

She turned her back to stare out the window. If the harassment from the Caldwells ended, she would be most grateful. *Please, God, make it so.* Perhaps Duke would take it a step further. Hadn't he said he wanted them to be friends?

Her cheeks warmed. She tried to dismiss the idea but it had developed tenacious roots. Seeing him on that big horse, hearing Billy talk of being rescued by Duke, recalling the way he'd teased her when they were kids—

Enough. He was a Caldwell. Even without the feud between them, they were a whole universe apart. A rich rancher and an adopted daughter of dirt farmers—no one would ever imagine them together. But the idea dogged her as she helped serve the meal and later as she went to her room.

Two empty beds stood side by side next to hers. Cora and Lilly were married. She still found it hard to believe. For some reason, she thought they'd always be together.

Her earliest memory was of the three of them standing on the dusty prairie watching a wagon drive away and waving bye-bye to their papa. Then she and Lilly had each clutched one of Cora's hands, their big sister who had promised to take care of them.

That's where Ma Bell had found them. Lilly had gone eagerly into Ma's outstretched arms but Cora had hung back. Rose had stuck firmly to Cora's side.

"My papa is coming back. He said to wait," Cora had insisted.

"Your little sisters are tired and hungry," Ma had

said. "Come with me and let me feed all of you. We'll be in town. Your papa will know to look for you there when he comes back."

Thinking of that day, Rose smiled as she prepared for bed.

"Ise not tired 'n' hungry," she'd stoutly insisted, standing bravely at Cora's side and knowing that if Ma Bell had mentioned milk or bread or cheese, she would have faltered. Instead, Cora had nodded and allowed Ma Bell to lead them home.

Fifteen years later and their birth father had never returned. Rose could remember nothing more about her father and nothing at all about her birth mother. Cora had told her that their mother had died and Cora had promised to take care of the twins.

Rose wished her sisters were still there. They could have discussed what Duke had said. Though she knew they were likely to trust his words. Her sisters had certainly mellowed since meeting their husbands. Was that what love did to a person?

Rose hadn't changed. Except to finally accept that they would never learn anything more about their birth parents. She was happy enough, but inside, a hole remained. A lack. She knew Ma and Pa loved her and she loved them and was happy they had adopted the three little girls abandoned on the prairie, yet somehow, when Rose looked within, a hungry emptiness clawed at her insides. It wasn't a large hole but it went deep and persistently made itself known. She had no family history. No knowledge of her real background. No assurance there wasn't something mighty strange about a man who'd abandoned three little girls in the middle of nowhere. The few times she'd let a boy escort her someplace, they had acted as though her lack of background allowed them to take liberties with her. She'd soon set them straight on that score.

She sat on the edge of her bed and, as was her practice, read a chapter in her Bible and then said her prayers, adding a special request. *God, show me what to believe about Duke. I don't want to trust his every word out of loneliness and weakness. Yet, if the feud is over, well, I'll thank You wholeheartedly.*

She wakened with a jolt the next morning, her heart pounding as she bolted from her bed. Something had startled her from her sleep. Hopping on the cold floor, she rushed to look out the kitchen window into the gray, predawn light. Cows, pigs, sheep and chickens milled across the yard. The cows mooed. The sheep baaed and ran around in crazy circles, making the chickens fly up with startled squawks. The pigs rooted through the spot where she occasionally emptied the slop bucket.

She hurried back to her room and donned warm clothes, then grabbed her coat and headed outside to again corral all the animals.

Only once did she stop to stare in the direction of the Caldwell buildings. So much for ending the feud.

Duke had not told her the truth. What else was false? His claim that he wanted to be her friend?

A cold wind whistled down the hill, stinging her eyes, causing them to water. There was no other reason for the tears she dashed from her eyes.

Duke's emotions tangled as if they'd been caught in the wind. Disappointment, anger and helpless hope formed a rope that twisted tighter with every breath.

He'd ridden over to the Bells' so certain Rose would be overjoyed at his announcement. Instead she had questioned his sincerity. She suspected his motives.

Come to think of it, she'd always been on the suspicious side. If he took her an apple, she'd check it for worms. If he found a pretty rock and gave it to her, she'd toss it aside wondering aloud if he meant to insult her.

Mrs. Humphrey had noted his distraction when he'd returned yesterday. "Who you mooning over, Duke?"

Duke had forced a boisterous laugh to his lips. "I'd never moon over anyone. You ought to know that."

He tried to hold on to that sense of injustice this morning.

Over breakfast Mrs. Humphrey considered him in her motherly way.

He met her doubtful look without blinking as he had last night. "Good breakfast," he said after a moment of measuring each other.

"Duke, I hope you can manage on your own a few days. I want to visit my son."

"By all means." It would be a relief not to have to endure her probing looks. "We can certainly manage." He included Billy, who sat across from him at the table. "You can always go to the cookhouse and eat with the men if you get hungry."

Billy made a sound of distress. It hadn't taken him long to discover how harsh the cowboys' teasing could be.

"We'll be fine."

Not long after breakfast, when she was ready, he arranged for one of the men to take her to town in the wagon.

He wandered through the house; stood in his father's

office. He was in charge now, but it didn't seem all that exciting. He returned to the kitchen where Billy sat with his papers and pencil.

"Billy, let's go visit Rose."

Billy cheered. "She said I could visit the cats anytime I wanted." He gave Duke a sideways look. "I like cats."

Was Billy asking to have a pet? Duke had no objection but would wait to check with Rose before he said anything.

They saddled up and were soon on their way.

It had grown colder in the past couple of days. Winter could not be avoided. Father was away and Duke wondered if there was something he needed to be taking care of. Though Father had assured him Ebner knew what to do.

Duke wanted to help. He wanted to work. But when he'd asked Ebner what to do, the foreman had waved him away.

"I got it under control. I always got it under control. I don't need some young buck messin' things up."

Duke had stared after the man. Young buck? Is that how Ebner saw him? Duke shouldn't be surprised. Ebner had never been all that friendly to him.

Forget Ebner. Sooner or later he'd learn to respect Duke.

His thoughts flitted ahead to this visit with Rose.

Perhaps if he'd been paying more attention he would have been prepared when a rabbit jumped out in front of King. The horse snorted, reared and got the bit. Knowing he was in control, King bucked.

Duke hung on through the first three bucks but he was off balance, unprepared for King's behavior, and went flying, his arms windmilling. The ground rushed toward him and clouted him on the forehead. He closed his eyes and gasped for breath. Darkness pushed at the edges of his brain but he fought it off and sat up. The world tilted and spun. Something dripped into his eyes and he rubbed it away.

His hand came away bloody.

The black pushed closer.

"Billy." He looked around for the man... Where was he? He lifted his head and squinted to focus his vision.

Billy galloped away, leaving Duke alone.

The blackness overwhelmed him.

Chapter Three

"Rose! Rose!"

She turned at the sound of her name. Her heart leaped to her throat as Billy raced toward her on horseback, bouncing as though he'd come unseated any moment.

As Billy reached her side, she grabbed the horse and steadied it. Her heart beat a frantic tattoo against her breastbone at the sight of his tearstained face. "Billy, are you hurt?"

"No. No." He blubbered out the words.

"What's wrong?"

Billy's mouth worked and a few garbled words came out, but nothing she could make sense of.

The muscles in her neck started to spasm. She glanced around, searched the horizon for any sign of danger. It took only a few seconds to assure herself there were no cows racing toward them, no cowboys watching from the crest of the hill. At least with the skiff of snow the risk of fire had been dealt with. She shuddered. Fire was her biggest fear.

She helped Billy to the ground and patted his back, trying to calm him. One of the half-grown cats rubbed around her ankles, giving her an idea. She scooped it up and put it in Billy's arms. The cat purred and pressed its face to his chest.

As she hoped, the animal calmed Billy and he sucked in a deep breath.

"Billy, what's wrong?"

A shudder shook the man from head to toe. "Duke." He choked and couldn't continue.

"What's he doing?" Did he have some kind of mischief planned and Billy meant to warn them?

"Hurt," Billy said, his mouth working as he tried to explain. "Duke hurt." He patted his head.

"He hurt his head?"

He nodded. "Fell."

She stroked the cat, pulling Billy's attention back to the animal.

Billy shuddered again but petting the cat helped him relax. "Duke fell off his horse. Hit his head." A sob caught in the man's throat. "Blood. Lots and lots of blood."

Rose quickly analyzed the information. If Billy had come to the Bells, did that mean Duke was near? She again scanned the horizon, this time looking for either a wandering animal, though King had likely headed for the barn, or an unusual lump on the ground. She saw neither.

"Billy, where is Duke now?"

He turned and pointed.

"Do you remember where?"

He nodded, then his face wrinkled. "Maybe."

"Wait here while I saddle Hope." Never before had she clung to her horse's name but now she did.

Ma stepped from the house wearing a warm jacket. "Is something the matter?"

Rose quickly explained. "Billy's upset. Can you stay with him?" She introduced the pair and Ma spoke softly and soothingly to Billy.

He wouldn't go anywhere as long as Ma was there to watch him.

She returned in a few minutes with her horse saddled.

"Everything okay?" she asked.

Her ma nodded. "Billy was telling me how much he likes cats. I asked if he'd like to own this one even if he has to leave it here."

"I'll call her Patches 'cause she's all patchy with different colors." He rubbed his cheek against her fur.

Patches purred and licked his face.

Grub sat nearby watching.

Billy put the cat down and patted the dog. "I like you, too."

Relieved that Billy had calmed down, Rose led both horses to his side. "Why don't you show me where Duke is?"

"Wait a moment." Ma hurried back to the house and returned shortly with a small sack. "I've put in some bandaging and other things you might need."

"Thanks, Ma."

Rose indicated Billy should mount up and then swung into her own saddle.

Ma tsked and shook her head but didn't say anything. She and Pa had long ago given up trying to make her ride sidesaddle.

For a few hundred yards Rose easily followed Billy's

back trail before it disappeared in a mess of cow tracks and trampled snow.

"What direction now?" she asked him.

He looked around, twisting in his saddle to glance back in the direction of the farm. "We just came that way, didn't we?"

"Yes, Billy. That would take us back to my home."

He nodded. "I rode there as fast as I could." His whole body quaked. "I was so scared."

"Yes, when you saw that Duke was hurt." She gave him a moment to sort through his thoughts. "Where did Duke fall?"

"On the ground."

She hid her grin. It was a stupid question. "Was he over there?" She pointed to the north.

"Maybe."

Good. "Then let's go find him."

"Or maybe he was over there." He pointed south.

"I see." In other words, Billy didn't know. Maybe he'd remember something else. "Where were you planning to go?"

"For a ride."

"Of course. Why didn't I think of that? Were you going to see someone?"

Billy grinned. "You."

"Me?" Why would Duke want to visit her? She hadn't been exactly welcoming yesterday and didn't much care to see him again after she'd spent several hours sorting animals and getting them into their proper pens this morning. "Why?"

Billy ducked his head. "'Cause he likes you."

She sputtered. Then forced herself to relax. This was Billy talking. He saw what he wanted to see. She sat back and considered her surroundings. The most direct route between the two places would be over that hill. She nudged her horse in that direction.

From the crest of the hill she could see no sign of Duke or his horse. "Did you come this way?"

"Maybe." A cry choked off the word.

He didn't know and couldn't tell her. She'd have to figure it out herself. She took a deep breath. *Think.* This was Duke. Would he take the most direct route? No. Not anywhere near. He'd take the most dangerous, the most challenging. That meant he'd ride along the escarpment and cross the coulee that lay to the west.

She reined her horse in that direction. She had to confess it was one of her favorite places. From the top, she often observed deer feeding in the coulee and hawks circling overhead. There'd been a nest she'd looked down on in the early part of summer to watch the baby hawks.

She reached the coulee. Some vicious rocks lay scattered across the snow-crusted slopes. If Duke had hit his head of one of those—

She shuddered. She'd imagined finding him injured but perhaps his injuries were beyond help.

Her breath whooshed out when she didn't see a body anywhere. Perhaps she'd been mistaken in thinking he'd come this way. "Do you remember this place?" she asked Billy.

He nodded. "Maybe." Then his eyes focused. "Duke wasn't with me."

Rose tried to understand what Billy meant. Had they been on this route but Duke had fallen before they reached this place? Only one way to find out.

She made her way across the coulee and climbed the upward path. From there she could see several miles in every direction, clear to the trees filling the hollow toward the Caldwell buildings. And there was no sign of Duke.

Billy jumped to the ground. "He was here." He pointed. "He's gone." He turned his face upward, his eyes wide. "He's gone to Heaven."

"No, Billy. I don't think so." At least not from this spot because there was no body.

She dismounted and bent to examine the ground where Billy stood. There was a rock and a large dark spot. Blood. Lots of blood. She shivered. Duke might be a Caldwell and a royal pain, but she had no wish to see him dead. She looked around.

Her heart clinging to the back of her throat, she went to the edge of the cliff and looked down. But there was no sign of Duke or his horse. Had the horse remained with him and Duke was now riding homeward?

She swung into the saddle, indicated Billy should do the same, and rode toward the Caldwell Ranch. She veered to the right of the trees.

A movement caught her eye. Something was in there among the stark branches and dark shadows. It could be a deer or even a bear. Or perhaps Duke's horse. Should she check? She didn't want to waste time but neither did she want to neglect caution. She reined in and peered into the shadows.

There it was again; something lurching from shadow to shadow. She blinked hard. "Duke?"

Billy hit the ground running. "Duke, you ain't dead."

The figure folded to the ground.

Rose dismounted and hurried after Billy.

By the time she caught up with him, he'd squatted beside Duke who was struggling to sit up.

Blood covered his face and soaked the front of his coat. He rubbed his eyes to clear the dripping blood and squinted up at them. But it was plain that he couldn't bring them into focus.

She squatted in front of him and took his chin to bring his gaze to her. "Duke, do you hear me?"

"Loud and clear."

Which was more than she could say about his answer. He sounded as if his tongue had gone to sleep.

"Don't die, Duke. Please don't die." Billy sobbed the words.

Duke pulled his legs up and tried to get to his feet. "Got to go home."

Yes, she needed to get him back to the ranch where he could get warm and have his wound tended.

"Billy," she said calmly, "can you bring the horses?"

He got started on the assignment without answering.

She turned back to Duke and gently pressed him back to the ground. "Relax. We'll get you home."

He nodded, groaned at the movement and grabbed his head. "Hurts."

"I expect so." She touched his forehead, trying to see the cut through the blood. It looked deep, deep enough to mar his handsome features. Could he handle knowing that?

Billy led the horses forward.

Rose considered her options. She'd like to put Duke on Billy's horse and let Billy hold him on the ride to the Caldwell Ranch, but Billy was scrubbing tears from his face. She couldn't count on him to know what to do.

She pulled Hope close. "Help me get Duke on my horse," she instructed Billy.

Between them they pulled Duke upright. He wobbled so badly she staggered under his weight. "Grab the saddle horn," she told him as she wrapped his fingers around it. "Hang on." She and Billy boosted him into the saddle and she climbed up behind him. She sat back, reluctant to hold him as intimately as this ride would require.

He listed to the south. Billy grabbed him. "What if he falls again? I don't want him to go to Heaven today."

"He won't." She wrapped her arms around Duke and pressed tight to his back. "He won't." Though whether she meant fall or die, she wasn't prepared to say.

He groaned and tried to reach his head but his arms were firmly pinned at his sides.

"You're okay now," she soothed. "I'll soon have you home."

He grunted and leaned into her hold as she urged Hope to move forward.

Billy followed on horseback. "Is this my fault?"

"Of course not. Why would you think that?"

"'Cause I'm stupid and do stupid things."

"Oh, Billy, don't you believe that. Besides, we all do stupid things at times." Anger twisted inside her, both at the knowledge that this gentle man had been made to feel that way and because Duke had chosen to ride a horse that almost killed him. "Such as how smart is it to ride a horse you can't control?"

Duke mumbled something but she couldn't make sense of his ramblings.

"You'll soon be home safe and sound," she murmured.

He mumbled again and seemed to snuggle into her arms. It sounded as though he'd said, "Nice."

Heat stole up her cheeks. Surely he didn't mean hav-

ing her arms around him. It was only to keep him from
falling on his head again. She marginally relaxed her
hold but he swayed and she fought his weight to keep
him in the saddle. She had no choice but to hold tight.

The ranch buildings came into sight. She glanced
around. Now would be a good time for that obnoxious
foreman, Ebner, to show up and offer a hand. Or any-
body.

But apart from the neigh of King who stood outside
the corral wanting in, there wasn't another living, moving being to be seen.

She rode up to the front of the house and stopped at
the steps. This was only the second time she'd been this
close to the house. Once, she and her sisters had come
with Ma in the wagon. She and Lilly had been eleven
or twelve, which would have made Cora fourteen at
the time. Ma had heard Mrs. Caldwell was ill and had
done the neighborly thing and brought over a hot dish.

Cora had protested. "Ma, do you think they'll welcome us? Most likely they'll chase us off with a shotgun."

Lilly had clutched her hands in her lap. "They might
be really mad."

Rose smiled as she recalled how fiercely she'd reacted. "They don't deserve Ma's help."

Ma had shushed the girls. "We will do what is right
and good, and not let the actions of others determine
our own."

A woman who wasn't Mrs. Caldwell had come in
answer to Ma's knock and, with a friendly smile, had
thanked Ma for the dish. Rose learned later the woman
was Mrs. Humphrey who worked for the Caldwells.

They'd been informed Mrs. Caldwell was indisposed, and no invitation had been offered for them to step inside.

Ma had smiled as if there had been no insult and said to tell Mrs. Caldwell they'd pray for her recovery.

Rose had been so impressed with her ma's attitude that she promised herself to be more like her. All too often her anger dictated how she acted, but today would be one time she actually succeeded in doing what was right despite her feelings.

"Billy, help me get Duke off the horse." She slipped to the ground as she and Billy steadied Duke, then he slid into Billy's arms. Billy would have crashed under his weight if Rose hadn't taken a portion of it.

Together they guided Duke up the steps. Billy pushed the door open.

Rose released Duke and stepped back. She'd never been in this house, knew she wouldn't be welcome. Any more than she had welcomed Duke into the Bell house.

Billy staggered under Duke's weight and glanced back at Rose. His expression drooped. "Rose, don't go. Don't leave us."

Duke's head came up. "Rose…" She understood that word well enough. "Help." And that one, too.

She could not resist a call for help from anyone.

She stared at the door and swallowed hard. If anything symbolized the difference between the Bells and the Caldwells, this door did—big, heavy-looking paneled wood with a fine brass handle. The door to the Bells' house was a plain slab of wood with a black knob.

Billy wobbled. She pushed aside any insecurities and grabbed Duke's arm, lifted it over her shoulder and edged through the door.

They were in a kitchen about the size of the entire

living quarters at home. A big wooden table, several inches thick, stood in the middle of the room. Half a dozen chairs were pushed up to it.

At one end of the room a fireplace lay with wood ready to light. A huge black stove occupied the opposite side of the room. Cupboards and shelves filled the walls.

"He needs to lie down," she told Billy.

"Through there." He pointed to one of the three doorways and they shuffled into a sitting room. Her eyes scanned a burgundy sofa and several armchairs, each with a table and lamp beside it. But she didn't see anywhere she could rest a person dripping in blood.

"Is there a blanket or towel to cover the sofa with?"

Billy hurried to fetch something, leaving Rose to hold Duke up on her own. He turned unfocused eyes on her and grinned crookedly. "Hi."

She laughed. "You wouldn't sound so welcoming if your brain wasn't scrambled."

"Yes, I would." He nodded, causing him to almost lose his balance.

"Whoa! Take it easy." They sidestepped a bit before she got him steadied.

Billy trotted into the room with a heavy gray blanket.

"Spread it on the sofa."

He did so, meticulously smoothing it into place.

She edged Duke to the sofa and eased him down. She stood over him, studying him. "About the best I can say for you at the moment is you're alive."

He wiped his eyes. "That's not such a good feeling right now."

"You're not gonna let him die, are ya?" Billy wrung his hands.

Duke cracked open one eye. "Are ya?"

Why did his question bring such a rush of emotions? Regret, determination and wild wishes all tangled together.

"Of course not. I need to get some water." She rushed from the room, pressing her cold hands to her hot cheeks. What was the matter with her? One glance around the room answered her question. She didn't belong here and, should Duke be in his right mind, he'd be the first to tell her so.

And yet…

Didn't it feel good to have him need her?

She shoved the thought away and concentrated on the task before her, dipping hot water from the reservoir on the stove, filling a bowl, opening drawers until she found towels. She searched through them, looking for a ragged one that would serve to clean up Duke's blood. All she found was one towel that had a slight stain. She took it and a couple of others with her back to the other room.

She pulled a stool up to the sofa and carefully began to wash away the blood on Duke's face. The wound continued to bleed. With barely a hesitation that she was about to ruin a beautiful tea towel, she pressed it to the wound and held it in place while she gently washed his face.

Once the blood was cleaned from his eyelids, he opened his eyes. Aware that his gaze locked on to her face, Rose avoided meeting his eyes. She dragged the towel over the blond whiskers along his jaw to his hairline. She couldn't help noting how golden his hair was. Slowly she cleaned toward the wound and lifted the cloth. The bleeding had slowed enough she could see that it was deep, but thanks to the amount of blood he'd shed, it was clean.

"Billy, will you please get that sack of things Ma sent with me?"

He dashed away to do so.

Duke continued to stare at Rose and she tried to ignore him, keeping her eyes glued to the wound as if by doing so she might meld the edges together.

His hand wrapped around her wrist.

She jerked her attention to the hand, then slowly brought her gaze to his. Not for a moment did she doubt he was clear in his mind. So much so he threatened to mentally overwhelm her. She couldn't pull away from his gaze, couldn't talk reason to herself.

He smiled somewhat crookedly as if his mouth hurt. "I'm glad you're here." His hand fell to his chest and his eyes closed.

"Duke, wake up. Don't you dare fall asleep." Ma had taught her well. If he slept, he could easily slip into unconsciousness and from there to—

He was not going to Heaven today. Not if she had anything to say about it.

Cool fingers brushed his cheek. The touch pushed back the thick fog that threatened to enclose him.

"Duke, wake up. Stay awake."

The voice seemed concerned. He tried to think about how to reassure the person. Who was it? Rose Bell. He smiled and fought his way to the surface.

"What are you doing here?" His tongue staggered under the weight of the words.

"Open your eyes."

"Okay." Easier said than done.

"Duke, open them."

She sounded as though she cared. He must be dreaming. "I am."

She chuckled. The sound tumbled through his brain. More evidence this was only a dream. "And yet they are still closed. Come on, I need to see your eyes."

"They're blue." His voice sounded thick even to his own befuddled brain.

She chuckled again.

He had to see if this was a dream or if she was actually there, so he raised his eyebrows in an attempt to force his eyelids up. The simple movement hurt. "Ow." His eyes opened and he stared into a beautiful, concerned face. "Hi."

Her smile fled. Or had he only dreamed it in the first place?

"You've got a nasty gash on your forehead."

"I can feel it clear to my toes." He watched emotions flit across her face as she leaned closer to look at his head. First, concern and then worry. Worry? Rose Bell worried about Duke Caldwell? It didn't seem possible. Her gaze returned to his and he caught a flash of something he almost believed to be tenderness. For him? Hardly. The Bells were known for helping the sick and injured. That's all it was.

A tiny grin tugged at her lips and amusement filled her eyes. "Your handsome face will be forever marred."

"I can live with that."

"You're fortunate to be alive." Her eyes snapped with anger. "Why are you riding a wild horse around the country? Don't you know you might have been killed?"

He was caught in the green flare from her eyes.

"Seems you should be happy about that. You haven't exactly thrown out the welcome mat to me."

Her expression slowly hardened, grew impassive.

He missed being able to read her emotions.

She sat back and pulled her hands to her lap. "That doesn't mean I want to see you dead."

"Good to know." His eyelids drifted closed.

"Duke, don't you dare go to sleep."

He answered without opening his eyes. "Doesn't seem like I'm going to get a chance with you constantly calling my name."

He heard footsteps and then a worried voice. "Here it is. Is he alive?"

Duke opened his eyes to see Billy hand Rose a sack. "I'm okay, Billy. Don't you worry. It will take more than a skittish horse to kill me."

Rose pursed her lips. Her disapproval of his horse was evident.

Billy patted Duke's arm. "I prayed and prayed and prayed ever since you got hurt. God helped me."

Duke's mind cleared enough for him to remember trying to find his way home. "How did I get here? And what are you doing here?" he asked Rose.

"Billy came to the farm to get my help."

It took a moment to digest this information. "You came?"

She pulled back. "I'd never refuse to help anyone in trouble."

He held her gaze. "Anyone? Even a Caldwell?"

She nodded. "Even you."

"Ouch. You make it sound as though that's the worst possible thing ever."

Her expression softened again. "I'm sorry. I didn't

mean it that way." She opened the sack and pulled out bandages and a tiny jar. "I'm going to fix your cut as best I can." She considered it. "I suppose I could sew it up."

He laughed but cut it off as pain ripped through his head. "Never mind sewing anything unless it involves fabric."

The gust of air she released told him she was happy not to have that option. And yet she'd offered. What a strange woman she was.

She pulled the stool closer and gently stroked his hair back from his forehead.

He closed his eyes as a thousand sensations of pleasure and delight flooded his skin and tingled in his fingertips. This feeling was new. And not unwelcome. In fact—

"Ouch."

"Sorry. But I need to pull the edges as close together as I can."

"Don't hurt him." Billy sounded about ready to cry.

"It's okay," Duke assured him. "It hardly hurts at all. I just wasn't prepared."

"I should have warned you. Now I'm going to put a dressing in place to hold it." She bent over him, her scent bringing to mind summer pastures filled with wildflowers. Her touch was gentle yet firm. Not unlike the lady herself.

"There. That will keep it for now."

"Thanks." His voice came from a long distance.

"Duke, you must stay awake."

Why must I? "You'll stay?" He pulled the words from the fog.

"Until I'm sure you're okay."

So long as she was there, he'd be safe. And he let the fog drift closer.

A faint breeze, a sense of aloneness, forced his eyes open. "Rose?"

She stood by the sofa. "Billy, stay with him while I clean up these things. And keep him awake."

Billy perched on the stool that Rose had vacated and patted Duke's hand. "You'll be okay now. Rose fixed you up good. I knowed she would. That's why I got her to help."

Duke grunted a time or two to indicate he listened as Billy rattled on and on, but he barely heard a word the man said. His thoughts had followed Rose to the kitchen. Would she leave without saying goodbye? The thought of being alone except for the frightened Billy sent his pulse into a fury.

From the depths of his heart he prayed. *God, please convince her to stay.*

Chapter Four

Rose stood in the middle of the kitchen, her hand pressed to her throat. What was there about this place, this situation, about Duke, that unraveled her thoughts until she could hardly remember who she was?

She went to the stove and lifted the kettle. It was full of water. A cup of tea would set her to rights. She pushed wood into the stove and stirred up the fire. While she waited for the kettle to boil, she searched for tea. Every cupboard she opened increased the tightness in her head. Would she be accused of snooping? But Mrs. Caldwell was away, so she wouldn't know. Still, Rose's sense of intrusion increased.

As did her growing awareness of the vast difference between her as a Bell and Duke, a Caldwell.

She found a canister of tea and a fine china teapot and closed the cupboards firmly and with a sigh of relief.

She warmed the pot, then measured out a handful of tea leaves and added the boiling water.

A good look around the kitchen gave her cause to think that Duke didn't cook for himself. The place was far too tidy. Did Billy cook for them? Did a housekeeper come in and prepare meals? Or did they go over to the long building down near the barn she took for the cookhouse?

Duke would never make it that far in his present condition.

She poured tea into three matching teacups, put them on a serving tray and carried it to the other room.

Billy jumped up as she entered the room. "I'd of helped if you called."

"Thank you, Billy, but I managed fine." She set the tray on the nearest table. "I thought tea might hit the spot."

Duke pushed himself upright, grimacing.

She hurried to his side. "Lie back."

"Can't drink tea lying down."

She could practically hear his teeth creak from the way he clenched them.

He swung his feet to the floor and gave her a lop-sided grin. "I'm fine. Really."

She stood in front of him, her hands planted on her hips. "About as fine as snow in July." It was on the tip of her tongue to say being a Caldwell didn't make him impervious, but the pain and determination in his face made her hold back her words. Instead she almost commended him for the strength he showed.

He lifted his face to her. "I believe I'll have that tea now. Thank you." His crooked smile made her grin.

"Yes, sir." She carried a cup to him and hovered close as he took it. The tea sloshed so wildly, she caught his hands to steady them.

His eyes bored into hers.

A part of herself broke free and seemed to float

above her as she looked into his eyes and held his hands. If only…

"You must find it hard to do this."

"Do what?" His voice settled her wandering mind.

"Coddle me."

"Am I doing that?" Her words came out soft and sweet, from a place within her she normally saved for family. "Seems to me all I'm doing is helping a neighbor in need."

"It's nice we can now be friendly neighbors."

This was not the time to point out that friendly neighbors did not open gates and let animals out.

Duke lowered his gaze, freeing her from its silent hold. He sipped the tea. "You're right. This is just what I needed. I'm feeling better already." He indicated he wanted to put the cup and saucer on the stool at his knees. "I haven't thanked you for rescuing me. Thank you." He smiled.

She noticed his eyes looked clearer. He was feeling better. The tea had been a good idea.

"You're welcome." She could barely pull away from his gaze. Why did he have this power over her? It had to be the brightness of those blue eyes…

What was she doing? She had to stop this. Resolved to not be trapped by his look, she pulled her gaze away and managed to gather her wits about her. "Do you have a housekeeper coming in to make your meals?"

When he didn't answer right away, she clarified, "I ask because if you've been taking your meals at the cookhouse, I don't think you'll make it tonight."

Billy answered. "The cowboys eat at the cookhouse." His voice lowered. "They stare at me."

That didn't exactly answer her question. What were they doing for meals?

Billy brightened. "I like it best when we go away and have a campfire. Duke knows how to cook lots of things over the fire."

Her eyebrows rose. "Is that a fact?"

"Yup. He showed me how to do biscuits on a stick."

Duke leaned his head back on the sofa. "Don't look so surprised, Rose. I'm a lot handier than you think."

She forced her expression into blandness when she looked at him. "I doubt you know what I think."

"I'm guessing you think I'm a useless, spoiled rich kid."

"Hmm." Let him believe that. Far better than knowing the truth that she wished she could go camping with them to see him make biscuits on a stick.

His mouth tightened. He closed his eyes as if to hide his hurt from her.

She'd rubbed some ointment on the edges of the wound that should relieve some of the pain, but remnants always crept through. "You should take it easy."

"What do you call what I'm doing?" His words were lazy but she didn't miss the edge of pain.

She made up her mind. "There's no way you are going to make it to the cookhouse. Nor are you in any shape to be cooking over a campfire. If you'll allow me, I'll prepare a meal for you."

That brought his eyes open in a hurry.

"If you don't object to me doing so," she added.

"Object? I'd be forever grateful."

Billy grinned from ear to ear. "Can we eat in the

kitchen?" He slanted a look at Duke. "I kind of don't like the dining room."

Duke chuckled softly. "I'd enjoy eating in the kitchen, myself."

"Then it's decided." Rose gathered up the teacups and tray and marched back to the kitchen to stare around. She didn't know where anything was, or what sort of staples a place like this would have, but from peeking in the few cupboards she'd opened looking for the tea, she guessed anything she needed would be available. She'd make something simple that would be easy for Duke to eat.

Ma's potato soup could never go wrong and Billy's story of biscuits on a stick helped her decide on biscuits to accompany it.

She found a bin full of potatoes and was removing some when Duke, leaning on Billy's shoulder, came into the room. She straightened and favored the man with a scolding look. "What happened to the part about taking it easy?"

He pulled out a chair from the table and sat. "There. I'm taking it easy."

Billy sat beside him. "Duke wanted to watch you cooking. He said there's nothing prettier than a gal in the kitchen."

Duke rolled his eyes. "Billy, I didn't mean for you to repeat that."

Billy lowered his head. "I'm sorry. I'm stupid."

Duke gave him a playful punch on the shoulder. "Billy, you aren't stupid. And don't you forget it."

Billy sucked in a long breath. "If you say so."

Rose turned away to hide her expression. Her admiration for the way Duke dealt with Billy left her struggling for equilibrium.

"Billy Boy," he said, "I fear the horses are still tied at the rail. Would you take care of them, please?"

Billy set out on the task immediately.

"Billy seems an odd friend for you." Rose kept her attention on peeling the potatoes as she spoke, but she couldn't resist darting a glance at Duke to see his reaction.

He wiped a hand across his face. If she wasn't mistaken, he tried to remove regret. Regret from Duke Caldwell? It didn't seem possible.

"Billy said you saved his life. Sounds as though he tried to drown himself."

"It was my fault." The agony in Duke's voice brought her attention to him.

Her heart twisted at the look on his face. "What did you do?" she whispered.

"I stood by while so-called friends teased him."

The horror ground through her insides. "Let me guess. They called him stupid?"

"Among other things." Each word seemed to scrape from inside him. "They were very cruel. To be fair, I was on my way to some silly play and I didn't think I had time to stop and tell them to leave him be. I should have."

"Oh, poor Billy."

Duke wiped his hand across his face once more.

"He tried to drown himself because of what they said?"

Duke's gaze clung to her, full of despair and sorrow. She pressed her hand to her chest in a vain attempt to quench the same emotions rising within her. "You rescued him?"

Duke nodded.

"He saved me." Neither of them had heard Billy re-enter the room. He rushed to Duke's side and hugged him. The movement caused Duke to flinch with pain but he patted Billy's back and smiled.

Billy continued, "He almost drowned, too. You're a good man, Duke."

A silent communication passed between Rose and Duke. She understood what he hadn't said. He saw only his failure in not intervening when he could have.

She wanted to grip his shoulder and say his good deed cancelled out his failure. Instead she turned her attention back to the meal preparations.

Who was he? Truly? A manipulator who said the feud was over when it obviously wasn't. A hero who almost drowned rescuing someone weaker than him in every way.

He was a curious mixture of strength and vulnerability. Could he be both at the same time? What was she to believe?

Was he a feuding neighbor, the arrogant son of the rich rancher?

Or a kind, noble man?

She tried to dismiss the questions. What difference did it make to her? She had only come because he'd been injured and Ma had taught all the girls to never refuse to help a sick or injured person.

Apart from that, she was Rose Bell and he, Duke Caldwell. That was all she needed to know about him.

But her fierce admonitions did not stop the churning of her thoughts.

* * *

Duke had confessed his shame. She'd understandably been shocked and had turned away to prepare a pot of soup. Why had he let her see his weak side?

His only explanation was that his head hurt, making it hard to think straight.

Rose filled the soup pot and mixed up a batch of biscuits and popped them in the oven.

Putting aside his regret over confessing his sin of omission regarding Billy, he sat back and enjoyed watching Rose flit around the kitchen. His mother didn't cook. Back east all the meals had come from the kitchen, prepared by a cook and served in a dining room. When Mrs. Humphrey prepared meals in this room he'd only been allowed to watch. Hence, cooking over the open fire had been learned by trial and error. Being able to share the kitchen with a young woman was a new experience. One, he decided, he quite enjoyed.

Rose brushed strands of hair out of her face. She wore her red hair in a braid down her back and it danced in sunshiny waves as she moved.

"Billy's right," he murmured half to himself. "Your hair is pretty."

She ground to a halt and slowly came around to face him, her eyes narrow and challenging. She held the big stirring spoon like a weapon.

He held up both hands in a gesture of retreat. "Hey, it's a compliment."

Slowly the spoon was lowered. "Thanks," she mumbled.

Billy went to her side. "How come you don't like people saying your hair is nice?"

"Mostly because they don't mean it." She kept her back to both of them.

"I mean it." Billy sounded hurt.

"I know you do."

Duke waited, hoping and wishing she might turn to him and say the same thing. When she didn't he couldn't leave it alone. "I mean it, too."

She stiffened. Then she slowly set the spoon on the cupboard and turned to face him. "'Redhead redhead, fire in the woodshed.' Remember that? I do."

Her accusation ripped through him like a tornado, twisting, turning, filling him with tangled regret. He pushed to his feet, ignoring the dizziness, and crossed to her. He longed to touch her, to smooth her hair, to assure her in so many ways. "I was a foolish kid who didn't know how to express his admiration."

"Admiration?" Her eyes dripped disbelief. "For what?"

"Your hair is beautiful. You are beautiful."

Her eyebrows reached for her hairline.

In for a penny, in for a dollar. He might as well say it all. "You are about the kindest, wisest woman I've met."

She snorted. "Haven't met many women, have you?"

He grinned. "Met some." Indeed he'd met a lot of young women while back east. "None of whom would rescue an injured man. None who would likewise prepare him a meal. Rose Bell, you are something special." He had the satisfaction of seeing pleasure flicker through her eyes before he returned to his seat.

Let her muse on that a while, he thought.

Billy chuckled. "Duke sure does like you, Rose."

Rose jerked around and stirred the soup rather vigorously. "He hit his head too hard."

A few minutes later she put two bowls on the table.

He caught her wrist. "Which one of us isn't eating?"

She didn't pull away but her face revealed a wealth of confusion. "I made the meal for you and Billy. I'll ride on home." She glanced out the window. "It will soon be dark."

He looked out the window, too. "You have time to eat with us before you go. Billy and I will do the dishes so we don't keep you."

She glanced around as if seeking escape or excuse.

"Please eat with us, Rose."

Not until she nodded did he release her wrist.

She scurried to the cupboard for another bowl. Put it on the table then ladled out soup and set out a plate of golden biscuits.

She hesitated only a moment before she sat in the chair opposite Duke. Only then did she lift her eyes to him.

He smiled at the expectant guardedness of her expression. "I'll ask the blessing."

She bowed her head and he did likewise. His heart was so filled with gratitude that his throat tightened and his words came out husky.

"God, bless this food. Bless those who share it at this meal. Thank You for Your many blessings. Amen." Silently he added thanks for Billy, for Rose and for being safe at home with only a minor cut on his head. And for Rose being willing to share his table.

"Amen," Rose and Billy echoed.

They were quiet a few moments as the biscuits were passed and the soup tested.

"That is so good." Duke indicated the soup. "You'll have to give me the recipe."

Rose stared. "Why would I do that?"

He shrugged. "Maybe Billy and I will make it our-selves."

Rose leaned closer. "I could tell you but then Ma would come after you with a fry pan and demand you forget you ever heard her secret ingredient." She nod-ded with a hint of warning in her eyes. "So for your sake, I better not."

He stared at her. Beside him, Billy shifted in his chair.

"Duke, you might get hurt."

Duke knew she was joshing him but decided to play along. He widened his eyes in fake surprise. "But... but—" A sputter or two would help convince her that he bought her story. "I saw you prepare the soup. I saw what you put in." He'd watched all right, but his atten-tion had been on the cook, not the ingredients. He gave a shudder that he hoped seemed real. "I can hardly for-get what I saw. Can I?"

Billy pushed his chair back and sat forward, prepar-ing to run.

Duke rested a hand on Billy's arm. "Don't worry. I don't think anyone is going to hurt us." Time to end this farce. "In fact..." He leaned over the table and fixed Rose with a narrow-eyed look. "I remember your mother as a kind, gentle soul. I'm quite certain she'd never threaten to hurt me."

Rose blinked and then amusement flooded her eyes. She leaned back and laughed. "I thought I had you wor-ried but you were only teasing."

Billy let out a gust of air. "You were teasing?" he asked Duke.

"We both were," Rose said. "Sorry if we worried you, Billy."

Billy looked from Duke to Rose and back again, confusion wreathing his features. Then his expression cleared and he nodded. "That's how my friend, Andy, acted around his girl."

Rose's grin fled. "It's not like that."

Duke's pride nose-dived at her quick denial. Then it rebounded. Had she responded too quickly, as if afraid, or surprised, at the truth in Billy's words? He grinned at the idea but said nothing.

Instead he talked about how glad he was to be back in Montana. "I didn't much care for city life."

She nodded, though he wondered if she was even listening to him.

He tucked a secret smile inside. Perhaps even now she was wondering if there could be a hint of attraction between them.

A few minutes later, Rose glanced across the table. "Are you finished?" At his nod, she started to gather up the dishes.

He waved her away. "I said Billy and I would clean up."

She nodded and sank back, her gaze on the dressing on his forehead. "You really should be resting."

"I'll be fine." He didn't get to his feet, knowing dizziness would assault him.

With an uncertain nod, she pushed away from the table and rose. "Then I'll be on my way." But she stood there watching him.

He lifted his gaze to hers and had to blink at the concern darkening her eyes. "Rose, I'm fine. Thank you for everything. Rescuing me. Taking care of me…" His throat tightened at all she'd done. Perhaps it was only out of duty and concern for mankind, but her touch, her concern, her smile all wound through his heart with the feel of a personal gift. "And for the delicious meal." When he said the last words, a thought struck him and he laughed.

She blinked. "The meal was funny?"

He sobered but amusement made his words round and pleasant on his tongue. "Normally a guy takes a gal out for a special dinner. At least that's been my experience. But this has been the nicest dinner I've ever shared with a gal."

"And you expect me to believe that after you've spent a year in Philadelphia?"

"It's true. Guess it's the company that makes the difference."

"More likely it's the bang on your head that has scrambled your thoughts."

He had never been more certain of anything despite the throbbing of his wound.

She slipped into her coat and stuffed her hair under a big hat.

Why did she cover her hair? He wanted to yank the hat from her head.

She turned. Something in his look made her hands grow still.

The air between them filled with a wealth of things that needed to be said.

"Rose—" But words were not adequate.

She turned her back and reached for the door handle. "I must go. Goodbye." She fled the room. Billy had left her horse tied to the rail. Within seconds the thud of hooves rattled through his head.

He rubbed his chin. Why did she remain so prickly when he'd succeeded in getting Father to end the feud?

Did she find him unlikeable?

He considered how often she'd blushed while talking to him, how her eyes had locked on his and then skittered away.

He would not believe she found him unappealing.

Chapter Five

Rose sat in front of the mirror. She undid the braid that held her hair and let her locks fall across her shoulders. Waves of red dulled in the low lamplight. She began to brush her hair.

Billy admired the red color.

Duke said he did, too. She tended to believe him because of the way his eyes had flickered with admiration. But his words didn't unknot the tension she felt every time her hair was mentioned. She hated her hair. People constantly made comments about it.

She brushed mindlessly, letting scenes from the day flit through her mind.

Billy's loyalty to Duke.

The way Duke had clung to her as she'd tended his wound. She smiled at her reflection. Had she ever imagined she'd be needed or wanted by a Caldwell?

Her hands grew idle as she continued to stare at herself.

Okay, she'd at least tell herself the truth. There was something about Duke that intrigued her. Perhaps it was only a need to find out how sincere he was.

Or perhaps it went deeper than that. There was something in his probing gaze that touched a spot deep within her, like the gentle strumming of a guitar string. It sang soft and quiet in her heart. What would it be like to hear it wild and exuberant? Her pulse beat faster as if fueled by the beat of a drum.

She set her brush aside and braided her hair for the night. She was Rose, the practical sister who meant to stay home and care for her parents. Where did thoughts of wild and exuberant belong?

In someone else's life, to be sure.

In bed, she picked up her Bible to read a chapter as she'd done since Ma and Pa had given the girls each a Bible of their own when they were twelve years old. On the flyleaf of each Bible, Ma had written a verse and blessing for each of the girls.

Rose looked at the well-worn page. The verse Ma had chosen for her was Psalm 139:14: "I will praise Thee: for I am fearfully and wonderfully made."

She sighed at the words Ma had written.

Rose, my beautiful flower, I pray for you to continually walk in the joy of who God has made you to be.

Some days she rejoiced in who she was. She loved her family and her life on the farm. The work brought her deep satisfaction.

But she had to confess that she didn't always experience that contentment. Sometimes she questioned why God had given her red hair, why He had allowed her to be born into a family that abandoned her. Still, she never ended that thought without a prayer of gratitude for Ma and Pa adopting them.

She read a chapter and turned out the light to say her prayers. *God, keep my feet on a straight path. Guide me to make wise choices.*

Duke simply did not belong in that prayer.

Her thoughts settled. Duke was a neighbor who'd needed help. Whether good neighbor or bad, it made no difference. She was foolish to think there could be more. She would not be so unwise as to let her emotions get involved.

"Morning, Ma. Morning, Pa," she called as she hurried from the bedroom the next day. She tramped to the barn, shivering in the cold to feed the animals. She pulled the collar of her coat closer against the winter wind.

She sang as she did the chores, then returned to the house. No cows were milking now, but they had frozen milk to use throughout the winter. They had a good supply of butter stored in the garden shed, as well.

"You're cheerful this morning," Ma said as Rose joined them for breakfast.

"What's not to be happy about?" She grinned at both parents, happy to see Pa sitting at the table. "I have two wonderful parents, a barn full of healthy animals, storerooms full of produce and the snow has held off." It had snowed heavily after Christmas but only drifts remained. "God is good."

"Amen." Pa reached for her hand and she reached for Ma's as Pa said grace, adding his thanks for the many blessings of their lives.

After breakfast, as she helped Ma with dishes, Rose

grew thoughtful. "I think I should go check on Duke. That cut was deep. It could get infected."

Ma gave her a long, considering look. "Yes, I suppose you should."

"Don't stay long," Pa said. "It could snow. I feel it in my bones."

Pa's bones had gotten real accurate at forecasting the weather.

"I'll be back long before dark." Her return depended on what she found when she got to the Caldwell Ranch.

Ma handed her some medicinals. "Just in case."

She saddled up, wrapped a warm woolen scarf around her neck and rode to the ranch. A man was feeding the horses but other than that, she saw little sign of activity. No doubt the cowboys had gone out to check the cows. She knew from previous years that the cows were herded down to lower pastures for the winter and the cowboys herded them to keep them closer to home.

No one appeared at the door as she rode up. Her nerves tensed. Hadn't they heard her? Or was Duke feverish?

Her heart kicked into a gallop at how sick he might be. Pausing only to slip the reins around the hitching post, she hurried to the door and knocked.

No one called out an answer.

She sniffed. Did she smell smoke? Was that smoke drifting beneath the door? It was. She threw the door back and coughed at the gray billows greeting her.

Duke and Billy stood at the stove. Duke fiddled with the damper while Billy wrung his hands.

"Are you on fire?" she called, her voice full of the same fear that burned along her nerves.

They both turned to face her. Tears ran down Billy's

cheeks. She couldn't tell if he was crying or if his eyes watered from the smoke. Her eyes stung and started to tear. She coughed and waved her hands to chase the smoke from the room.

Duke's eyes watered, as well. "Guess the damper wasn't open." He barely squeezed the words past his coughing.

"It's my fault. I'm so stupid," Billy wailed.

"You were only trying to help." Duke patted him on the shoulder. "No harm done." He dragged Billy toward the door and pushed him and Rose out into the fresh air. "Let's wait for the smoke to disappear." He turned to confront Billy. "You are not stupid and I don't want to hear it again."

"Yes, Boss." Billy hung his head. He sniffed and wiped his face on his sleeve. Then he glanced at Rose. "Do you think I'm stupid?"

Her heart ached for the pain this young man had endured because he was different than most his age. "Oh, Billy, you aren't stupid in the least. You're helpful and kind. Even the animals recognize that and you know they're real smart about people."

"They are, aren't they?" He wiped at his face again, leaving streaks. "I'll try not to be stupid again." He went to Hope and pressed his face to the animal's head. "You're a nice horse. Why do you call her Hope?"

Rose smiled at him. "Five years ago someone brought us this colt that had been injured. They said we could have him if we saved him. Ma took a look at his injuries and how thin and unhealthy he was and shook her head. I knew she thought he was a lost cause. I don't know how many times I said, 'It isn't hopeless.' And it wasn't." She lifted one shoulder. "So when he grew up big and strong, we called him Hope."

Billy laughed. "He's a nice horse."

Rose nodded. "He's a very good horse."

Duke pulled a handkerchief from his pocket and wiped his eyes. "Didn't expect to see you." He sounded less than welcoming.

Had she expected he would be eager to see her?

She pulled herself up tall but it was hard to appear distant and unconcerned when her eyes stung and her lungs burned. "I thought I should check on your wound. Just being neighborly." She added the latter lest he get the notion she was doing anything out of the ordinary.

He leaned over and coughed until she thought his lungs would come out.

"That's going to start you bleeding again if it hasn't already." She pushed him toward one of the porch chairs. "Take it easy."

He sucked in air slowly and managed to take a breath without coughing.

"That's better. Now you sit here while I go check the kitchen." Most of the smoke had drifted outdoors. She opened a window by the stove to clear the last of the acrid air. She found a potholder and lifted the lid on the stove. They'd used way too much wood. If it began to burn it would overheat the stove and maybe start a real fire that might get out of control. She grabbed the potholder and pulled the top pieces out, dropping them in the ash pail. Thankfully, they hadn't even started to smolder.

In a few minutes she had a merry little fire going. Soon the room would warm up. She closed the window and turned to call the others in so she could shut the door.

"I was going to make breakfast," Billy said.

"Good for you. That was a nice idea. What were you going to make?"

"I can make porridge."

"Good. You get started while I look at Duke's head." If they stayed in the kitchen, she could supervise Billy without being obvious about it.

Duke turned a chair to face her and sat. "My head is just fine."

Billy giggled. "That's 'cause he has a hard head."

Rose laughed at his humor.

Duke groaned. "Don't you start picking on me."

Billy's expression changed so suddenly Rose stared. "I would never pick on you. Never ever ever." He rushed to Duke's side. "Please. I'm sorry."

Duke caught Billy's fluttering hands. "I was joshing. It was a good joke. Didn't you think so, Rose?"

Rose nodded. "One of the best. I really enjoyed it. How smart of you to notice that Duke has a hard head."

Smiling, Billy returned to the cupboard where he meticulously measured water into a pot and just as carefully measured oats. Seems someone had taught him that task well.

Duke touched the back of Rose's hand, bringing her attention back to him. "It was a good joke but don't enjoy it too much. I might take it personal."

Their gazes locked as she recalled how he'd teased her when they were young.

He looked right into her heart as if he saw and understood. "I'm sorry," he whispered. "I only wanted to get your attention."

Her fingers trembled. She jerked her gaze from his. Why would he need or want her attention? He was a Caldwell. He usually had people laughing at his jokes and encouraging his sometimes rash behavior.

Why did his confession leave her so shaken? "Let me look at that wound." She had to unwrap the bandage. It required that she lean close to Duke. It meant nothing, she told herself. She was only tending a wounded neighbor.

But never before had her fingers trembled. Or her muscles twitched. Nor had she ever before had this delicious yet frightening awareness of touching someone.

She clenched her teeth. *Stop being so foolish. You've helped with head wounds before.* Yes, on old Mr. Angus and four-year-old Sonny and two school boys. Never on a man who had her thoughts as scrambled as a broken egg.

She edged closer to him. Felt the warmth of his body and the smell of smoke so strong she barely managed to stop a cough. With firm fingers, she slowly unwrapped the bandage. The wound had bled in the night and the bandage was stuck. "I'll have to soak this to get it off." If she ripped it free she would likely start the wound bleeding again. She filled a dish with warm water and pulled another towel from the cupboard. Perhaps she should take the soiled ones home and wash them.

As she returned to the table, she stumbled against a chair leg and Duke caught her at the waist to steady her.

Something inside her wrenched at his touch. She couldn't move. Couldn't talk. Couldn't think. What was wrong with her? This, she reminded herself firmly, was Duke Caldwell. Douglas Caldwell, she corrected herself, hoping to put distance between them. With a sinking sensation she realized she neither thought of him as such nor called him by that name anymore. But never mind if she called him Duke or Douglas. She only wanted to see if his head was okay.

Above all, she had no intention of letting her heart be affected by tending him.

He was a Caldwell. She was a Bell. He was rich. She was not. They came from different spheres. Nothing could change that.

Her heart must understand.

He slowly released her and dropped his hands to his knees. He'd been aware of her quick intake of air, the stiffening of her muscles. Did she object to his touch or had it seared through her thoughts as it had his?

Even with his hands pressed hard to his knees, he couldn't shake off the way his insides had lurched.

He tried to bring his thoughts into focus but with Rose so close at his side he felt her in every pore. She filled every thought.

Even past the sharp smell of the recent smoke in the kitchen he caught a familiar scent of wildflowers and fresh hay. Rose's own delightful perfume. He recalled how it had caught at his senses when he'd passed her in church or in the store or had the pleasure of sitting next to her at a church social.

Her cool fingers brushed his forehead as she pressed a damp cloth to his dressing.

He closed his eyes against the sweet torture of her touch. Even welcomed the sharp pain as she pulled the last of the bandage free.

"It looks not too bad." She sounded both cautious and hopeful.

He chortled. "Not too bad? Is that good or do you mean it could be worse?"

"Exactly." No mistaking the teasing in her voice.

"You're saying I'll live?"

Her fingers stilled. No answer came.

Even though he dreaded to see that she might regret the fact, he turned to look into her face and his thoughts stalled.

She blinked as if trying to hide her expression, but he'd seen enough to want to shout victory and joy.

He knew without a doubt that he'd caught a flash of some emotion so deep, so foreign, that it startled her.

As it did him.

And why should he exult in such knowledge?

It was beyond understanding.

"You'll live." Her voice was gravelly. "For good or ill, you'll live."

Did he detect a tremor in her words?

She grabbed a fresh bandage and moved behind him to rewrap his wound, but he caught her wrist and forced her to face him.

"Good or ill? What's that supposed to mean? It sounds like you see me as a bad egg. Is that true? Is that how you see me?"

She lowered her gaze, refusing to look at him. "You overlook the fact I also said for good. Isn't the choice yours?"

He released her wrist. "I persuaded my father to end the land feud. Does that not prove I'm a good person?" He wished he didn't sound so needy but, oh, how he ached for her to see him for who he was—a simple man with simple needs. He wanted home, love, and to be valued for himself. Not valued because he was a Caldwell.

Nor devalued for the same reason.

She shifted so she stood behind him and he couldn't see her expression. "The gates were all opened yesterday and the animals were all out."

How did that involve him? Then it hit him what she meant. "You suspect someone did it intentionally? You think I'm lying about ending the feud." He let bitterness drip from every word. After her visit yesterday he'd allowed himself to believe she viewed him differently.

He thought she cared about him. He maybe cared about her just a little, as well.

Hadn't he vowed to guard his heart?

After a moment's pause Rose answered. "I guess it will take more than words."

He threw his hands into the air in defeat. "Am I to be held responsible for everything that goes wrong at your place? That hardly seems fair."

She wrapped the bandage around his head, her gentle touch at such odds with her harsh judgment of him.

Done, she came around to face him, her eyes as dark as the winter spruce outdoors. "It's complicated." She swallowed hard.

He sensed her struggle to explain herself and hardly dared breathe, afraid to move or to speak lest he cause this fragile moment to crash into splinters at his feet.

"I'd like to believe you. Nothing would make me happier than to see the feud over. But the gates didn't accidentally fall down." She challengingly held his gaze.

He struggled to find an explanation. "It has to be someone else. Father told the cowboys the feud was over."

She grabbed the soiled dressing and hurried across

the room. She put away her things, scrubbed her hands and turned to help Billy at the stove.

"Why, that looks perfect," she said. "Billy, who taught you to make porridge?"

"My aunt Hilda. I lived with her for some time." He forgot about stirring the pot and stared at the wall behind the stove. "I can't remember how long."

Rose patted Billy's shoulder. "Well, thanks to Aunt Hilda's lessons and your good memory, you are about to enjoy a hearty breakfast. Why don't you put out some of those biscuits that were left from last night while I dish up the porridge?"

Billy hurried to do her bidding as Rose pulled out two bowls.

"Two?" Duke said. "I count three people."

Rose kept her attention on spooning porridge into the bowls. "I ate before I left home."

If he wasn't mistaken, she avoided looking at him. "Then have coffee with us."

"I don't drink coffee."

"Then we'll have tea. I know you drink tea." He didn't want her to leave. "My head might start to bleed again. Then what will I do?"

That brought her attention to him. "No reason it should unless you do something foolish." Her green eyes flashed with challenge.

"You half think I would, don't you?" He narrowed his eyes and silently challenged her.

She grew very interested in scraping the sides of the pot. "Well, there is that horse of yours."

"It was my fault. I wasn't paying attention and with King I have to keep my mind on what I'm doing."

"What distracted you?"

"I can't rightly recall." He knew his gaze was a mite sheepish. She'd never guess the truth that his thoughts had been on visiting her.

"I see." A slight widening of her eyes caused him to think she knew exactly where his thoughts had been. Did he detect a hint of color staining her cheeks? His chest swelled to think he might have been the cause.

Emboldened, he asked, "Rose, would you please stay and have tea with us?"

Their gazes caught and held. And for that one brief space of a heartbeat there was no one else. No expectations from parents. No feud between the families. Just he and Rose and a world of possibility.

"I'll make some while you and Billy eat." But she didn't move. Dare he hope she was as imprisoned by the moment as he?

Chapter Six

Rose could see her hands at the end of her arms but she couldn't feel them. She couldn't make them move. Her feet, too, refused to budge from the spot. Her thoughts were so tangled she couldn't grab a single one and follow it to an end.

He'd been thinking of her when his horse tossed him? Not that he'd come right out and said so, but she knew she wasn't mistaken in understanding his meaning. And why did she have the distinct impression that his thoughts had been pleasant?

Billy sat at her elbow. "I'm hungry."

His words jolted her into action. She spun away and returned to the cupboard. As she put the pot to warm, she fought for control of the confusing storm of her emotions. How could she reconcile his interest in her with the continuing feud? Had it simply been a last final act like cowboys thumbing their nose at the Bells? If only she dared to believe it.

Would she then be able to let her heart have its way?

Duke said grace and the two of them started their meal while she sloshed the hot water around the inside of the china teapot. A spray of painted roses circled the fat belly of the fine china pot. Gold trimmed the lid and handle. She stared at the fancy vessel. This was their everyday teapot? No doubt they had a sterling-silver one for finer occasions.

She put the pot on the cupboard and dropped her hands to her sides. What if she dropped this fine piece of china and broke it? What if she chipped a cup? She'd never considered herself clumsy but then again, she'd never handled anything but plain dishes. Don't be so foolish, she chided herself. It was just a teapot and likely nothing special to the Caldwells or it wouldn't be in the kitchen cupboard. She only had to make tea as she did so often she could do it with her eyes closed.

But she kept them wide open and took extra care.

She reasoned that all these fine things and this unfamiliar kitchen had overstimulated her senses, causing her to think, even believe, things that had no basis in fact.

For instance Duke had not said thoughts of her had distracted him.

She'd only imagined a warm look in his eyes that suggested he enjoyed thinking about her.

Pshaw. She was Rose Bell, redheaded woman of uncertain heritage. Of course, he wasn't thinking of her in a pleasant way. If his thoughts had been on her at all.

She only spent time here because she was genuinely concerned that Duke's head wound not get infected. She'd never be accepted by someone like Duke and certainly never by his family. Not that she wanted to be. She would stay at home with Ma and Pa and look after them knowing her heart would be safe.

With her thoughts and emotions reined in, she carried the teapot to the table, along with the matching cups and saucers.

"I'll get the sugar," Billy said and sprang from the table. He returned with a matching sugar bowl, again trimmed with gold and filled with—

She stared.

Neat little squares of sugar. She'd heard of this Vienna sugar but to serve it at the kitchen table! This, even more than the teapot, signified the difference between her and Duke. She would do well to remember it before someone saw fit to point it out to her. Her insides shriveled—a coil pulling back from external pressure.

Duke must have sensed her withdrawal. "Is there something wrong with the tea?"

She realized she stared into the contents of her cup. Forcing a smile to her lips, she looked up. "No, nothing."

His gaze caught and held hers, and she read the truth in his eyes. He knew she didn't speak honestly. She couldn't say how she could be so certain but she knew she was correct.

"There is something wrong." His soft words dropped into her heart like sweet nectar.

He was a Caldwell, she was a Bell, she reminded herself. Forcing her gaze from his powerful look, she shifted her attention to the cupboard door—behind which stood so many fine dishes. "Nothing you'd understand." The words no sooner escaped her mouth than she wanted to yank them back. Why hadn't she said instead that it was nothing that concerned him? Or something equally dismissive.

"Try me. You might be surprised." Again, his soft words called to her heart.

Would he understand? How could he? He lived in the lap of luxury. "What was it like back east?" No doubt it was even more lavish than this ranch home.

He spent a moment stirring his porridge.

"I'm sorry," she said. "I'm keeping you from your food."

"Let me finish here, then I'll tell you about it."

"It's not important." Why had she even asked? Now she felt obligated to delay her departure so he could answer.

"I don't mind." He concentrated on his food for a moment and she drank her tea.

Billy finished his porridge and downed four biscuits with a berry jam that Rose guessed the housekeeper had made. Where was the housekeeper? She voiced the question.

Duke grinned widely. "What makes you think we need one?"

Rose slowly and deliberately looked around the room, letting her attention rest on the polished stove top, the orderly cupboards.

He laughed. "I suppose it is obvious. Mrs. Humphrey is visiting her son. I assured her we could manage quite fine without her services for a few days."

Billy looked up. "Good thing Rose came by to cook a meal for us. Say, could you make us dinner again? I really liked your soup. But it's all gone." He sounded so mournful, Rose answered without thinking.

"I'd love to make dinner for you if no one objects."

"I'd appreciate it very much," Duke said. If she wasn't mistaken he looked as happy as Billy.

Why had she promised such a thing? Yet she didn't regret it. Not yet anyway.

As soon as he finished, Billy insisted he would do the dishes. "My aunt Hilda said I was the best dish-washer ever."

Rose and Duke looked at each other and then their glances slid toward Billy.

"Where is your aunt Hilda now?" Rose asked.

Billy examined a spoon as if it held the answer. "I forget. Maybe…maybe she wasn't really my aunt and I only pretended it."

Rose glanced at Duke, her eyebrows raised, wondering if he understood what Billy meant.

Duke gave a tiny shake of his head.

She slowly brought her gaze back to Billy. "But there was an Aunt Hilda, wasn't there?" Surely he hadn't made it up, though she'd heard of children having pretend playmates and Billy wasn't much more than a child in his mind.

"She had lots of children. But I couldn't stay." He lifted his dark eyes to Rose and considered her.

"Why?" She didn't blink away from his intensity, understanding that he searched his mind and perhaps needed her silent encouragement to do so.

Finally he released a pent-up breath. "I was too big. I had to go to work for a man."

Perhaps Aunt Hilda cared for orphaned children. That would explain why he'd had to leave as he got bigger. Rose sadly acknowledged the fact that children in their own home with their own parents were also often forced to leave as they got older. Some were even abandoned at a young age. Why? The question wailed through her thoughts. She pushed it back to the depths of the dark cave within her.

Billy shook his head so hard his hair flung across his face. "I did not like that man. He did not like me. He hurt me." Billy's face wrinkled up as if the pain still existed.

"Oh, Billy. I'm so sorry." She rubbed his shoulder until he smiled.

"It's okay 'cause now I got you and Duke for friends. I like you."

"You're a good man, Billy Boy," Duke said with a gentle smack to Billy's back that made Billy's smile widen.

"You're a good man, Duke." Billy gave a manly pat to Duke's shoulder. "Now I'll do the dishes while you—" He looked around as if searching for something for Duke and Rose to do.

"Why don't you show Rose the house? That's a good thing to do." Billy carried the dirty dishes to the cupboard. "When you get back you'll see how good I do."

"Rose, can I show you around?" Duke stood at the side of the table awaiting her answer.

She hung back. "Billy, don't you want some help?"

His face creased. "Do I need it? Maybe I do."

She hadn't meant to make him think he couldn't manage on his own. "I don't expect you need any help whatsoever." Glad to see the smile return to Billy's face, she turned to Duke. "Lead the way, Mr. Caldwell." She hoped she sounded teasing but she meant the words to remind her of who she was and how much separated them.

Duke waited for her to fall in at his side and led her from the room to the one she'd been in the day before. He pulled back heavy drapes on the windows.

Light flooded the room and Rose's eyes grew wide. She'd expected heavy furniture and—

She wasn't sure what, but she surely hadn't expected this.

A bright room full of books and inviting nooks. A fire crackled in the fireplace.

Duke stood with his hands crossed over his chest, watching her reaction. "This is my favorite room in the house."

She turned full circle, pleasure growing at every detail she took in. "I can see why." She moved to his side and looked out the window. The view allowed them to see anyone approaching the ranch but also the trees to the right of the trail, their bare branches now frosted with snow. To the left, the rise and fall of the land led to the river though from here only a dark shadow indicated its place. "It's a beautiful view."

"You haven't seen the best. Come along." He led her through an archway on the far side of the room and she gasped.

"Oh, my."

He chuckled. "Nice, isn't it?"

They had entered a library. Or was it a sun porch? Though—despite all the windows—it lacked the wintery chill of a porch because of the potbellied stove to one side.

Rose couldn't resist walking along the bountiful bookshelves, reading the titles. "Have you read all these?"

"Would you believe me if I said I had?"

She studied him, unable to tell if he was serious or mocking. "I don't know. It's a lot of books." Wouldn't Pa enjoy something new to read?

"Feel free to borrow one. Or as many as you like." He tipped his head and grinned, which had a rather unsettling affect on her breathing. "I have only read a handful of them myself."

"Thank you. Pa would really enjoy a book." Should she accept this offer or did it cross one more line that she should be avoiding? Her heart called out a warning. Too often she trusted people only to discover they could as easily forget her as the snow of last winter.

She rubbed her palms along her thighs. "Maybe later."

"Don't forget." He crossed the room and again pulled aside the drapes. "Come and see the view."

Rose had been about to exit the room, not because she wasn't interested in seeing more but because she found it so incredibly appealing. She had not once thought the Caldwells would have such a beautiful home. From the dark green wood floor to the wide, wooden book shelves to the wicker chairs and blue cushions to the scattered afghans—there wasn't a thing about this room that failed to please her senses.

She couldn't resist his invitation and joined him at the window. "Oh, my." She pressed her hand to her chest.

"I agree."

It was a perfect view of snow-covered mountains and white pastures dotted with trees and cows placidly grazing.

"It's like a picture postcard."

"It's nice all right." He leaned against the window frame, watching her.

She could barely tear her gaze from the sight but neither could she stand there forever with Duke grinning at her. She knew an incredible sense of peace and contentment, which was at such odds with the tension and annoyance she normally felt around Duke. She should be alarmed. But at the moment she wasn't.

"There's more to the house." His voice rang with teasing but not in a way that stole from the moment.

She reluctantly left behind the view and followed him to a door that led to a dark hallway. To her right were wide doors to the outside—no doubt the main entry. She'd been coming in the kitchen entry, apparently.

Across the hall a door opened to the ranch office with a big mahogany desk and leather furniture. This room was what she'd expected from the house—dark, forbidding and full of shadows.

Duke didn't invite her into the room but led her down the hall and pushed open double pocket doors. "The dining room." He stepped aside to let her enter.

She wasn't sure what to make of this room. In the center was a large table of gleaming, dark wood on which someone had placed a white runner with a pattern of intricate cutwork and a basket of bright red and silver balls. Leftovers from Christmas perhaps? A huge sideboard held a silver tea service. Windows looked out on the same mountain scene from the other room, though most of the view was obscured by heavy drapes partially drawn. This room provided another reminder of the difference between the Caldwells and the Bells. She would do well to sear the picture into her brain.

A narrow door beside the sideboard revealed a tiny pantry with a door she knew would connect to the kitchen. She crossed to stand in the pantry. Safe in the servants' quarters. She had half a mind to slip through the connecting door, back to the kitchen. A sigh passed her teeth. Had she forgotten Duke offered to show her the house? She was a guest. She had every right to be here.

Determination and resolve in place, she turned and considered the dining room again, trying to assess her feeling. It was large and formal yet not unfriendly.

Duke stood in front of her, looking into her face. "What's wrong?"

"Nothing. But I can't decide what to think of this room. I loved the— Do you call those first rooms a library?"

"Library or sitting room."

She nodded. "They are beautiful and welcoming. The office is…well, it's not."

He laughed. "My father doesn't intend it to be welcoming. I think he wants people who meet him there to be intimidated."

She chuckled. "I'm sure it works." She glanced around. "But this room is not like either of those. It's…" She shrugged again.

"Well, let me tell you, it can be very cheerful on the right occasion. Or intimidating on others."

"I believe it." She returned to the hall.

He stopped at her side. "Rose, is the house what you expected?"

She considered her reactions. "I have to say it isn't."

They faced each other, so close she fell into the intensity of his gaze as he searched beyond her words to the depths of her heart.

"What did you expect?" His words seemed to ask for assurance.

She tried to make herself realize how foolish such a notion was. But his gaze was so demanding it burned the backs of her eyes. It made her heart stick to her ribs and forget to work. It caused her tongue to seize so she couldn't speak even if she'd been able to pull a word from her befuddled brain.

He repeated his question.

"I—" She would not stammer. "I expected it to be more like your father's office than the sitting room." Words suddenly burst from her mouth. "You are rich and powerful." She meant the Caldwells in general. "Your house is big. I thought it would be like its owners. Cold and forbidding. I guess I just never thought it would have appealing aspects."

His expression flattened. The blue of his eyes grew icy and he shifted his gaze away.

"I'm sorry. I spoke hastily."

"You judge us Caldwells rather harshly."

The truth could not be avoided. "I've had cause, wouldn't you say?"

"Perhaps you did." He emphasized the final word, then moved down the hall toward a flight of stairs leading upward. His hand rested on the ornately carved baluster as he turned to confront her. "Rose, is it possible that we can forget about the feud between our fathers and just be friends?"

The idea enticed her. She would like a friend who lived close by. Someone she could enjoy visiting with. But was it possible? Especially if he continued to insist the feud had ended when she saw no evidence to support his belief. To the contrary, she had seen plenty to make her certain it wasn't over. She shivered. Even now the Caldwell cowboys could be up to mischief. If Pa saw them, he'd try to stop them and with his injured ribs… *Please, God, protect Ma and Pa.*

"Never mind." Duke took a step upward but before he got further, Billy dashed into the hallway.

"Come and see. Come and see." He waved them to follow and trotted away.

"What's wrong?" Rose called, but Billy disappeared down the hall and back to the kitchen without answering. She pressed a hand to her throat. "Did he sound frightened?" She wasn't sure.

"We better go find out." Duke caught her elbow and together they rushed after Billy.

Duke restricted his grasp on Rose's elbow to a mere touch when he wanted nothing more than to drag her around to face him and demand why she couldn't accept his offer of friendship.

Was she unwilling to forgive the things done in the past to the Bells by the Caldwell cowboys? He'd have to ask her what she thought about forgiveness.

Right now, though, he had to find out what had upset Billy.

They reached the kitchen where Billy stood in front of the west-facing window. "Oh, no. Oh, no. Oh, no." Each word caught in his throat.

They rushed to his side to see what upset him.

"Oh!" Rose gasped. "Billy, don't look."

A wounded deer.

Blood leaked from a wound in its shoulder where someone had shot it.

Bile burned up Duke's throat. "Whoever did this should have finished the job." He strode toward the door and reached for the rifle.

Billy spun around. "You're going to shoot her?"

"Billy, I have no choice. The animal is seriously wounded."

"No, don't. You can't. She's just a poor little deer." He flung around to Rose. "You can fix her, can't you? Like you fixed Duke."

Rose caught Billy's shoulders. "She's suffering, Billy."

Billy flung away. "I'll help her." He darted past Duke and out the door without bothering to take a coat.

Rose rushed after Billy. "We better stop him."

Duke grabbed his jacket and handed Rose hers.

They barely made it to the step before a shot rang out.

Rose gasped. "Who's shooting? What if Billy—" She didn't finish but lifted her skirts and ran.

Duke's heart kicked into a gallop and so did his feet as he raced around the side of the house at Rose's heels. His pulse thundered in the cut on his forehead.

Side by side, they rounded the corner.

"Billy." Rose's cry filled the air.

Billy lay across the animal, now lying quietly in the snow, relieved of its suffering.

Not ten feet away Ebner stood, a rifle at his shoulder.

Duke ground to a halt and grabbed Rose as she made to pass him. He wasn't about to run blindly into the sights of a loaded gun.

"Billy!" Rose shrieked.

"What's going on here?" Duke spoke calmly although his insides boiled.

Ebner slowly lowered the gun. "Just putting the creature out of its misery."

For a moment Duke thought he meant Billy and his hands balled into fists.

"I didn't see your stupid friend until he burst around the corner. Coulda got hisself shot."

"Could have?" Rose tore loose from Duke's grasp and rushed to Billy. She shook him and called his name. When Billy turned his tear-streaked face toward Rose, Duke released pent-up air.

"She's dead," Billy wailed.

"I know. Come, let's go inside." Rose tried to pull him to his feet.

Seeing her efforts, Duke went to assist her. "Come, Billy. There's nothing we can do for her."

Together they managed to get Billy standing and turned him toward the house.

Duke glanced over his shoulder at Ebner. "See that you move that right away." He could just imagine Billy watching out the window, crying over the poor animal's death.

Ebner signaled to a cowboy in the corrals to bring a horse.

At the house Billy paused. "Is she in Heaven now?"

"She could be, all right," Duke said.

Billy shuddered. "Then she'll be happy."

They guided him inside.

"Why, look at the time." Rose glanced at the clock. "I need to start dinner. Billy, would you help me? My. Look at how clean the kitchen is."

Billy beamed. "Did I do a good job?"

"It's as clean as brand new."

Duke filled a glass with water and downed it, giving himself an opportunity to glance out the window. Already the carcass was gone, leaving only a faint pink color in the snow.

He turned, caught Rose's questioning glance and

nodded. She flashed a smile so full of gratitude that his lungs momentarily forgot to work.

"What are you going to make?" Billy asked.

She shifted her gaze to him. "What would you like?"

"I liked your soup yesterday." He grew thoughtful. "But Duke really likes potatoes and gravy. Maybe we should make that."

"That's a fine idea. Is that the pantry?" She indicated the door past the stove.

Duke pulled it open. "Mrs. Humphrey is very efficient. I'm sure you'll find everything you need."

"Billy, can you get half a dozen potatoes?" She dove into the pantry and began examining jars. "Ah, here we go." She chose canned beef Mrs. Humphrey had done in the fall.

Duke leaned against the cupboards watching her scurry around. Her assessment of the Caldwells—of him—still stung his insides, but watching her work in the Caldwell kitchen, seemingly at home, eased the burn of her words. If only they could corral the moment. Them together. No animosity between them. His insides coiled. How long would it last before she'd remember he was a Caldwell and remind him of the fact? Seems she couldn't look past that.

She stepped back into the kitchen. "Billy, what's wrong?" He stood over the potato bin without moving.

"How many is half a dozen? I forget."

"Six."

Billy carefully counted them out and began to wash them.

Rose opened the jar of meat and emptied it into a pot.

"What can I do to help?" Duke asked.

Rose's head jerked up, her eyes round, her mouth agape.

Her surprise scratched at his innards. "When will you stop treating me like I'm useless?" Did she think being a Caldwell meant he was unable to do anything practical?

If he wasn't mistaken, she looked confused.

"Duke, somehow I don't think you belong in a kitchen."

He moved closer so he could enjoy her scent. "Rose, I'm a cowboy at heart. Nothing more. Nothing less." Being a Caldwell was only where he'd been born.

She nodded. Opened her mouth as if to speak, then closed it again and turned back to the stove.

His heart ached. How he longed for her to see him for who he was.

"Rose, give me a chance." He didn't care that his words revealed the depth of his need.

Billy looked from one to the other, his face twisted with worry. "Rose, you gotta tell him he's not stupid."

She slowly straightened. Took her time about setting the big spoon aside and even more time to face Duke.

His breath caught in the back of his throat and lodged there as he waited for her to speak.

Her expression shifted from guardedness to resignation in slow degrees and then she smiled, and his lungs remembered to do their job.

"Duke Caldwell."

Did she have to emphasize his surname as if to remind them both of how much lay between them?

"You aren't stupid." Her gaze darted to the bandage around his head. "Well, maybe with one exception. Riding a horse you can't control."

He laughed with both delight and resignation. "You'll never let me forget that, will you?"

Her smile widened. "I think you'll get plenty of reminding every time you look in the mirror."

"Really?" He crossed to the little mirror above the cupboard and rolled back the bandage.

Rose gasped. "You'll start it bleeding again."

Indeed he had, but he didn't for one moment regret it.

She hurried to his side, saw the fresh oozing and ordered him to sit at the table so she could have a good look.

He gladly obeyed her.

As she leaned over to check the wound, he grinned. "It's nice to know you care." He tried to make the words sound teasing but they cried from the depths of his heart and he caught his breath, waiting for her reaction.

"Just so long as you don't blame me for your scar."

He'd wear it with joy, remembering her gentle touch and the pleasure of having her in his house for the first time in his life.

How odd that was. Their closest neighbors had never been in this house. Nor had the Caldwells been in the Bells' house. No wonder she was guarded around him.

"Rose, can you ever forgive the Caldwells?" *And me by extension?*

Chapter Seven

Rose forced her fingers to remain steady as his words exploded in her head. This wasn't just about a neighbor needing the help of one of the Bells and some of Ma's medicinals. He wanted her to forgive the Caldwells.

Could she?

How many times had she wanted to do something retaliatory when the Caldwells damaged the garden or threatened the animals?

"Once I was raising a pumpkin that would surely be the biggest in the area. I planned to enter it in the fall fair. But the Caldwell cows mysteriously stampeded over the garden. All that was left of my prize pumpkin was pig food."

She'd wanted to do something, anything, to get even.

"Pa wouldn't let me do anything to even the score. He said God expected us to forgive. Ma said we would act like neighbors should. Our behavior did not depend on how others behaved."

She grew silent. Her fingers lingered on the bandage without applying it. She wasn't ready to face him or to answer his question.

"I'm sorry." That was all he said. Then he sat there, silent, as if understanding she needed to consider her answer.

She enjoyed visiting him more than a Bell should enjoy time spent with a Caldwell.

Well, of course she did. It made sense if she stopped to think about it. Her sisters had married and left home. She simply longed for company her own age.

Duke grew tired of waiting for her to respond to his question and turned to face her.

It was on the tip of her tongue to say she couldn't forgive until the feud ended, but either he truly believed it had or he was a lying scoundrel. But that seemed at such odds with the way he watched her, his eyes softly pleading, that she couldn't think it possible.

Ma and Pa had taught the girls Christian principles. The girls had memorized many scripture verses and one washed through her mind. A passage from Matthew, chapter 6. "If ye forgive not men their trespasses, neither will your Father forgive your trespasses." God had forgiven her much. She must do the same.

Finally she whispered, "I'm trying to forgive and forget."

He lifted a finger to her cheek. "Thank you."

"Do you want me to put the potatoes to boil?" Billy asked, jerking Rose's attention from Duke's warm touch on her face.

"Would you? And could you stir the meat?" She would let it heat, then thicken the gravy.

The moment broken, she tended to her task.

She fixed the bandage on Duke's head and stepped back, though even three feet didn't free her from the awareness of his presence or his power, especially when he fixed those blue eyes of his on her and smiled.

"Thanks. Now what can I do to help?"

It still surprised her that he wanted to assist in the kitchen. But she couldn't say the idea displeased her and she hurried to the pantry and selected a jar of green beans. "You could open these and dump them in a pot."

While he did that, she thought of dessert. Did he expect a sweet at the end of the meal? What could she make in quick order? She brightened. Ma's sauced butterscotch pudding was just the thing.

It took five minutes to mix it together and then she stuck it in the oven. It would be ready to eat by the time they finished dinner.

A short time later they gathered around the table. Rose bowed her head, expecting Duke to say the grace as he had before.

But silence filled the room.

She peeked at him. Her heart rushed up her throat at the soft look in his eyes.

Before their gazes touched, he lowered his head and began to pray.

Her eyelids froze at half-mast. What had he been thinking? Thoughts of her? Pleasant thoughts?

As she closed her eyes, a smile warmed her lips. Something about that unguarded look poured sweetness into her soul and she ignored the warning call of her heart that clamored, *You're headed for a heap of hurt*.

When he said "Amen," she sat straight and strong.

"You sure are a good cook," Billy said after a few mouthfuls. "Best ever."

"Why, thank you." She smiled at Billy, then let her gaze slide to Duke.

He grinned. "I sure do appreciate all your help."

Was it only her imagination that his voice was husky?

"You're welcome." Smelling the delicious aroma of her butterscotch, she sniffed the air. "I do believe dessert is ready." She hurried to the stove and pulled the pudding from the oven, then set it on a hot pad on the table so Billy and Duke could help themselves.

They finished the main course and took a generous portion of dessert. Both took second helpings, which pleased her no end.

It was nice to be appreciated.

"I'll do dishes again," Billy said when they finished.

"But, Billy, you did breakfast."

"I like doing dishes."

She quirked an eyebrow. "I don't intend to argue with that." With more reluctance than she should be aware of, she planted her hands on the tops of her thighs. "Then I should be on my way."

Duke shook his head. "Uh-uh. Not yet. We have unfinished business."

The well-being of the pleasant meal slipped from Rose. What did he mean?

"I was in the midst of giving you a tour of the house. And I said I would tell you what it was like down east."

"Oh, you don't need to bother. I don't want to take up any more of your time."

"I don't mind. I find your company stimulating." There was a definite husky sound to his words.

Her heart swelled at his comment and then clenched tight with caution. She should leave while she was still in control of her emotions.

"I have something I want to show you." He rose and waited.

"Very well." She could no more resist his invitation than she could ride his wild horse, even though a warning sound blared in the back of her head. This was the Caldwell home. This attraction was only make-believe on her part. She didn't intend to throw her heart open only to have it trampled. She'd learned that lesson well enough. Or at least she should have. Hadn't she readily given her affection to George? And what had she gotten in return but pain and disappointment? How much sense did it make to go down that path again?

None!

But without protest, she accompanied Duke through the sitting room and down the hall to the foot of the stairs where he stopped and turned to face her.

She met his gaze, wondering at the dark intensity of his eyes.

"See this?"

She moved closer to look at the large black-and-white picture hung in the stairwell. "Looks like part of an old castle."

"It's the remaining tower of the Caldwell castle in Scotland. The original was built in the thirteenth century."

The thirteenth century! Imagine being able to trace your family roots back that far. She had a mere fifteen years of family history with the Bells. In comparison, it seemed so small and insignificant. It shouldn't matter. Like Ma and Pa always said, it was how a person acted that counted.

Yet somehow it continued to bother her.

Duke sat on the stairs and patted a spot for her to join him.

If she had half an ounce of sense she would flee this

place. What was she thinking? She didn't belong here. Never would. Not that she had ever considered the idea.

He patted the spot again and smiled up at her. Her doubts subsided, momentarily forgotten, and she sat at his side.

The stairs were wide but still their arms brushed and it seemed as if they shared a special moment.

"My father told me about the Caldwell castle, of course," he said. "The Caldwells lived by a motto. Honor Above All."

Honor above all? How did that fit in with trying to drive the Bells from their land? She would never understand why their small stretch of land mattered so much to the Caldwells.

Duke went on. "My grandfather is rabid about maintaining what he calls 'the Caldwell dynasty.' Every time he said the name, his chest would puff out." Duke sat back and expanded his chest to illustrate.

Rose laughed though a part of her found this talk of dynasty and landownership a little off-putting.

Duke's chest flattened and he leaned over his knees. "You asked about my trip east. There were some wonderful parts. Getting to know my grandparents and aunts and uncles and cousins was nice. Visiting places where our constitution was hammered out was great. I loved the library and museums."

"Do I hear a *but* in your voice?"

"I guess you do. People seemed eager to meet me and to get to know me. I fancied myself quite a popular fellow." He seemed regretful of his status, so she waited, sensing he had just begun to explain.

"I even fancied that a certain girl—Enid Elliot—had a special fondness for me." His glance toward Rose was half mocking, half embarrassed. "I suppose I only saw what I wanted to." He sighed deeply and stared at his hands where they rested on his knees.

When it seemed he didn't mean to continue, she asked gently, "What happened?"

He worried his lips. "Turns out she was only interested in being associated with a Caldwell. She likely would have married me just to get the name." His voice grew hard. "I was just a Caldwell to her. Not Duke. Not me."

How often had she yearned to be seen as Rose? Not the red-haired, abandoned child adopted by the Bells. Just Rose. But it never entered her mind that Duke, with his vast history and privilege, might experience something similar.

She reached over and rested her hand on his forearm. "If it's any consolation I think of you as Duke." She wasn't sure when it had become so but it was.

He shifted so he could look into her face. "Not Douglas Caldwell?"

She squinted as if considering the question. "Who is that?"

He laughed and squeezed her hand. "I perceive you have a faulty memory."

He meant his words as a joke, but they stung her conscience as sharply as a slap to the face. What was she thinking? Indeed she had a very poor memory if she thought she could forget that he was a Caldwell and that they tried to drive the Bells from their farm. As far as she could tell, despite Duke's words to the contrary, they still wanted to. She sprang to her feet. "I really must go or Ma and Pa will be worried about me." Her feet carried her toward the kitchen as fast as she could go without trotting.

"Wait," Duke called. "You haven't seen the upstairs."

"It would be unseemly for me to visit the bedrooms with you," she called over her shoulder, her cheeks burning at the idea.

She rushed into the kitchen.

Billy stood waiting, an expectant smile on his face.

She slowed her frantic rush to glance around the clean room and murmur approval to Billy. Then she caught up her coat.

Duke plucked her hat and scarf from the hooks and pressed them to his chest. "Rose, what did I do? What did I say to send you running?"

She took a steadying breath and slowly brought her gaze to his, hers guarded and a little accusing, his confused and perhaps a mite hurt. She relented marginally at his look. "Duke, it's time for me to go." Back to her home. Back to her life as a Bell. Back to dealing with a stupid feud. It was on the tip of her tongue to ask if he truly believed the feud was over. But she couldn't bring herself to mention it. She couldn't explain why, except she didn't want to deepen the hurt in his expression.

"I have to go." She took her hat and scarf from his hands. "Goodbye. Goodbye, Billy."

Duke followed her outside and to her horse. "Thank you for everything."

She thought he'd meant to say more but he rubbed his lips together and stepped back.

"Take care of your head." She reined Hope around and made for home.

She was almost there before the tension in her body finally relaxed.

She should have asked him about the feud. But she didn't want to lose all the pleasant moments they'd shared over the past two days.

She reached the top of the hill and looked down on the farm. Smoke curled from the chimney and steam rose from the animal pens. Grub sat on the doorstep, oblivious to her approach, as always.

A movement off to her far right caught her attention. Ebner sat astride his horse, watching her. Her scalp tingled. He was too far away for her to see his expression but she knew he would be scowling, hoping for a way to make their lives miserable enough they would leave. She stared at him for several moments before he rode away.

Until next time.

Her gaze returned to the farm.

No matter what Duke said, the feud was not over.

Duke stared out the window a long time after Rose left. He'd said something to send her into a headlong flight, but as he reviewed the conversation in his mind, he could find nothing that he thought would have had such an effect.

They'd been talking about the Caldwells. She'd assured him she saw him as Duke. The confession had brought a swell of something so sweet, so elemental inside him that he didn't have a name for it.

And then she'd run.

Finally he turned from the window to see Billy watching him, his face wreathed in worry.

"Was she mad at you?" he asked.

"I don't know."

Billy nodded. "Sometimes it's hard to know."

His simple answer was so full of wisdom that Duke chuckled. "It is indeed. Come along. Let's go sit in the other room." He led the way to the sitting room that Rose had admired. In reality it was two rooms but the archway connecting the two was wide enough to make it seem as one.

He went to the second room, picked up a book and sat to read.

Billy liked to draw and had a selection of papers and pencils in a satchel. He opened it and set to work.

Duke looked around. Rose had admired these rooms, especially the books— He sat up as the memory struck. "I promised she could take some books home. She forgot and so did I."

Billy didn't even glance up from his work. "Can we take them over tomorrow?"

"Indeed." He sat back. It was the perfect excuse to see her again. Maybe he'd find out why she'd hurried away from him. He looked forward to the possibilities that the visit offered.

"Oh." Billy turned back to his papers. "She wants you to rest. You should listen to her, you know. She's real smart, especially about things like that."

"You're right, Billy." She was also smart enough to read between the lines. He just wished he knew what message he'd inadvertently given. He could ask her again but he doubted she'd tell him.

Rather than read the book he had selected, he went to the shelves and picked out half a dozen to take to Rose and her parents.

He couldn't concentrate on anything but his upcoming visit.

* * *

The next morning the fire started without the smoke. Billy made porridge again and offered to clean up. "I don't want to go out there—" He nodded toward the barn.

Duke understood Billy didn't care to encounter any of the cowboys, especially Ebner. He went out to tend to chores himself while Billy washed the dishes.

No one else had been to the barn yet so he fed the horses, then grabbed a fork and set to work cleaning the floor.

Four cowboys entered. One chewed a toothpick, one sucked on a pipe and the other two belched.

Seems they had enjoyed breakfast.

Duke leaned on the fork. "Morning." He called them all by name.

"Morning, Duke," they replied as they saddled their horses.

"What are you doing this morning?" Ebner never consulted him, never informed him of the plans. It made Duke feel like a visitor when, with his father away, he was boss.

"Ebner wants us to check that north slope and make sure no cows are hiding in the trees. Says if a heavy snow comes they'll starve." The four of them led their horses out of the barn and Duke continued cleaning the floor.

Ebner stepped inside. Without any greeting, or an acknowledgment of Duke's authority, he barked, "Does your father know you're entertaining one of the Bell girls?"

"I don't see that's any concern of yours. This is Caldwell property and I'm a Caldwell." He hadn't meant to sound so high and mighty but Ebner rubbed him the wrong way.

Ebner spit. "Good ranch land fenced and broke up. Soon the whole country will be hacked up and fenced off. I sure hope I don't live to see the day."

Was Ebner talking about the Bells or about the settlers who came west in a steady stream? Did he carry a special dislike for the Bells or settlers in general? Not that it mattered. Father had told the cowboys to end the feud. "People have to live somewhere."

Ebner crossed to within three feet of him and jammed his fists on his hips. "That sure don't sound like a Caldwell. Living down east has turned you into a sissy." He stomped off and minutes later led his horse from the barn without giving Duke a chance to argue.

He was no sissy. He was Duke, an ordinary cowboy.

He jammed the fork down hard enough to send a shudder up his arm.

An ordinary cowboy with hopes and dreams of his own. Someday people would see it.

He finished cleaning the barn, saddled King and a horse for Billy and returned to the house. "Are you ready to go?"

Billy grabbed his coat. "I can't wait. Mrs. Bell said I could have Patches for my own."

"Patches?"

"My cat. She's so nice. I love her and she loves me."

As they rode toward the Bells, Duke heard a lot more about Patches than he could hope to remember. The wind caught them as they passed the grove of trees and he pulled up the collar of his coat. January could produce nasty storms or unexpected warm spells as they'd had for the past few days. This cold wind reminded him this was a Montana winter.

They crested the last hill and he came to a halt. The Bell farm looked calm and peaceful. No sign of the Caldwell cowboys anywhere. He let out a relieved sigh.

Rose would soon see the feud was over.

Would she be glad to see him?

In his mind things had shifted between them since she rescued him and tended his wounds, but it could be the feeling was one-sided.

"You gonna change your mind?" Billy asked. "'Cause if you are, I'm going anyway. I want to see Patches and Rose and her ma and pa."

"I haven't changed my mind."

He rode down the hill.

She would no doubt hear their approach. Would she run out to ask them to leave or open the door and invite them in?

He reached the front of the house and dismounted before the door opened.

Rose stepped out, a coat hanging crookedly from her shoulders and unbuttoned as if she'd donned it hastily.

"Are you okay?" she asked. At the look of concern in her face, Duke felt a little smug. Her gaze went to the bandage on his forehead.

He touched it. "I'm fine. But you forgot to get books. I brought you some."

Air whooshed from her in one long exhalation. "Books? You rode all the way over here just for books?"

"He misses you," Billy said. "Can I see Patches?"

Rose's eyes widened. "You missed me?" Her gaze held his like a vise.

He hadn't said so but realized it was absolutely true.

The house had seemed empty and silent after she'd left. "Winter days tend to be long."

Only the way the corners of her eyes crinkled gave him an indication that she was pleased at his admission.

Billy shifted from foot to foot and sighed deeply, calling Rose's attention to him.

"Come along. I'll take you to see Patches." She pulled her coat closed and tramped toward the barn. Their dog, Grub, followed on her heels.

Duke stood rooted to the spot. Was he invited?

She glanced over her shoulder. "Aren't you coming?"

"Sure am." He tied up the horses and caught up to her.

At the barn Rose called, "Kitty, kitty." And the place exploded with half a dozen cats. She squatted and let them rub against her.

Billy plopped to the floor and pulled a motley-colored cat into his lap.

Duke leaned against the nearest stall and glanced around. Though much smaller than the one on his ranch, the barn was new enough the boards were still yellow. Cows chewed their cuds contentedly, while a horse neighed a greeting. In one corner he spied a tack room that was orderly and neat as the rest of the barn. The place was warm and welcoming—not a thought he normally entertained in a barn. It was like drinking sweet hot cocoa.

Rose eyed him, her eyes flashing. "You don't like cats?"

Billy's head came up, shock widening his eyes. "You don't?"

"I like cats just fine." To prove it, he hunkered down to the floor and scooped up a black-and-white cat. It rumbled a greeting and pressed its face to his chest. "Friendly, aren't they?" The cats at the ranch were wild things. Once when he was younger he'd found a batch of kittens and spent time playing with them. When his father discovered what he was up to, the batch of kittens was moved.

"You're spoiling them," Father had said by way of explanation. "The cats have a job to do."

Duke had not petted a cat since. But now he found it a pleasant experience.

Billy smiled his approval but Rose continued to study him in a challenging way.

"What?" he asked.

She shifted her attention to the cat she held. "Nothing." A beat of waiting silence. "It's just that I'm having a hard time thinking of you with a cat as a pet."

Her words, though gently spoken, stung. "Again, the poor opinion of me. Can't you see me as just Duke?" He couldn't say if it was anticipation or dread causing him to hold his breath. Or both.

She continued to stroke the cat, as if it demanded her complete attention.

Billy followed Patches into the tack room and found a length of leather to pull across the floor for the cat to chase.

Prepared to have his question ignored, Duke released his breath slowly and quietly.

Perhaps not as quietly as he thought for she looked at him and at the uncertainty in her face his hands grew still.

She rocked her head back and forth slowly. "It's impossible to forget you're a Caldwell."

She pushed her hat from her head.

He kept his gaze riveted to hers even though the fall of red hair enticed him.

"You're a Caldwell," she repeated. "You have a picture of a Caldwell home that was built in the thirteenth century. You know who you are." Her forehead wrinkled, making him want to reach out and smooth it. Smooth away her worries at the same time. "I don't know who I am."

"You're Rose Bell."

"But who is that? A child found on the prairie. That's all I know about me." She pressed her open palm to her chest.

"I don't think that's completely true. Rose, I've known you most of my life. And there is so much more to you than that."

Her hungry eyes begged to be fed with evidence.

"I don't even know where to begin. First, you are a loving, loyal, protective sister and daughter." A memory made him chuckle. "Remember the time young Morty stole Lilly's lunch pail and wouldn't give it back? He had Lilly in tears. Your eyes flashed like hard green rocks. I almost warned Morty he better be careful but I figured he needed to be taught a lesson and you were the one to do it."

She waited, her eyes wide, letting him tell the story as he remembered it.

"You marched up to him, your fists bunched at your sides, until you were practically eyeball to eyeball with him. Poor Morty didn't know what to do. He raised the pail as if he meant to hit you with it but you yanked it from his hand." Duke chuckled. "He backed away but you kept pressing forward until he ran into the schoolyard fence. I'll never forget what you said. 'You leave my sister alone or I'll rearrange your face so even your own mother won't recognize you.'"

Duke tipped his head back and roared. When his amusement was under control, he grinned at her. "I'll never forget the look on your face." He pretended to shudder.

She shrugged one shoulder as if to say it didn't matter. "All I remember is how angry I was and how afraid Ma and Pa would be upset with me."

"Were they?"

"I don't think they ever knew." Her shoulders sagged.

"There's more." He had to convince her to see herself as others did. "You're a good neighbor. Why, you'd even help someone you didn't care for." He couldn't put his name in the "someone" category even though he knew that's how she viewed him—not a friend, not a good neighbor, just a person who needed help. One she didn't much care for. How he wanted to change that.

"You tend the wounded—both animal and human. If you see a person in need, you do what you can to change that. You have a smile that lights the room and a laugh that lifts the heart."

Her eyes widened.

Had he gone too far? It was true and he wouldn't retract the words.

Another memory—this one less welcome—surfaced. "Say, weren't you and George Olsen seeing each other when I left? Has he asked for your hand yet?"

"No." She lowered her head.

Relief rushed through his veins, though why it should be, he wasn't prepared to say.

"Why not? Is the man stalling?"

"We aren't seeing each other any longer." So much

pain and disappointment filled her words that Duke squeezed his fists until the knuckles whitened.

He sought for a way to ask for an explanation but before he found one, she lifted her head and her eyes bored into his. He held his breath at her intensity.

"His mother convinced him I was not a good prospect."

He didn't move a muscle for fear of ending this moment that felt as fragile as a freshly fallen snowflake on warm ground.

"After all," she continued, each word strained. "I quote, 'What does anyone know about who she is? No one can vouch for her background.'"

He understood how the words had seared her heart. "Oh, Rose." He touched her cheek. "People say cruel things that have no truth in them. I used to tease you and I'm sorry. I just wanted you to notice me. I wanted to be seen for who I was and not just a Caldwell." He cupped her face with his hands. "Your hair is beautiful. You are beautiful—inside and out. You shouldn't let anyone make you believe otherwise."

Did she realize she leaned ever so slightly into his hand as she clung to his gaze? The air between them filled with expectation and—

Hope?

He couldn't say what sort of hope, nor what it would look like if fulfilled, but it overflowed his heart.

The cat on his lap demanded attention and the moment ended. He almost wondered if it had ever happened.

Rose pressed her face to the cat in her lap and looked at him through the curtain of her eyelashes.

If he wasn't mistaken, she wore a pleased expression.

Was it possible his words had encouraged her? He could ask for nothing better.

It didn't matter that she was a Bell and he a Caldwell. All that mattered was that she believed him when he said she was a beautiful woman—both inside and out.

Did she see him as Duke, an ordinary cowboy, or did the Caldwell image still cloud her thoughts?

Chapter Eight

Rose pressed her face to the cat's soft fur. Duke's words caressed her insides every bit as much as the cat's fur did her skin.

He considered her strong. Beautiful.

It didn't matter that he had teased her when they were younger. Today he'd given her something no one before had. A blessing.

Billy ran by, chasing Patches and laughing. Grub loped after them, woofing enjoyment at the game.

Rose laughed, too. As much from her inner joy as amusement at watching Billy.

Her gaze slipped unbidden to Duke and stalled there as he smiled. The air between them shimmered with the thought that he liked her. Even more, he approved of her. Saw her with strengths and abilities.

Then Billy ran by again and her cat took off after the cord Billy dragged.

Duke's cat escaped, too.

Duke got to his feet and held out a hand to help her up.

His hand enfolded hers. He didn't release her even

after she gained her feet but smiled down at her in a way that claimed her heart.

He might be a Caldwell, might even be part of an ongoing land feud between their families, but at the moment she wanted only to cling to his hand, to drink in his look of appreciation and—

Whoa. If she wasn't careful she'd be throwing caution to the wind and hugging the man hard enough to make him protest.

"Rose." Ma's voice came from the house, the distance reducing it to a mere whisper on the wind. "Dinnertime. Bring your guests."

Rose slipped her hand away and put a good six feet of distance between them, her cheeks burning. Ma hadn't seen her, but Rose's conscience always caused her to imagine that Ma or Pa or both sat on her shoulder watching. What would they think of her being so captivated by Duke's few simple, kind words when they'd offered those same sentiments time and time again and they hadn't impacted her so profoundly?

"You heard my ma. Join us for the meal."

Billy scooped up Patches. "Can I bring her?" He obviously took Duke's acceptance of the invitation for granted.

Ma didn't much care for cats in the house, though she would likely allow an exception for Billy. But—

"Patches might not like it. She's never been in the house. The barn is her home."

"Okay." He put the cat on the floor. "I'll be back."

Rose's cheeks had cooled. Her thoughts were under control and she let her gaze go to Duke. "You will come in?" She really wanted him to and not just out of neighborliness. Nor because Ma would scold her if she let them leave when a meal waited for them. Not even because he'd brought a book or two.

She wanted to cling to the gift he'd given—a feeling of being seen as Rose. It might well be a temporary feeling and only words from a gilded tongue, but for now she basked in the glow.

Duke glanced toward the door then let his gaze roam the interior of the barn. "It's nice in here."

She laughed. "Are you afraid of my folks? Besides, it's even nicer in the house." Doubts assailed her. The house was simple. Why, the whole thing would fit into the Caldwell kitchen. Would he find the house small and confining, their lives simple and awkward? "It won't be fancy but Ma is a good cook and you'll get a hot meal before you return home."

Billy waited at the door, anxiety on his face.

Duke's gaze didn't quite meet Rose's but rested on something over her shoulder. "Do they know your guest is a Caldwell?"

Her heart tipped sideways at his question and she recalled how he had on more than one occasion wished to be seen as Duke—not a Caldwell. Could she return the generous gift of approval he'd given her?

"Duke, it would make no difference to my parents. Their hospitality is always generous." She would have added that the strain between the Bells and Caldwells was not due to Ma and Pa. Ma, especially, thought bad feelings between neighbors was wrong. But Duke slowly brought his gaze to hers. The uncertainty in his eyes pinched the back of her heart and she couldn't bring herself to say or to do anything to deepen the doubt in his gaze.

She took two steps toward him and patted his arm.

"She'll be hurt if you refuse her invitation." So would Rose. Though for the life of her she couldn't explain how and when she'd stopped seeing him as a Caldwell whom she should avoid.

"Very well." But he sounded anything but certain.

Billy pushed open the barn door and let in a blast of cold air. The sky was heavy with gray clouds.

Rose escorted them across the yard.

A succulent aroma made them all sniff the air before they reached the house.

"Smells yummy," Billy said.

"Ma's split-pea soup."

Duke stopped at his horse to remove a sack.

Sure looked like more than two books, she thought. Wouldn't Pa be pleased?

They stepped into the house.

"Ma, Pa, you remember Duke?" They'd already met Billy.

"Of course, welcome to our home." Ma wiped her hands on her apron and held them out to welcome the guests.

Pa got up slowly from his chair.

Rose held her breath as he straightened. If only his ribs would heal. Ma assured her they would in time.

His steps firmer than she'd seen in some time, Pa crossed the floor to shake hands with Duke and Billy. "Good to see you." He waved them to chairs on one side of the table as Ma dished out the soup.

Rose took a seat across from Duke and glanced around the table. She took in the well-worn wooden table, simple bowls, mismatched pieces of silverware, and the brown teapot. Everything was simple and plain but cheeriness filled the room. At least in her mind.

What did Duke think of it?

She studied him openly, perhaps a bit challengingly.

He met her look with a mirror image of her own. "This is very nice. Thank you for inviting us to share your meal." He spoke to Ma then brought his gaze back to Rose, his eyebrow slightly arched.

Her eyes stung and she ducked her head. She was doing exactly as he accused others of doing—judging him on the basis of being a Caldwell. How unfair of her. She faced him and smiled, hoping he would understand and accept her silent apology.

He tipped his head slightly and gave a narrow smile.

"I'll ask the blessing," Pa said.

Rose reached for her parents' hands on either side as Pa reached for Duke's. Ma and Billy already held hands and Billy grinned as if he'd received a great gift.

Rose sensed Duke's hesitation. Would Pa forgo the hand-holding this time? No. He waited until Duke lifted his hand to the table and let Pa squeeze it.

Duke's eyes widened and turned a paler blue.

She ducked her head and smiled. Pa's acceptance of Duke had clearly surprised him.

Pa asked a blessing on the food and on their guests. "May they be filled with the bounty of our table and may we be blessed by each other's company. Amen."

Rose glanced up in time to catch a look of wonder on Duke's face. *See?* she wanted to shout. The Bells aren't bad people. You might learn to welcome them as neighbors. Wouldn't that be great?

The thick, satisfying soup and freshly baked bread occupied everyone for a few minutes, then Ma brought forward an apple pie.

"These are apples from our own trees," Rose said

after Duke had taken a bite and closed his eyes in delight.

Duke's eyes popped open. "You grow apples here?"

"Pa's been experimenting."

Pa's eyes glowed. He explained how he grafted apple-bearing stocks to hardy native trees. "Every year I see more success." His expression clouded momentarily and Rose guessed he thought of the most successful tree that had been badly damaged in the latest stampede over their farm. But he didn't say anything. Duke hadn't been home at the time. They could hardly hold him responsible in any way other than he was a Caldwell.

She was doing it again. Judging him for his name rather than seeing him for who he was.

She studied him as he and Pa talked. He seemed sincerely interested in Pa's work with the apple trees.

"Wouldn't it be something to grow apples on the ranch?" Duke's gaze included Rose in his look of amazement.

The meal was over and Ma served tea.

Duke had brought in the sack of books and had dropped it to the floor beside his chair before the meal. Now he lifted the bundle to the table. "I told Rose she could borrow some books but she forgot to take them."

A nicer explanation than she had run away in haste.

"So I selected some I thought all of you would enjoy." He removed them from the sack and handed two to each of them.

"*Around the World in 80 Days*." Pa sounded so pleased. "I can't wait to read this." He glanced at the second title. "This one, too."

Rose looked at her titles. "*Ben Hur* and *Treasure Is-*

land. Thank you." What fun it would be to read both of them. And Ma and Pa's books, too.

Ma read her titles aloud. One was a book of poems. How could he possibly have known how much Ma enjoyed poetry? The other story was about a farm in Africa. "I shall enjoy these very much. Thank you."

Billy begged to help with dishes but as a guest in their home, Rose couldn't let him do them alone. As she washed the dishes and handed them to Billy to dry, her attention was on the conversation between Duke and Pa, centering on a multitude of topics, including the books.

Their talk was cut short by a powerful gust of wind that rattled the window and made the door creak.

Pa looked up. "That sounds wicked. What's going on outside?"

Rose peered at the window and wiped away frost. "It's snowing."

"I felt it coming." Pa seemed satisfied his prediction had come true.

Duke bolted to his feet. "Billy, we have to get home." He slipped into his coat and helped Billy into his.

The wind increased in velocity, wailing around the house.

Pa limped to the door and pulled it open. Snow blasted in and the wind blew frigid temperatures into the house. He pushed it shut. "You won't be riding home in that. It's too dangerous. But you're welcome to stay here until it blows over."

Rose saw Duke's hesitation. Did he object to spending more time with the Bells?

He made his way to the door. "I'll hunker down for a bit but I need to do something with the horses."

Rose's uncertainty gave way to respect. He'd only been thinking of the animals.

"It's coming down something fierce. You're apt to get turned around out there." Pa turned to Rose. "You know what to do."

She did know, having lived through more than one Montana snowstorm. She went to the closet and pulled out a length of rope, then bundled up from head to toe. "I'll put the horses in the barn."

She opened the door but when she tried to close it, Duke held it and stepped out.

"I'm coming," he yelled against the noise of the wind.

"You'll have to hang on." She attached the rope to a hook beside the door, then wrapped the set of reins Duke handed her around her fist. He held his own horse. "Now hang on." He gripped her shoulder as she lined up her sights for the garden shed.

She could do this with her eyes closed but Duke's touch distracted her. Did she lean into his hand? She closed her eyes and concentrated, focusing on the ground beneath her feet, noting every change in texture to inform her if she veered from the well-worn, snow-covered path. She must keep her destination fixed in her mind, allow nothing to distract her.

The wind buffeted her and she stumbled, then righted herself.

Duke's hand had fallen from her shoulder. She stopped. He bumped into her—a dark shadow in the swirling whiteness.

"Hang on," she yelled.

"Don't fall," he shouted back.

She grinned as she paced off the distance. The dark shape of the building appeared ahead of her. She secured the rope in another steel hook, then leaned against the wall, out of the wind for the time being.

He stood in front of her, grinning. "You're covered with snow." He brushed her hat, her shoulders, her cheeks.

Her face grew warm enough to melt every bit of snow.

But she couldn't resist letting him continue his task.

"That's better," he said.

"You're snowy, too." Feeling very bold, she brushed snow from his hat, his collar and although the snow on his face had melted, leaving his cheeks damp, she wiped her mittens across his face, feeling the grate of his whiskers on the wool.

Their gazes melded together. The snow blowing around the little shed enfolded them in a tiny, private world. How easy it would be to stay right here forever.

But King snorted impatiently, breaking the fantasy.

"We best move on." She led them past the shed and followed the fence beside the garden until her hand reached the corner post and she knew it was time to veer toward the barn. First, she wrapped the rope around the post and double-checked that it was secure. This was her last refuge. If the rope came loose, she could easily get blown off course on her return journey.

Carefully, she positioned herself, not letting the swirl of the snow confuse her sense of direction. Closing her eyes helped.

She patted Duke's hand on her shoulder to signal him to hang on and then she plunged away from the fence.

Duke gripped Rose's shoulder. He couldn't see two feet in front of him. If he lost contact with her he could wander around until he bumped into something but still he'd have no idea which way to go in this unfamiliar location. Not that he was completely helpless. He'd heard plenty of tales of cowboys caught in a storm that had pulled their horses down who had found shelter against the animal.

Unfortunately not all the stories had happy endings.

He tightened his grip on Rose. He was completely at her mercy, yet the thought brought only comfort.

Five steps. Ten. Fifteen. How far was it to the barn?

Beneath his hand she strained forward, her arms outstretched, feeling her way.

He curled his fingers, hoping he wouldn't leave a bruise on her shoulder but not willing to lose contact with her.

Then a dark shadow loomed in front of them and he let out a gust of air. They were safe. Thank God for His guidance. And Rose for her courage and ability.

They edged along the wall to the corner, then faced the brunt of the wind as they made their way to the door.

Duke reached past her and pushed the door open, taking both horses and leading them inside as she secured the rope to the final hook. Then she tumbled inside and Duke pushed the door closed.

"Brr. That wind has a nasty bite. Are you okay?" He brushed the snow from her back as she wiped it from her face.

She laughed. "What an adventure."

He stared at her. "I think you enjoyed that."

"Now that we're safe and sound, you have to admit it feels good to have faced the storm and survived."

He shook his head. "You'd fit right in with Phileas Fogg."

"Who?"

"The character in *Around the World in 80 Days*. He liked a good challenge, too." He tried to sound as if he disapproved but doubted that he succeeded. There was something about Rose with her cheeks all rosy and her eyes flashing with victory that filled him with admiration.

He didn't realize how long they'd been staring into each other's eyes until King bunted him in the back. He jerked away. He had enjoyed those delicious moments of brushing the snow from her clothes, of laughing over her boldness. Longing rose within him…a feeling so rich and bold it almost felt like pain.

He led King to the end of the barn and removed his saddle and gear, then set to brushing him. Rose did the same with the horse Billy had ridden over.

They'd known each other all their lives yet he knew so little about her. Oh, he knew she could grow fierce if her sisters were teased. He knew she liked to be the first to recite the times tables. At the church suppers, he'd discovered she fancied lemon pie. He'd seen her out riding enough to guess she enjoyed that activity. But now he wanted to know everything. What were her favorite activities? What did she fear the most? He'd be sure to keep such a thing from her if he could. What had she been like as a child? How did it feel to have a twin sister? Any sort of sister? He'd grown up an only child, finding company in kindhearted cowboys on the ranch.

The wind tore at the barn, rattling every door. "It sounds strong enough to strip bark from trees," he said.

She chuckled. "You'll be here until this is over."

He couldn't see her face to tell if she found pleasure at the thought or if she regretted the need.

"Billy and I could stay in the barn." He spoke cautiously, not welcoming the idea but determined to give her the option.

She came around the horse and faced him.

It didn't take any imagination to know she didn't like what he'd said. Her eyes flashed just as they had so many years ago when she had challenged Morty. But he refused to back away as Morty had done.

"You would sooner stay in a cold barn with only animals for company than share space with the Bells?" Anger edged every word and she closed the distance between them until they were toe to toe.

He wasn't afraid of her. In fact, he kind of enjoyed this side of Rose. All sparks and fire. A slow grin pulled at his mouth and widened until she blinked.

He brushed his knuckles over her cheek. "Of course I wouldn't. But won't we crowd you?"

"Not in the least. We're used to small quarters. But you're used to a big house. Will you be comfortable?"

"A house is a lonely place without good company, which I expect to enjoy in your house."

From the look in her eyes, he knew her anger fled, replaced with confusion.

It pleased him to have confounded her.

"Good company?" She swallowed hard. "You mean my pa."

"I expect he's very good company. We will surely find lots to talk about. I'm particularly interested in how he's growing apples here. But that isn't who I had in mind." Why was he teasing her this way?

Because he reveled in the emotions flitting across her face. Her confusion now gave way to surprise.

"Ma is a good one to talk to. She's very wise. Knows

lots about medicinals and healing plants, and Bible truths and cooking. She has some wonderful recipes."

He placed a finger on her lips to silence her. "I'm sure she does. I'll be sure and consult her should I need medical treatment. But haven't you forgotten someone?"

Her eyelids fluttered. Her lips pursed as if she enjoyed his finger on them. She swallowed loudly. "Who? Billy?"

"You. I intend to enjoy your company." He meant it sincerely.

Surprise filled her face and she took three steps backward before she stopped.

"Why are you so surprised?" he asked.

She made a protesting noise without answering even though he waited expectantly. He longed for her to acknowledge the growing attraction between them but she didn't. After a moment he picked up the brush and resumed brushing King. She returned to caring for Billy's mount. Neither of them spoke as she brought a ration of oats to each horse.

He took his time about putting away the saddle and bridles, about setting the curry brush back in the tack room. If not for Billy he'd remain in the barn simply to avoid the cold feeling her silence caused.

"The trouble is, you are a Caldwell." She stood in the doorway. "For the past eight years I've had to be on guard against your family and your cowboys. Suddenly you say it's all changed…but I'm afraid my old habits remain." Her voice fell to a whisper. "I'm afraid if I let my guard down we'll be caught unawares. A stampede, a fire, our animals hurt, even killed—or worse, Ma or Pa hurt."

Every word she spoke burned a path through his

thoughts. She didn't believe him. He shouldn't have stayed in the tack room, giving her an opportunity to corner him. He stubbornly kept his back to her and didn't answer. What could he say? She was right. He was permanently branded with the Caldwell name and the Caldwell feud. She would never see him as anything else. He couldn't change the fact. But for a few delicious hours he'd thought she'd seen him as Duke.

Was he to forever be judged by his name and not by his merit?

Chapter Nine

Rose searched for words to explain what she meant. "It's not that I don't see you as Duke, but that doesn't change the fact you are a Caldwell. For eight years they've been set on driving the Bells from our land. Don't you see how big a jump it is for me to see you as a friend when we've been adversaries most of my life?" The words wailed a protest within her head, though she congratulated herself on keeping her voice calm and reasonable.

He shrugged and kept rearranging the curry brushes.

She closed the distance between them but still he kept his back to her. Fine. She could talk to his back.

"You say the feud is over but perhaps you are mistaken. Yesterday, when I returned, Ebner was watching the farm. Surely you can understand why that would put me on guard."

He flung around at that. "It seems to me that if we're friends—" a world of doubt hung on that one word "—you have to believe me about ending the feud. I spoke to Father about it before he left and he told the cowboys it was over. We have to be prepared to forget the land feud." He rushed on before she could protest. "Otherwise friendship is impossible." His eyes filled with so much disappointment that her heart beat a protest.

He returned his attention to the items on the shelf.

She grabbed his arm and pulled him fully around to face her. "What if you misunderstood?"

He looked past her, his jaw muscles bunched. "Seems you're accusing me of deceit. Or perhaps my father."

"I truly wish I could be confident it is over," she offered in her most conciliatory tone. Oh, how she wished it. For her family. For the security of their farm. For their peace of mind.

And also because she enjoyed Duke's company.

But the facts refuted Duke's insistence that it had ended.

There was nothing more to be said. She turned to walk away but he caught her shoulder and stopped her.

"Are you saying you don't wish to be my friend?"

The longing in his eyes, the plea in his voice, drove away her caution. "I think it's too late for me to make such a claim." Despite her uncertainty about the feud, she would never see him as an enemy again.

The meaning of her words dawned in his eyes. He squeezed her shoulder gently, an action that made her knees limp. His gaze drifted along her cheeks and returned to her eyes. He smiled. He might as well have hugged her for the effect it had on her. Every argument fled. Every bit of caution faded.

He chuckled. "Then let's enjoy our friendship."

She ignored the questions hammering in the back of her brain. What was Ebner doing watching the farm?

She dare not let her guard down. But that didn't mean she couldn't enjoy Duke's company. "Yes, let's."

His smile filled his eyes with such crystal blue she almost thought the sun had broken through the clouds. "Good. Now are you ready to go back to the house?"

Part of her longed to stay here, sheltered and hidden in the barn where real life could be ignored. But Ma and Pa would worry and the last thing she wanted was for Pa to bundle up and come looking for her.

She pulled her coat closed, did up the buttons and wrapped her woolen scarf around her head and neck. He did the same thing. They pulled on their mittens.

"Now you stay close and hang on tight to the rope," she instructed. "I wouldn't want you to get lost out there."

They stood at the door, listening to the wail of the wind and the snow pelting against the barn. She hated to venture into the storm but she had no choice.

Duke pushed the door open and she grabbed the rope. He closed the door tight and the rope twitched as he grabbed it. They stayed close together as they fought their way back to the house.

The golden glow in the kitchen window welcomed them seconds before her hand hit the wall. Ma's doing, to help guide her home.

She fumbled with the door handle. It gave as Pa pulled it open.

"You're back safe." He unwrapped her scarf and took her coat from her shoulders.

She turned to check on Duke. He'd removed his outerwear and was shaking his head to get rid of the snow clinging to his hair. His blond locks sparkled with moisture.

Her mouth grew dry as she stared.

"Let's put your things to dry." Pa gathered the coats and the scarves and mittens and hung them over chairs next to the stove.

Ma stood by watching.

Billy sat at the table, a piece of paper in front of him. "Is Patches okay?"

"She's buried in a nest of hay, safe and warm." Rose hurried to the stove, lifting her hands to the welcome warmth.

Duke did the same.

Pa hovered nearby. "You made sure Grub was in the barn?"

"Yes, Pa. He was curled up next to one of the cows when we left."

"Good. Good." He limped to the table and sat heavily.

Ma hurried to pour tea and put out a plate of cookies, nodding at Rose for them to sit.

Rose touched Duke's elbow. "There's hot tea and fresh cookies."

He smiled; the white bandage on his forehead a reminder of how they had reached this tenuous friendship. She touched the material. "It's only a little damp. It'll be okay." She pulled back and tucked her hand against her stomach. She was grateful she didn't have to change the dressing in front of her parents. She was afraid they would notice her strange reaction to Duke.

She sat at the table across from Pa, who was twirling his cup round and round. What was wrong with him? She sent an inquiring glance to Ma.

Ma shook her head. "Bert, stop fussing. Everyone is safe and sound."

Tension raced up Rose's spine. Ma only used Pa's Christian name when she was deeply concerned.

Pa's fingers stilled. He stared at his cup for a moment then let out a long sigh that shuddered through Rose.

What was wrong? Were they concerned because she had spent so much time with Duke? Did they see some warning sign she didn't see? Or that she purposely ignored?

Pa looked down the table to Ma, his face lined with worry or concern or both. "Every storm reminds me of my father."

"I know." Ma sounded so mournful that Rose put her half-eaten cookie down, unable to swallow.

Pa turned to Duke. "My father froze to death in a storm like this."

Rose's mouth dropped open. Fifteen years as his daughter and Pa had never so much as hinted at this tragedy though it explained why he was so insistent that they be well prepared for a storm. He'd cut the rope to the right length and had the girls practice making it to the barn and back while blindfolded.

Rose had always thought he was simply being cautious.

Why had he never told her and her sisters? And why had he chosen to tell Duke? Rose tried to decide how she felt about that. But wasn't this exactly what she wanted? To see the Caldwells and the Bells learn to be friends. Yet her thoughts remained troubled. Would friendship invite more harassment? The wind rattled the house. They were snowbound. None of them had any choice but to shelter together. No one would misconstrue that fact.

Her mind settled and she listened to Pa relay the details to Duke.

"He insisted he must go check on the stock even though my mother begged him not to. I will never forget her standing at the window, looking into the swirling snow, a lamp in her hand, praying aloud for him to return. Darkness came and she insisted I go to bed, but I couldn't sleep. Pa had been gone way too long. The snow ended midmorning the next day and my mother went looking for Pa. She returned to check on me and get warmed up, then went out again. She did that hour after hour, until finally she sank to the floor and wept." Pa closed his eyes and pressed a hand to his chest as if it hurt to breathe.

Rose realized she had also pressed her splayed fingers to her chest as if she could ease the pain that had woven between her ribs.

She couldn't take her eyes from Pa and wondered if everyone else felt the same way.

"Ma slowly came to accept that Pa was dead. Vanished in the storm. Neighbors found his body that spring three miles from home in the middle of the prairie."

"What a sad tale." Duke's voice sounded thick and Rose shifted her gaze toward him.

The look on his face held so much pain and concern.

Billy wiped his eyes. He appeared to have no family except Aunt Hilda, and Rose was convinced she was likely a caregiver.

"How old were you?" Duke asked.

"I was ten years old. I had to grow up fast." He sighed, then sat straighter, as if he'd forgotten the past. "I lost my father on the prairie but I found my girls there." He smiled at Rose.

The way he spoke of finding them always flooded Rose's heart with warmth.

"Have you ever heard how we found them?" he asked Duke.

"Only bits and pieces."

Rose groaned. "Pa, no one wants to hear that story." She certainly didn't want reminders of her lack of family background, especially in front of Duke with his thirteenth-century castle.

"I'd like to hear the whole story," Duke protested. "I've never known how much of what I knew was fact and how much conjecture."

"My wife tells it better than I." He smiled at Ma.

Ma nodded. "Mr. Bell had taken me out to gather roots and herbs. He decided to load some firewood at the same time so he was in the trees while I wandered around on higher ground. I heard this strange sound. A shrill wailing. I thought an animal had been hurt and looked around trying to find it. I thought I might be able to help it should it allow me to."

Rose had heard this story many times. She turned her face toward Ma but watched Duke from the corners of her eyes. She wanted to judge his reaction.

He looked at her, his eyes full of sorrow and sympathy.

She blinked. Did he understand how it hurt to have been abandoned? But how could he?

Ma continued her story. "I saw a movement some distance away and called to Mr. Bell that I was going to investigate."

"I was afraid she might encounter something dangerous so I hurried after her," Pa added.

"I couldn't believe my eyes when I made out three wee little girls. The two littlest ones wailed."

"Lilly cried the most." Rose didn't know why she wanted to make that clear, except she didn't want Duke to think her weak—not even as a child.

Duke chuckled. "And you stuck out your chin and decided to be tough."

Rose blinked. It was so close to the facts. How could he possibly know?

Ma laughed. "You're almost right. I looked all around to see if they'd wandered away from their folks. Not a person in sight. So I went up to them. Cora—she was five then—insisted her papa was coming back to get them. I asked a few questions and discovered they'd been there overnight." She shook her head. "I don't know how they managed. I asked if they'd like to go with me and get something to eat. Lilly came right to my arms and said she was hungry. But Cora insisted they must wait. Rose stood staunchly at Cora's side. I had to promise them we would find their papa."

"Did you ever find him?" Billy asked.

"I'm afraid we didn't, though we searched thoroughly and the sheriff sent notices everywhere. No one claimed the three girls and eventually we adopted them. What a joy they've been to us."

Ma and Pa beamed at Rose so fiercely that she felt her cheeks warm.

"Lost my pa to the prairie but found my girls there," Pa said again, almost crowing with delight. "Wish my ma had lived to enjoy them."

Ma pushed from the table. "Pa, you need to rest a spell."

They normally napped after lunch but Rose knew they had waited anxiously for Duke and her to return.

The two of them headed for their bedroom.

Billy sighed. "I gots no ma and pa, either."

Duke gripped his shoulder. "But you have friends who care about you."

Billy beamed. "You're my friend, ain't ya?"

"I am indeed."

"And Rose's, too?"

Duke's gaze caught Rose's and held it with steady assurance. "Yes, Rose's, too."

Billy nodded. "And Rose is my friend, too."

"I am indeed," she said.

"Can I draw now?" Billy indicated the paper that had been moved aside to serve tea.

Rose smiled. Ma had known what Billy needed and given him drawing things. "You go right ahead."

Rose gathered up the tea dishes and took them to the cupboard where she remained, watching the thick snow pelting the window.

Duke moved to her side. "I never stopped to realize what it would be like to be left alone on the prairie."

She shifted so she could look at him.

His eyes sobered. "But you found something many people don't have." A beat of silence passed between them.

"I can't think what you mean."

"Parents who love and adore you."

She nodded. "I've never doubted their love."

His blue eyes bored into hers, seeing what she did not say. "Yet it isn't enough?"

"It must be hard for someone with a thirteenth-century castle to comprehend."

He grinned as if the idea was vastly amusing. "I don't have a castle. I don't have much of anything except my horse, my saddle and the clothes in my closet. The rest is my father's."

"You have history. Roots."

"That's true. So do you. You just don't know them."

"Whether they be good...or ill." How often she'd heard that.

"Rose." His voice caressed her. "You are you. Isn't that what matters?"

She knew how dearly he wanted to be seen as Duke. "And you are you. Is that enough?"

They studied each other soberly. Searching past the surface to the secrets beneath. The longings hidden deep within.

The corners of his eyes crinkled; a sign of contentment. "I guess it is." He lowered his head for a moment and then looked at her again. "Is it enough for you?"

His voice was so quiet, so full of concern, that she felt herself yielding to him. She had to yank her senses into order before she could answer. "I suppose it is. Except—"

"Except what?" he prodded when she paused.

"I would like to know who my parents were. For good or ill." She rushed on. "Cora says our mother had died. But that leaves our papa. Where is he? Is he dead or alive?" Her voice grated from her raw throat. "What kind of man would abandon three little girls? Do you know how many times I've asked myself that question?" She rushed onward, unable to stop the flow of her words. "Cora says we should forget it. She says he didn't want us when we were little and we don't need him now. Lilly says I should forget it. I might not like what I discover." She shook her head. "But I can't forget it."

He squeezed her shoulder gently and his touch calmed her mounting frustration. "Any more than I can forget being a Caldwell?"

"Exactly."

"But what if you did find the truth and it was unpleasant?" His hand still rested on her shoulder, giving her the strength to face such a possibility.

"It seems to me that knowing is better than not knowing, no matter what I discover."

"Maybe not."

She shook away from his hand. "How can I expect you to understand? You know your ancestors so far back you can't even count."

"And yet in the long run, it doesn't matter. It isn't my name that I care about or that I want others to recognize. It's me."

She sighed. "You are Duke. I am Rose. Let's leave it at that."

He grinned and chucked her on the chin. "Don't make it sound like a fate worse than death."

Duke didn't understand why it mattered so much to Rose. As he'd said, he got a little tired of being a Caldwell. Being seen only for his name. There had been times he wished he could become nobody—a man with no past, no history. He ached to make Rose see her history shouldn't matter. "I don't care where you came from or who your family was."

She nodded, her eyes dark with uncertainty. "That's nice to know."

"But it's not enough for you?"

She smiled, though it barely reached her eyes. "It's enough for today." She gave another glance out the window. "It seems this storm is going to last a while. What would you like to do?"

"Do?" He had no idea what she had in mind.

She tipped her head and regarded him with a teasing light in her eyes.

A tension in his shoulders he'd been unaware of until now slipped away at her change from worried to playful. "What would you do if you were home and stuck indoors during a storm?"

"I've had the experience a time or two."

"So what did you do?"

"I read. I helped my mother roll up yarn." At the widening of Rose's eyes he shook his head. "She's a fine seamstress and knits special baby sweater sets."

Rose's eyes widened. "Did she make those sweater sets in Mr. Frank's store?"

Duke nodded slowly. "Don't say anything. She doesn't want anyone to know."

"They're beautiful. I've always admired the craftsmanship."

"She'd be thrilled to know it."

A fleeting doubt crossed her face as if she didn't believe his mother would care about her opinion. "What else did you do?"

"Played checkers with my father. I begged Mrs. Humphrey to show me how to bake cookies but she shooed me from the kitchen." He was a Caldwell, she'd said. He didn't need to cook his own meals or bake his own cookies. Duke had slipped away feeling as if being a Caldwell was a punishment rather than a privilege.

Rose gave him a long, considering look.

He squinted at her. What sort of plan was she hatching?

"Would you like to learn now?"

"To bake cookies?"

She nodded.

"You'll teach me?"

"I'll try. I can't say if I'll be successful."

He rubbed his hands with glee. "You teach and I'll learn."

Her eyebrows quirked. "It's a deal."

She opened a cupboard. "You'll need a mixing bowl, a wooden spoon and—" She listed off ingredients and equipment and stood by letting him flounder around locating everything. He put it all on the table.

Seeing what they were about to do, Billy put away his drawing and came to stand across from Duke. "I can make cookies." He gave a little grin. "If someone tells me what to do."

"Then listen up, my friend," Duke said. "I might need your help."

"What kind of cookies are you making?" Billy asked.

Duke stared at the ingredients. "Rose didn't tell me but I'm going to guess gingersnaps of some sort."

Rose bumped him with her elbow. "That's correct. Now the first step…"

He learned how to cream butter and sugar and add eggs. He learned to measure flour and other dry ingredients, then mix them in with the butter and egg mixture. He wouldn't admit it but the mixing was hard work. Why didn't they invent a machine to do this?

He stirred a little too hard and some of the dough flew out of the bowl. A piece landed on the back of Billy's hand. He ate it.

"Yum. You're a good cookie maker, Duke."

"Thank you." He scooped up the scattered bits and dropped them back in the bowl, darting a glance at Rose to see what she thought.

She grinned. "You're learning fast, Duke Caldwell."

He kind of liked the sound of his full name on her lips. "Why thank you, Rose Bell."

The cookie baking momentarily forgotten, they nodded to each other, silently acknowledging that history or lack of it, land feud or not, didn't matter while the storm raged around them. In this house they were themselves. Nothing more. Nothing less.

"You gonna bake them?" Billy asked.

Duke turned his attention to the task. "Is that what's next?"

"I think so. Isn't it, Rose?"

"You are right, Billy." She told Duke where to find the baking sheets and instructed him on greasing them.

He dipped his fingers into the dough and pulled out some. He was about to plop it to the pan when she caught his hand and held it over the bowl.

Her touch was sweeter than any cookie dough. He gave himself a mental shake. Best keep his thoughts on the task at hand.

She handed him a spoon. "Take out a size somewhat larger than a walnut and make a ball." She illustrated. "Try to keep them about the same size."

He did four and looked to her for approval.

She nodded and smiled. "Good job."

He felt his chest swell just as Grandfather's had when he'd talked about the Caldwells. This was much more fun than a Caldwell history lesson.

He continued making balls and arranged them in neat rows on the baking sheet.

"Now you flatten them with a cup dipped in sugar."

He did as she instructed and she had him place the tray in the oven. He'd just filled another when Mr. and Mrs. Bell came out from their bedroom.

"It smells like ginger cookies," Mrs. Bell said.

"Rose is teaching me how to make them." Duke knew he grinned widely but he couldn't help it.

He noticed that Mr. Bell looked refreshed and several years younger than when they'd left the kitchen. The man pressed a hand to his ribs as if they hurt. Rose said he'd been injured when Caldwell cows had stampeded through the farm. She'd left no doubt in his mind that it had been intentional. Thankfully she didn't need to worry about it happening again.

But what had Ebner been doing watching the farm? There were no cows nearby. No reason to be there. Duke would be sure to keep an eye on Ebner and remind him the feud had ended if the man should show any sign of wanting to continue it. The older couple sat in wooden rocking chairs with a small table between them. Mrs. Bell picked up a basket of mending while her husband opened the book Duke had brought. He smiled his gratitude at Duke, then began to read.

Duke could tell from the expression on the man's face he enjoyed the story.

"Time to check the cookies." Rose made him do everything himself and a few minutes later, a dozen sparkly cookies cooled on a rack.

He'd done something completely new and out of his realm of experience, and it pleased him no end. Come to think of it, this was not the first time he and Rose had done something together that had been a little challenging.

"Remember when we were on the same team at church?" Their class had been divided into three groups and each group had been given a challenge. Theirs was to memorize fifty Bible verses, do a group project to help someone and prepare a presentation for the whole class.

"You didn't learn the verses."

"I always had trouble with memorization." He waited for her to meet his eyes. "You helped me."

"I couldn't have our group failing because of one weak link." She grinned in a teasing way that took away any sting from her words. "I wanted to be able to go on the picnic Mr. Benson promised."

"Thanks to you, we didn't miss out." She'd made a game out of memorizing the verses. Showed him how to find connections between the words and phrases.

"You're a good teacher," he said.

"You're a good learner." She didn't even reveal surprise. She tipped her head to consider him. "You taught a good lesson to the others, too."

He ducked his head. "I think I was a little forceful."

She chuckled. "You made your point."

"Really?" He studied her, liking the way her eyes sparkled. "Exactly what point did I make?" He raised his eyebrows and silently challenged her.

"You think I don't truly remember, don't you? But you're wrong. You spoke from one of our memory verses. James, chapter 1, verse 27. '"Pure religion…"'"

He joined her in quoting the verse and earned a smile of approval.

She continued. "'To visit the fatherless and widows.' You told the class about our project of gathering toys and books and taking them to the widow Willa Simmons and her four children."

"The kids were so pleased."

"Mrs. Simmons was even more thrilled when you fellas fixed her broken door and chopped a bunch of wood."

"It was a good day."

"I think the whole class was encouraged to find more people to help. You spoke very powerfully."

They studied each other silently and in that moment something sweet and eternal filled a corner of his heart.

"Can I have a cookie?" Billy asked.

She jerked her attention away from Duke. "Of course." She tasted a cookie. He did, too.

"Delicious," they said in unison and grinned openly at each other.

She'd given him a gift. Not just the fresh cookies. But…

He sorted through his feelings until he found the word he wanted. Friendship. Friendship and acceptance.

The storm continued to roar outside but inside was warm and cozy.

He glanced around. The Bells had opened their home to him even though he was a Caldwell. They were good and generous people.

Duke took in the interior of the house. Everywhere he looked he saw evidence of their hard work. The jars of preserves on the shelf; the pantry with rows and rows of homegrown and home-canned produce. The fruit trees Mr. Bell was so proud of. No wonder they didn't want to leave even when Father had offered them a generous amount of money to buy the place.

He turned back to his cookie making. Rose would

soon learn she no longer had anything to fear from the Caldwells. The two of them could continue to be friends. And maybe more? He smiled at the thought.

Chapter Ten

Rose had not enjoyed baking cookies so much since the first time Ma had helped her make them herself. No, she amended. This was even more fun. No offense to Ma but Duke's company was a lot more enjoyable than that of a parent.

The last batch of cookies cooled.

"You aren't done yet," she warned Duke as he stood with his hands on his hips, his chest puffed out as he admired his work.

He ran a finger around the edge of the bowl. "The dough is gone."

"The dirty dishes have to be cleaned up."

His eyes widened. He opened his mouth and then snapped it shut. "I have to wash dishes?"

Billy giggled, then covered his mouth lest Duke object.

Rose had no such qualms and chuckled. "That's how it works." At least at the Bell household. No doubt Mrs. Humphrey did any cleaning up required at the Caldwells'.

But he was at the Bells' and she meant to treat him

as she would any friend. Though when had she ever entertained anyone who made the hours fly by with a confusing mixture of pleasure and caution?

He'd reminded her of the time in church when they'd been on the same team. How had it happened that they'd been placed together? Perhaps deliberately. Mr. Benson taught about friendship, forgiveness and acceptance. No doubt he meant for Rose and Duke to apply the lessons in a practical way. Rose remembered that she had objected on principle but had found satisfaction in discovering something she was better at than Duke. And in helping him learn the verses. Her selfish satisfaction had changed to a sense of accomplishment when he quickly learned from her suggestions.

Duke held up a hand, bringing her thoughts back to the present. "I'm not objecting. I'm just…well, I guess it makes me feel less like a guest and more like a friend." The look he gave her warmed her clear to the marrow of her bones. He rubbed his hands together. "Show me the way."

She turned to the cupboard and filled the wash basin with hot water. She gathered the dirty utensils but Duke caught her wrists before she could dip her hands into the water.

"I'll do it."

She stepped back to let him tackle the washing up. Then she grabbed a towel and dried.

Why did it feel so intimate to do dishes together? George had visited a few times, of course. But he'd always sat at the table and watched whatever work had to be done. As if it was beneath him to help. And yet, a Caldwell with a thirteenth-century castle in Scotland worked at her side.

Just like Wyatt and Caleb!

The realization burned a hot trail through her thoughts. It had been part of her brothers-in-laws' courting routine as they'd spent time with her sisters. And now Wyatt and Cora were married and so were Caleb and Lilly.

Whoa! She slammed the door on her runaway thoughts. There was absolutely no similarity. Duke was here simply because of the storm.

A contrary argument rattled inside her head. What had brought her sisters' husbands to the farm?

Wyatt had stopped because he'd had a horse too heavy in foal to continue.

Caleb had only come by to get help with an injured pup.

Neither had come calling to start with.

She gave herself a mental shake as she put away the dried mixing bowl. Just because he wanted to be friends, wanted to do dishes, wanted to end the feud, did not mean he wanted to court her.

Duke wiped the table clean. "There. Am I done?"

"You are and a fine job you've done."

He grinned at her praise.

Ma set aside the sock she'd been darning and pushed to her feet. "I best start supper."

Pa glanced up. "Duke, you're welcome to look through my books. Perhaps there's one you care to read."

"Thank you."

Rose watched him kneel at their meager bookcase. What would he think of the poor selection?

He pulled out a well-worn book, one of Pa's favorites, and stroked the cover.

Her throat tightened though she was at a loss to understand the clog of tears. It was only a book, for goodness' sake. But something about his reverent gesture and his lack of criticism at Pa's few titles plucked at her tears.

He sat in Ma's chair and opened the book. His head dipped as he began to read.

As she helped Ma with supper preparations, the storm continued to batter the house. Duke and Billy would have to remain as guests for the meal and perhaps even longer. For now, the outside world, the feud, even the Caldwell family history and her own lack of history could be ignored.

Billy hovered at Ma's side. "I can help cook."

Ma moved over and indicated he should join her. She quietly instructed him when he needed it.

As Rose worked at the cupboard, she glanced toward Duke. When he watched her, she quickly returned her attention to her task. But time and again her gaze darted toward him. Did he even read the book on his lap? Every time she glanced his way his gaze was on her, intent and full of—

She swallowed hard. She must be mistaken. Why would he look at her with longing?

Difficult as it was, she didn't look at him again. But she remained aware of his eyes on her.

Why was he watching her so intently?

Perhaps he wanted a cooking lesson. She stifled a giggle at the idea. Having a Caldwell in their kitchen still seemed like a far-fetched dream. But wouldn't it be fun to prepare a meal together here?

Thankfully, Ma wanted her to make the gravy and

she focused her attention on something more solid than silly flights of imagination.

Billy set the table, each plate and piece of cutlery placed with precision.

"Excellent job," Ma said, and Billy's chest swelled three sizes.

When the meal was ready, they gathered around the table and formed a circle of clasped hands as Pa offered a grateful prayer for safety and plenty. Then they shared a comforting meal. How amazing that Duke fit so easily into their small quarters and informal ways. Her thoughts stung at how judgmental she sounded. Mr. Benson would be disappointed that Rose didn't do more than learn the verse "Judge not, that ye be not judged." God's word was meant to be lived. *Forgive me, God. I'm only trying to guard my heart. Guard it for me. I don't want to have it ripped to shreds again.*

When everyone had finished eating, Pa reached for his Bible. He turned to explain to Duke. "I read a portion every night. It's been my habit since the day I married Mrs. Bell."

Duke's gaze caught Rose's. She read his approval but caught a hint of something else that she again interpreted as longing. There was that word again. Why did she keep sensing it? Or was it her imagination run amok?

Pa opened the Bible. He often chose passages that he'd thought of during the day. She thought he might read about being hidden in the cleft of the rock, protected while the storm passed by.

"I've chosen Psalms, chapter 46. 'God is our refuge and strength, a very present help in trouble.'" He read to the end of the chapter but Rose's thoughts had stalled at that verse.

Did Pa sense that friendship with Duke would lead to trouble? Trouble so bad they'd have nowhere to go but God's arms? A shiver snaked up her spine. Could he see an oncoming emotional storm with the same accuracy with which he'd forecast the snowstorm?

She dismissed the thought. Yet she knew Duke's parents might not be as welcoming of a friendship with one of the Bell girls as Duke was. They, with their long line of history, and she with only the memory of that day on the prairie.

Pa held out his hands and the circle again formed as he prayed for safety for one and all in the storm. "And guide us safely through the storms of life, as well."

Again Rose shivered. Was she blindly walking into a storm? Was it too late to stop the direction of her choice?

Her thoughts were cut short by Ma pushing her chair back from the table.

"Ma, you go sit down. I'll do the dishes." Rose quickly gathered up the dishes. When she reached for Duke's, he waved her aside.

"I'll help."

She jerked back. Her heart skittered right past all her good intentions.

"Unless you object?" He wore a guarded look.

She realized that he might have interpreted her reaction as less than friendly—the reaction of a Bell toward a Caldwell. Enemies. But she didn't see him as a foe. Not today. The knowledge made her nerves twitch. "I never refuse help with washing up."

"Good to know." His face lit up.

She knew her grin was wide and likely a little silly

but she didn't care. Being successful in erasing his wariness made her giddy.

"I'll help, too. Or I could do them by myself," Billy said, waiting at the cupboard.

Rose chuckled. "Billy, you're so eager, someone might take advantage of you and let you do all the work."

"I like doing dishes."

Ma had retired to her chair. She watched the three in the kitchen. "Billy, I believe it's because you know you do a good job."

Billy nodded. "Nobody calls me stupid when I do dishes."

His words silenced the room. The only sound came from the fire crackling in the stove and the storm rattling against the walls outside.

Ma broke the stunned stillness. "You are capable of doing many things well."

Billy shook his head. "No, I'm not."

Rose and Duke exchanged helpless looks. They both knew Billy had heard far too many cruel comments about his limitations.

"I believe otherwise," Ma insisted. "So much so that I invite you to visit any time you can and I'll teach you how to do different things. That's all you need—someone to teach you. Once you've been shown how, you'll see you are an excellent worker with a keen eye to detail."

A plate hung from Billy's hand. His jaw worked as if he fought tears and confusion.

Ma continued. "Look at how well you do the dishes and set the table. That's how you'll do every job you're taught to do."

"You'll teach me?" The words sounded small, as if his throat had grown too tight.

"It would be my pleasure."

"Mine, too," Pa said.

Rose prepared the water and started washing dishes. She handed the first plate to Billy and he dried it.

"Your ma and pa don't think I'm stupid."

Rose wiped her hand on a towel and patted Billy's arm. "Neither do I."

Duke draped an arm across Billy's shoulders and squeezed him close. "You're just right the way you are."

Billy beamed at all of them.

Rose ducked her head as a flood of emotions washed over her. Billy had found something here he needed. The same thing Rose and her sisters had found. Acceptance, encouragement and love.

Duke nudged her.

She sniffed before she lifted her eyes to him. At the answering emotion in his eyes, a great hand seemed to reach into her heart and squeeze it near to bursting.

In that moment she realized how much she liked him—Caldwell or not.

But Pa's prayer at the end of the meal lingered in her mind. *Guide us safely through the storms of life.*

She would be foolish to walk out into the snowstorm and equally foolish to purposely create a storm in her life—in the life of the Bells.

Oh, God, give me wisdom and caution that I might not do anything foolish.

Duke would have gladly let the storm rage so he could stay sheltered with this family for the rest of the winter. He found Rose an enjoyable companion and her parents interesting and, at the same time, comforting. The way they'd taken Billy under their wings said so much about them.

If only his own parents had taken the time to get to know the Bells, this feud might never have happened.

In a few minutes the dishes were washed and put away.

Rose hung the damp towels and stood by the table, looking around as if uncertain what to do.

Duke's jaw tensed. His presence put these people in an awkward position. Their house wasn't big enough to accommodate two guests. He turned to stare out the window. The darkness had deepened in the past hour but he didn't need sight to know the storm persisted. The wind roared around the house. Wisps of snow blew in under the door.

He walked to the table. Couldn't think why and returned to the window.

"Son, you won't be going anywhere. The storm hasn't let up and dark has descended." Mr. Bell called him "son" in an affectionate tone.

Not "Douglas." Not even "Duke." Son. Duke didn't dare look at anyone, not wanting them to see his surprise and pleasure.

Mr. Bell continued. "We haven't much to offer but please stay for the duration of the storm."

Duke studied the wood floor at his feet. Painted brown, it showed signs of wear in front of the cupboard. Signs of home and belonging.

Rose had turned to him but he kept his head down.

It wasn't as though anyone would notice if he and Billy didn't return to the ranch. Slowly he raised his head and encountered Rose's fiery look. She'd misunderstood his hesitation.

He gave a weak smile hoping she'd let the imagined slight pass without accusing him of wanting to avoid the Bells. Especially when the truth was so different.

He turned to Mr. Bell. "Your hospitality is most generous and I accept. I hope you don't find me an awkward houseguest." He meant the last for Rose as much as anyone.

Both Mr. and Mrs. Bell waved away his protests.

"Not in the least, but you'll have to make the best of it." Mrs. Bell nodded toward the narrow cot along the wall. "That's all we have for guests."

"That's fine."

"Me and Duke sometimes sleep outside," Billy said. "On the ground."

Duke chuckled. Seemed Billy felt the necessity of pointing out Duke did not require a down-filled mattress and silk sheets to be comfortable.

"The cot will be warmer than sleeping outside on the ground," Rose said.

Duke couldn't tell if she was relieved he knew how to rough it or if she meant to point out the advantages of sharing the Bell quarters. He fixed her with unblinking consideration. "We'll be warm and safe and comfortable, thanks to the Bells."

Their gazes silently dueled for three seconds, then she relented. "Yes, you will." She went to the cupboard next to the cot and moved several items. She set aside a leather-bound notebook.

Duke eyed it. Did she keep a journal? Would it have something about him in it?

"Pa, where's the checkers game?"

"Top shelf." He didn't even look up, his attention again on reading the book Duke had brought.

Duke knew a degree of satisfaction that he'd chosen a book the man enjoyed. Bringing the books had been an excellent idea. Especially as it provided this opportunity to spend time with Rose and her family.

He crossed to where Rose pawed through the contents of the top shelf. "Is this your journal?" He touched the book.

"No." She pulled down the checkerboard and the markers. "Want to play a game or two?" She grinned at him.

He knew he wasn't mistaken in seeing a challenge in her eyes. Ah, so she thought she could beat him at the game, did she? Well, he hadn't played his father and grandfather and several uncles and cousins for naught. "Sure."

But still he eyed the leather-bound notebook. "Not a journal?"

"Nope." She carried the game to the table and set it up.

"You're writing a novel?"

She shook her head and arranged the board to her liking.

"Then it's an autobiography?"

She snorted and gave him a look so rife with disbelief that he didn't know if he should grin or hang his head.

Out of the corners of his eyes he watched her parents exchange a smile. That's when he realized she was egging him on. Fine. He could play this game.

"Okay. Let me guess." He pressed his finger to his chin and tried to think what she might write in that book.

Her gaze rested on his finger, her eyes warm as spring sunshine.

He forgot what he was supposed to be doing as he watched her.

Billy looked up from his drawing. "I know. It's a drawing book."

Rose shook her head. "Nope."

Duke's brain kicked into gear again. "Farm records?"

She rolled her eyes.

It was impossible to think when she teased him. He tossed his hands in the air. "I give up. It must be some kind of secret correspondence." He'd spoken without thinking, but as soon as the words slipped from his mouth he wondered if that could be a possibility. Perhaps she pasted in letters from a beau. It made him want to grab the book and toss it into the stove.

"Rose, show him the journal," Mrs. Bell said.

"Fine. Seeing as he'll never guess." She retrieved it from the cupboard and handed it to him.

Billy leaned over his shoulder as Duke opened the pages. On each page he saw drawings of plants and lists of the medicinal qualities of each, plus titles such as "Ma's remedy for gout." He stroked a page with an especially detailed drawing of a plant called deer tongue.

"These drawings are beautiful. Exquisite."

She blushed clear to the roots of her hair. "It's a record of Ma's medicinals."

Mrs. Bell rested her darning in her lap. "I have all the information in my head and have taught it to the girls, but Rose took on this project. I'm rather pleased to see what she's done."

Duke couldn't stop turning the pages and admiring both the drawings and the perfect penmanship. He grinned at her. "I see Mr. Daley's lessons had an effect on you."

Laughter burst from her. "Remember how he made us stand at the chalkboard until we could make each letter perfectly?"

"I spent hours there. I could never get my writing good enough to please him. One day he said I couldn't leave until I made my *G*s properly. He kept me so late my father came looking for me and was he ever angry. He said he thought something terrible had happened to me." Duke tipped his head. "That day I felt pretty important to my father."

"I'm sure you are." Rose planted her elbows on the table and rested her chin on the heels of her upturned hands. "I never knew he kept you after school, though. I guess I thought—" She shrugged. "Guess I was wrong."

"What did you think?"

"It doesn't matter now."

They considered each other, the air between them heavy with a thousand memories, almost as many misunderstandings and false judgments.

"Let me guess," he murmured. "You thought I would never be punished by a teacher."

The flicker of her eyes said he'd understood her reason. "I can't believe he dared to discipline a Caldwell."

He turned his attention to the game and made a move. "My life wasn't all that easy, you know."

She moved her checker piece and looked at him expectantly. Whether she meant for him to make a move or to explain his statement, he couldn't say. He chose to do the latter first.

"My father has very high expectations of me. He expected me to work alongside the cowboys so I'd learn every aspect of ranch life. I didn't mind, especially when Angus was our foreman. He treated me kindly."

"I remember him. He never harassed us."

"He quit and Ebner replaced him. Ebner has never treated me—" Would he sound like a whiner? "I think he delighted in making my life miserable." Maybe he still did. Duke moved his checker piece rather than meet her gaze, but when he sat back, there was nowhere else to look but at her.

Her eyes were soft as rabbit fur. Full of sympathy. "We've found Ebner to be rather unkind, as well." Her expression hardened. "But your father must approve of him."

The truth lay like a rock in Duke's stomach. Why did his father keep the man? Was it because he approved of the foreman's actions? Or did he even know? It suited Duke better to think his father didn't know, but how could that be? His father would have to purposely ignore all the evidence.

"It was Angus who'd first called me Duke." He'd been wanting to tell her how he got the name and now was the perfect opportunity.

She opened her mouth to say something and closed it again without uttering a word. From the look that flashed across her face he knew that what she'd been about to say made her feel guilty.

"It wasn't because I thought I ruled the roost."

Her smile didn't reach her eyes, proving to him she'd been thinking along those lines.

"I thought it meant you were next in line to the throne," she admitted.

He chortled but it didn't completely erase the hurt of her opinion.

"So tell me why Angus called you Duke."

Seems both of them were eager to leave behind her judgment.

"I was a little guy when he first came and he asked me my name. Well, I couldn't say Doug clearly and he thought I said Duke. That's what he called me from then on."

"That's sweet."

"I wish Angus hadn't left."

"Why did he?"

Duke pondered the question. "Let me see. I was eleven or twelve when he left. I think he and my father argued about something."

Rose sat straighter, her hands folded in her lap. "Wouldn't that be about the same time we moved here?" She spoke so low he had to strain to hear her.

He'd never thought of it. But now it seemed so obvious he wondered how he could have missed it. Had Angus quit rather than try to drive the Bells off their land? That meant his father had hired Ebner knowing exactly what sort of man he was. The idea sat like a hot rock in the pit of his stomach.

Rose moved her checker. "Your turn."

He understood she meant the game but perhaps it was his turn on other fronts, too. Maybe ending the feud wasn't enough. Maybe he had to get rid of Ebner, as well.

He'd need more than his suspicions, of course, though he wasn't sure how he'd get the facts to prove his theory.

If he did fire Ebner, would Rose finally believe that the feud was over?

Would she finally see him as more than a Caldwell?

Chapter Eleven

"I win." Duke sat back and grinned at Rose.

She had meant to beat him at the game but her thoughts hadn't been on checkers.

How could she concentrate with Duke sitting across from her, his blue eyes bright as a summer sky as he talked about Angus and how he got nicknamed Duke? A cute little story. Then at her suggestion that Angus had been dismissed to get someone who would harass the Bells, Duke's eyes had grown dark and stormy. She knew she wasn't mistaken in thinking he found the idea loathsome, but it wasn't as if he didn't know about the feud. Everyone did. She couldn't imagine what he objected to unless… A pleasing idea came and stayed. Unless he truly did find the feud unnecessary and wrong. Had he tried to end it as he said? Did his father truly ask the cowboys to cease harassing the Bells?

Oh, if only that could be so.

Not that it would make the impossible differences between her and Duke disappear. Besides, she'd seen no evidence the feud had ended. She'd seen Ebner watching the farm and that did not bode well for the Bells.

No, she'd not believe anything but the facts.

She brought her focus back to the game. "Best two out of three?"

At his nod, she set up the game again.

He made the first move then leaned back. "Do you remember that time at the church picnic when we got paired up in a three-legged race?"

She stared at him as the memory blared through her thoughts. Her cheeks warmed. "You complained my legs were too short and we couldn't possibly win a race because of it." He'd scowled fiercely at her as if it was her fault she was much shorter than he. Why would he bring it up? Did he mean to remind her of the friction between them?

He chuckled. "I figured there had to be a way to compensate so we could win the race."

She ducked her head and moved a checker with absolutely no thought to strategy. Had his scowl back then meant concentration rather than anger?

He grinned so widely it burned away any resentment the memory carried.

She tried to cling to her feelings. Tried to protect her heart.

"Do you remember what we did?"

She shook her head. It was empty of everything but the way his gaze probed into her thoughts.

"I told you to plant your foot on top of mine as I tied our legs together, then I held you around the waist and practically carried you. We won, remember? Each of us got a very nice peppermint stick as our prize."

Rose's face burned. All she remembered was embarrassment and resentment. "You thought it was fun?" she murmured, unable to meet his eyes.

"It was a hoot." He ducked his head, trying to see her face. "Didn't you think it fun?"

"I thought you were angry at me." She could barely push the words from her throat. Thankfully they were only a whisper so no one else in the room could hear them.

He leaned back and didn't speak.

She stole a glance from under the shelter of her eyelashes.

Was it her imagination? He looked hurt.

She brought her head up and faced him squarely.

They studied each other with wary, guarded eyes. The past was full of hurts and misunderstandings. The present, she realized, was warm and cozy and ripe with possibility. But the future— No, she would not rob today's enjoyment by borrowing from tomorrow.

A smile came from her heart to her lips. Her eyes felt as if a fire had been kindled inside and the warmth escaped from them. Would he see that she was sorry for constantly misjudging him?

He nodded and smiled back at her. "Good thing the past is past and each day is a new beginning."

"I like that." A promise of so many better things to come.

Twice more he beat her at checkers but she didn't care. What did it matter who won?

Ma brought some extra bedding from their bedroom, signaling it was time for bed.

Rose put the game away. "Good night." Her gaze circled the room to include everyone. It ended at Duke and lingered, caught by the intensity in his eyes.

Pa shuffled across the floor. "Good night, daughter."

She strode past Duke, avoiding his gaze. "I hope

you'll be comfortable." She hurried to her room and closed the door, leaning against it a moment to gather her senses. When had she ever been so scatterbrained? So blatantly confused by the presence of a man? Pa must think the wind had started to make her nervous.

When she glanced at the three narrow beds in her room, a coherent thought broke through the haze of her mind. In the main room was only a single cot, which meant either Billy or Duke would have to sleep on the floor. She guessed Duke would insist Billy use the bed. Why couldn't Duke and Billy sleep here and she sleep on the cot?

Immediately she reached for the door handle. But just as quickly she dropped her hand and stepped back. Pa would likely not allow it. Even if he would, the idea of Duke in her bedroom would forever make it impossible to forget him.

Instead, she turned to prepare for bed. The room was cold, buffeted as it was by the persistent north wind, and she hurried through her routine. Finally she lay in bed, the covers pulled tightly to her chin. She lay tense, straining to catch any sound from the other room. The only thing she heard was the wind and she relaxed and let sleep claim her.

She woke to the sound of Pa starting a fire in the stove. The frosty air made her burrow deeper under the covers. The wind still battered the house and she smiled. *One more day with Duke.* The thought was enough to make her throw back the covers and hurry to get dressed, dancing as her feet encountered the cold floor.

A few minutes later she stepped into the living area. Billy and Duke were standing at the cupboard watching Ma slice bacon and drop it into the frying pan.

Billy glanced out the window. "Don't you think the animals will be cold?"

"The barn is solid and warm," Pa assured him.

"But the little cats might be hungry." Billy wrung his hands. "What will Patches eat?"

Duke patted Billy's shoulder. "She'll be fine. Cats are smart, you know."

"But maybe she's afraid." He cocked his head. "Maybe she thinks the sound of the wind is a terrible monster."

"Billy, why don't you watch the bacon for me?" Ma handed him a fork and guided him to the stove where she explained what he should do. He concentrated on the task for a moment.

"I think she'd like a piece of bacon."

Rose sighed. "Billy, would you like me to check on Patches after breakfast?"

"Oh, yes. I'd like that." Then his face wrinkled with worried concentration. "But it's still storming. Maybe you shouldn't go out there."

"I need to check on the animals."

"Okay, then."

"You'll have breakfast first," Ma said. "Maybe by then the storm will be over."

Rose's heart sank. If the storm ended, Duke and Billy would leave. It would happen sooner or later, of course, but she would delay if she could. The snow and wind insulated them together, eliminated the outside world and its trials. If only she could hope to maintain the feeling after the storm ended. Now, that was an impossible idea!

"What are you making?" Billy asked. "Can I help?"

Rose took over the bacon as Ma taught Billy how to make pancakes.

Duke leaned against the cupboard next to the stove and watched her. "If I stay here a few days I might learn to rustle up a few decent meals."

"Here." She handed him the fork. "No time like the present to learn a few skills."

He expertly flipped the bacon, removing slices as they were perfectly crisped.

"I'm impressed, but I think you've done this before."

He grinned at her. "Mostly over a campfire. This is somewhat easier."

The pancake batter was ready and Ma insisted Billy make them. The first few spoonfuls he dropped on the griddle were misshapen but Ma showed him how to make them round and Billy soon had a stack of nicely browned pancakes ready.

Duke leaned close to murmur in Rose's ear. "Your ma is an excellent teacher with Billy."

Rose nodded. "Ma is always so patient." But it was more than that. Her ma instructed Billy softly and kindly, and Billy responded quickly.

Over breakfast, Billy returned to fussing about Patches.

Finally, Pa turned to Rose. "Why don't you bring that cat to the house when you return? If that's okay with your ma."

Ma patted Billy's hand. "Will that make you feel better?"

"Yes." Billy's voice broke. "I'll do the dishes every meal we're here. I'll sweep. I'll—"

Ma stopped him. "Billy, I don't expect you to become our slave."

Billy nodded.

Rose stole a glance at Duke to see his reaction and

caught him watching Ma with a look of respect. Rose lowered her gaze as he shifted, not wanting to be caught staring at him. But curiosity drove her to look again. Now he regarded Pa with the same awe and respect.

As soon as they finished, Ma said she and Billy would do dishes.

"I'll go to the barn then." Rose started to put her outerwear on.

"I'll go with you," Pa said.

Both he and Duke hurried to their feet though Pa did so much slower and with a groan. He pressed a hand to his ribs.

"These old bones feel the cold," he muttered.

Rose knew he hated to show any sign of weakness.

Duke planted a hand on Pa's shoulder. "Sir, you stay here and take care of your missus and Billy. I'll go with Rose. I've done it once already. I know what to do."

Pa sank back, his face drained of color as the pain he tried to hide grabbed him. "'Preciate that."

Duke turned away, his expression troubled, and pulled on his coat and scarf.

Rose grabbed the bucket of scraps for the cats and then the pair of them stepped out into the storm. Rose knew better than to let go of the door until she had a firm grip on the rope. This time it was snow-covered and cold, but she held on knowing her life—and Duke's—depended on it.

Moments later they reached the safety of the barn and staggered inside.

She stamped her feet and brushed the snow from her arms.

He pulled his mitten off and swept his hand across her hair, his touch lingering long after he'd wiped away the snow. Her heart urged her to lean into his touch, wishing for it to continue.

He brushed at her shoulders and down her back, then said, "My turn."

Her fingers tingled, not with cold but with awareness as she brushed his coat.

He faced her, inviting her to do his head.

As she looked into his eyes, she couldn't say for certain what she saw there. She blamed the low light of the barn. But she couldn't deceive herself with such explanations. He was inviting her to touch him…and she wanted to run her fingers through his blond locks.

But when she reached out to do so, he caught her hands. "Rose, I'm sorry about your pa, but surely no one meant any real damage."

The tender moment was broken. Instead a harsh sound burst from her. "You surely know that's not true."

"I can't believe my father knew what was going on."

She shook her head. "You said yourself he let Angus go. Angus never harmed us but as soon as Ebner came… well, it's never ended. Your father would have to be purposely blind and deaf not to know what's going on."

He opened his mouth, closed it again. Scrubbed at the back of his neck.

"Rose, what can I say except I'm sorry? But it's over."

"I know you believe it but I'm not ready to."

He pressed his lips into a frown and nodded. "What will it take to convince you?"

She held his gaze without blinking as her thoughts warred. She wanted to believe him. She had prayed for the feud to end. But she wasn't foolish enough to accept it, not as long as gates continued to be opened and as long as Ebner watched them.

"One way or the other, we'll soon know."

His heart barely beating, Duke prayed that Rose would believe that his father had spoken to the cowboys. She was right about one thing, though. Neither he nor his father could claim they didn't have any inkling about what Ebner had been up to. As she'd said, his father had likely hired the man because of his reputation and had given him specific orders to get rid of the Bells. On Duke's part, although he had never had an active role in the harassment except for his teasing of Rose, he'd overheard enough comments from the cowboys and seen enough evidence of what they'd done that he couldn't claim ignorance.

His only excuse was that he blindly believed his father had a right to the land because his father said so.

Rose let out a long sigh. "I need to feed the animals."

He grabbed her arm as she marched away. "Rose, don't you believe me?"

Slowly she came around to face him. "I don't know what to believe."

"That hurts." He dropped her arm. "All the hours we spent together… Is it only fake friendship?" He yanked the dressing from his head and tossed it to the floor. "Am I only a man with an injured head that you couldn't ignore?"

He had the satisfaction of seeing denial in her eyes but he wanted more. So much more. He cupped her cheek with his hand. At least she didn't flinch or pull away. "Was it all pretend?"

She shook her head, pressing her hand to his where

it lay against her face. "No, Duke. It is real. But I'm afraid."

"Afraid of what?" He let his gaze roam over her beautiful skin, now pink from the cold. With his other hand, he caught her braid and pulled it over her shoulder. What would it be like to loosen her hair and let it fall free in rich, red ripples?

"I'm afraid of what Ebner will do."

"I'm not going to let that happen. My father left me in charge. Ebner does what I tell him." However, he'd never given Ebner a direct order so he couldn't speak from experience.

The green in her eyes was like bottomless still water. She looked deep into his gaze, as if searching past the surface to the real Duke Caldwell.

She must have found what she wanted because she smiled and her smile flooded his heart and lit up the barn. "If you can convince me, it seems you can convince anyone."

He bent closer. "Does that mean I've convinced you?"

She nodded, her eyes so full of trust, his heart threatened to break from its moorings.

He caught her chin with one curled finger and lifted her face to him. The trust remained there…and something more. Longing. Wanting.

For him?

His heart kicked free and danced against his ribs. He lowered his head, intent on her full, inviting lips. He paused, giving her lots of time to pull back. Instead, she met him halfway. Their lips touched. Nothing more. It was barely a kiss. More of a sealing of something sacred and pure—his promise to ensure the land feud ended and hers to trust him. They lingered a moment, neither moving, and then they broke apart.

She looked at him in a way that made him feel as though he could walk without his feet touching the ground.

At the way he regarded her, she smiled and lowered her gaze. He didn't care that his joy poured from his eyes.

"I have to do the chores." She seemed somewhat confused as she went in one direction and then another before she decided to toss some hay to the cows and horses in the barn.

He followed and helped her, though he had trouble remembering what he'd meant to do with the pail of oats in his hands.

The land feud had ended days ago when he'd talked to Father about it. Father had seen the foolishness of continuing it, though maybe only because he was interested in becoming involved in politics.

But finally the feud between him and Rose had ended. He could ask for nothing better.

Except, perhaps, to know that Ebner would obey orders on this matter. Duke meant to see that he did.

Chapter Twelve

They'd kissed. Though barely. Still, it seemed a promise of things to come. Good things. Sheltered inside the barn, secluded by the storm, it hardly seemed possible that she and Duke had ever been enemies.

Hope whinnied and stomped a hoof, and Rose jerked her attention to the bundle of hay she carried.

"I'm coming, you impatient creature."

How long had she been lost in her thoughts?

She stole a glance at Duke. He stood at his horse, his gaze distant. She smiled. Had he found their kiss as surprisingly pleasant as she had?

He released a drawn-out sigh and moved away from his horse. He turned, caught her watching him, and their gazes locked.

She stood motionless. Aware of nothing but the shimmering air between them and the imprint of his lips on hers. She lifted a hand and touched her lips.

He smiled, triumph lighting his eyes.

Realizing what she'd done, she wheeled around and bumped into Hope's side.

The horse sidestepped but otherwise paid her no mind.

A cat jumped onto the stall wall and meowed.

"Where did I put that food?" She retraced her steps and found the bucket just inside the door. She didn't recall putting it down. The cat dish waited nearby and she dumped the food into it. "Kitty, kitty," she called and the cats tumbled from the loft, from the tack room and from a stall they shared with one of the cows.

Duke chuckled.

When she pushed to her feet, the power of his look held her like a vise, making it impossible to form a rational thought. She tried to yank her attention from him but found she could not.

She swallowed loudly.

He grinned. "Is Patches ready to go visit Billy?"

She turned her attention to the cat, both relieved and sad to be free of his look.

Against her better judgment she brought her gaze back to him.

He watched the cats, his expression unreadable— Did she see regret? Longing? Confusion? It bothered her that she couldn't say. Shouldn't he look pleased, satisfied, at having kissed her?

Had he found the kiss unsatisfactory? How could that be possible? She'd enjoyed it so.

Maybe she'd misread the meaning behind it. Maybe he hadn't meant it as a touching of lips, an opening of hearts. Another kiss would give her a chance to reassess the situation.

She took a step toward him.

"Do you realize how fortunate you are?" His words stopped her in her tracks.

"I am?" Because he'd kissed her? Didn't he realize

it worked both ways? He was fortunate she'd allowed him to kiss her.

"You're surrounded by pets." He scooped up one of the cats. "I never had any growing up. My father said cats had a job to do." He told her of finding a batch of kittens only to have them taken away.

As he spoke, her breathing eased. He wasn't regretting their kiss, only his lack of pets.

"You're welcome to take one of these cats or wait until spring when there'll likely be several batches of kittens."

"Several?" His eyes widened.

"We never have any trouble giving them away."

"Like I said, you're most fortunate." His gaze dipped to her mouth. "I am, too…more so every day." His voice thickened.

Her thoughts scrambled. Did he mean because of her? One of the cats meowed, bringing her thoughts back to reality.

Patches. Billy would be worried about his cat. "We should get back to the house."

The wind still rattled the barn doors. But inside she was warm and cozy and content. Even though a storm raged outside, they could hardly stay here forever.

It stunned her to think how she might be talking about their life. This moment was sweet and safe, but outside there was Ebner.

She shivered. "When do you expect your father back?"

"I'm not sure. I believe he expects to be asked to serve in some capacity in the new state legislature. He said not to expect him home for some time."

Had Mr. Caldwell truly spoken to the cowboys to end

the harassment of the Bells? If he had, did Ebner mean
to listen? It seemed that for Ebner, wreaking havoc
on the Bells was more than an order he had to carry
out. He seemed to get some personal delight out of it.
She'd always had the impression that Mr. Caldwell ran
things from the safety of his office and Ebner carried
out things in whatever way he decided.

Would Ebner listen to Duke if it came to that?

She shivered again.

Duke unwound from the wall and moved to the door.
"You're cold. We need to get back."

Thankfully he had misinterpreted her shiver. She
didn't want to tell him her concerns. He'd think she
considered him purely ornamental as a Caldwell. At
the moment she couldn't say how she felt about his role.

She scooped up Patches, tucked her securely inside
her coat and then squared her shoulders. Time to face
the storm.

Again she shivered, sensing her thoughts applied to
much more than the weather.

Duke squeezed her arm as if to reassure her. Though
whether or not he had the same unsettling thoughts,
she couldn't say and didn't mean to ask, preferring to
dwell in this little shell of seclusion as long as possible.

He reached around her and pushed the door open.

She gasped at the blast of cold air that stole her breath
and then grasped the rope. "Hang on," she called to him.
She didn't move until he closed the door and his hand
clamped next to hers on the rope.

As they crossed the yard she noted the snow had
abated enough she could make out the shapes of the
buildings, but still she clung to the rope as if it was all
that kept her safe. She meant no harm to man or beast,

but if only the storm would stay over the area for a few more hours perhaps she and Duke could find more solid ground between them.

Finally they reached the house and stepped inside.

Billy stood in front of them. "Is Patches okay?"

Rose unbuttoned her coat and handed the cat to him. He buried his nose against the warm fur.

"He's been fretting since you left," Ma said, sounding affectionate. She obviously wasn't fussed about Billy's sometimes odd behavior.

Pa lay beneath a quilt on the cot, snoring softly.

She and Duke slipped out of their snow-covered outerwear and hurried to the stove to warm up.

"I have tea waiting," Ma said. She kept her voice low so she wouldn't disturb Pa.

The four of them huddled at the stove, speaking softly as Rose gave a report of the trip to the barn. "The animals are safe and warm."

"So are we. Thank God for that." Ma glanced around the house with gratefulness. Her gaze came to Rose and she smiled. "We have been richly blessed."

Rose hugged her mother. There had never been a shadow of doubt that the three girls were welcomed and loved by the Bells. But as always, a little nag of dissatisfaction stirred at the back of her brain. What had her birth mother been like? Why would their birth father abandon them? She liked to think it was for a good reason but how could she be certain? And what reason was sufficient enough? And the most persistent question of all… Had Rose been such a difficult child she'd driven him away?

She'd once said something of the sort to Ma and Ma had cried out a protest. "Don't ever think you are to blame. Even if you weren't the sweetest, kindest, most loving child ever, which you are, children are not responsible for the decisions adults make." Ma had always said she believed something profoundly awful had prevented the man from returning.

Her insistence had never quite convinced Rose.

Duke nudged her. His gaze claimed hers. "I believe your mother means you are a blessing." He shifted his attention to the older woman. "Am I correct, Mrs. Bell?"

"You are indeed. Rose and her sisters are true gifts from God."

"There you go. You're a gift from God."

Rose ducked her head at the warmth in Duke's gaze and hoped Ma wouldn't notice the way he looked at her. For a fraction of a second she told herself that Ma's words and Duke's gentle look erased all her doubts. But remnants niggled at the back of her mind.

Would she ever be able to put them to rest fully and permanently?

Warmed, she moved to the table. Duke followed. Billy sat nearby playing with Patches while Ma went to her chair to work on her mending.

She thought of suggesting another round of checkers but knew her mind was too preoccupied to present a challenge to Duke.

When Pa groaned as he tried to sit up, Duke jumped up and went over to assist him.

"Thank you," Pa said. "How is the weather?"

They all cocked their heads to listen.

"Sounds like the wind has died down some," Pa said with satisfaction.

Rose went to the window. "The snow has almost

stopped." Try as she might, she could not inject any enthusiasm into her voice.

It was time to return to normal.

Only she wasn't sure what form normal would take now. Would things go back to the way they had been most of her life? Or would friendship with Duke change all that?

Duke watched Rose at the window. Did she look sad that the storm was ending? If they'd been alone he would go to her and assure her that things would be different from now on. He'd see to it personally.

He helped Mr. Bell to his feet. Mr. Bell headed for the window, which gave Duke an excuse to do likewise. He crowded close to Rose.

"A fair bit of snow," Mr. Bell said. "'Tis good for the land."

"The drifts are huge." Rose sounded distracted, as if she'd said the first thing that came to mind.

Duke tucked a pleased smile into his heart and dared hope she wished they could continue to be storm-bound.

"As soon as it clears up we'll be on our way." He hoped his words sounded calm and ordinary. Not full of the regret he felt deep in his heart.

"Give it a little longer." Mr. Bell went to his chair at the table. "Ma will make us tea while we wait." He signaled the others to join him and soon they were enjoying tea and some of the cookies Duke had made the day before.

Each bite filled his mouth with sweetness and hope. Surely this was the beginning of a new relationship between the Bells and the Caldwells.

"Tell us about Philadelphia," Mr. Bell said. "Did you

feel pride at being at the site of the First Continental Congress?"

"I did." He told them of the historic sites and the places he'd visited while down east.

"Don't you wonder if you might miss it?" Rose asked.

He hoped her question meant she might be concerned he would want to return. "I felt constrained by all the buildings, actually. I missed the open spaces and the mountains. Montana is my home."

Her eyes glistened and she smiled. "Good to hear."

Mr. Bell cleared his throat. "History is important. It is part of who we are and who we are to become."

A cold draft swept through Duke's insides as if the door had blown open. Mr. Bell spoke of country but Duke knew Rose would interpret her father's words personally. They would echo her doubts about who she was.

Sure enough, she pressed the knuckle of one finger to her teeth and stared down at the table.

He wanted to reach across the table and take her hands between his and assure her she was Rose and that was all that mattered. Aware that her parents might find such an action inappropriate, he stared at her, willing her to look at him.

Slowly her head lifted. Even more slowly, her eyes followed and he bit the inside of his lip at the doubt and sorrow that filled her eyes. *Oh, Rose, it doesn't matter where you came from, who your parents were or why your father abandoned you. What matters is your beautiful nature.*

He couldn't speak the words but he hoped she heard them just the same.

Mrs. Bell returned to the window. "I see blue sky."

Mr. Bell and Billy joined her, exclaiming over the clearing skies.

Duke stayed at the table, loath to leave. Things had changed between him and Rose. Between him and the Bells. He wanted to believe things had also changed between the Caldwells and the Bells, but he knew Rose wouldn't believe so until she lived it.

He especially didn't want to leave Rose with such a strong reminder that she had no history beyond when the Bells had found her and her sisters.

But it was time to leave. He pushed up from the table. "I'll go saddle our horses."

Rose gave a decisive nod. "I'll help you. Billy, you stay here until we bring the horses back."

"Okay. Patches doesn't want me to leave." He clung to the cat.

Duke and Rose donned their warm clothes and stepped outside. The sun made them squint.

"I guess we don't need to use the rope to guide us." He almost wished they did. It had bound their hands together in a fight against nature. But it had also bound their hearts together.

Inside the barn he caught her arm and turned her to face him. "Rose, your pa only spoke of our country when he said that about history."

"I know. But it's true, isn't it? History is important. It tells us who we are."

He planted his hands on her shoulders. "So does looking in the mirror."

She blinked.

He pressed on. "That's who you are. You go look in your mirror and tell me that any part of you is missing. You have all your body parts. You have a sharp mind and a good heart." He caught a lock of her hair that had escaped from under her knitted hat. Seems he always wanted to touch it, turn it to see the light catch it, watch it change color from red to gold to ginger. "You have a pair of green eyes like the finest emerald gems and your hair is so—" Would she laugh if he called it gorgeous?

"Red? Like fire in a woodshed."

He gave her a little shake. "Please forget I ever said that. I was a silly, thoughtless little boy looking for attention in all the wrong ways." A chuckle came from deep within. "And you gave it to me." He looked into her eyes; knew she saw more than his face. She saw clear to his soul.

"Maybe that's why I teased you so much. At least you noticed me."

Doubt and belief warred in her expression.

He didn't give her a chance to decide which to go with. "And, no, I wasn't about to say your hair was red like fire." His voice deepened. "I was going to say it is beautiful." Surely a better word choice than "gorgeous."

"It changes color with every movement." He turned the strand back and forth, mesmerized by the changes. "It goes from cranberry to gold to ginger to—" Realizing how foolish he must sound, he clamped his mouth shut.

She laughed; a throaty sound as if it was caught deep inside and only a whisper escaped. "Duke, when did you go from an annoying tease to a romantic poet?"

The tips of his ears burned with a mixture of embarrassment and pleasure.

She touched his lips. "I can't believe this mouth is the one that used to torment me so."

"And has now kissed you." Oh, mercy. What had

happened to all his senses that he blurted forth such things?

Her finger slid away from his mouth but her gaze lingered on his lips. Surely it was an invitation.

"I'd like to kiss you again," he murmured.

In response she closed her eyes and tipped her face up to him.

If he followed his heart he would wrap his arms around her and kiss her as though there was no tomorrow. But he forced himself to be wise and kept his hands on her shoulders. His kiss was chaste and quick, then he leaned back.

Her eyes begged for more but he had to be strong enough for both of them. "Didn't we come here for something else?"

Her cheeks colored pink and she stepped away. "We need to saddle the horses." She hurried to the tack room to retrieve Billy's saddle.

Duke followed at a slower pace to get his own. All too soon the horses stood ready to lead from the barn.

"Rose." He couldn't leave with her thinking he didn't enjoy their kiss. "This has been the best day of my life to date but I hope to have more just like this, only without the storm."

"It has? You do?"

He chuckled softly. "You have no idea how much I hope for it."

A slow smile curved her lips and she lowered her gaze. "Me, too."

Her shy response pleased him clear to the depths of his being. "Then count on it."

"I will." Her smile reached his heart and took up residence. He walked from the barn, his head high, his shoulders back, tall and proud. There was something about Rose. There'd always been something about Rose that made him want to shout her name.

He led the horses to the house and Billy stepped out, bundled up to leave. He still held Patches in his arms.

"I guess you have to put her down now," Duke said.

Rose leaned close and whispered in his ear, her breath tickling not only his cheek but his every sense. "He can take the cat if that's okay with you."

Duke tried to think but found it difficult with Rose leaning so close. Mrs. Humphrey often kept a cat in the kitchen. It had never been allowed in the rest of the house. He saw no reason Billy couldn't do the same.

"Billy, do you want to take the cat home with you?"

Billy looked ready to burst into tears. "Can I?"

Duke nodded. "If it meets with the Bells' approval."

All of them nodded and smiled. It struck Duke how generous they were. How they took pleasure in doing things for others.

"Goody, goody." Billy smiled so wide it must have hurt. "She can ride inside my coat." He tucked the cat in so only her head peeked out at Billy's neck. Patches licked his chin once then settled in as if she knew exactly what Billy expected of her.

Duke helped Billy into his saddle. They said their goodbyes and thank-yous, and rode away. At the top of the hill, he turned. Only Rose remained in the doorway. He lifted his hand to wave goodbye and she waved back. He watched her for the space of three heavy heartbeats, then, with a final wave, rode over the hill. He glanced back but the farm was now out of sight.

He turned his attention toward breaking a trail for them through the snow-covered track.

The sun reached its zenith before they approached the ranch. Duke sniffed. Was that cigar smoke? Had his parents returned? It would be an answer to his prayer if they had. He could ask his father for reassurance that the feud was over.

He went to the barn first and he and Billy took care of their mounts. When they were done and ready to cross the yard, Billy picked up Patches.

"Can I take her to the house?"

"She can stay in the kitchen. Mrs. Humphrey says a good cat keeps the mice away."

Billy was immediately defensive. "Patches is a good cat."

"I know she is. Now let's go to the house."

The smell of cigar smoke grew stronger and Duke threw open the door expecting to see his father. His greeting stalled in his throat. Ebner leaned back in a chair, his boots resting on the kitchen table, one of Father's cigars clamped between his teeth.

Billy skittered away to the farthest corner.

"So you survived the storm."

"We're here." The tone of Ebner's voice grated Duke's nerves, as did his posture. Did he have plans to move in and take over the Caldwell Ranch?

Ebner's boots clattered to the floor. "Where you been?"

"We found shelter."

"Let me guess. You just 'happened' to find shelter at the Bells'. Boy, your pappy is going to wonder whose side you're on."

"I expect my father would be grateful I am safe and sound. Besides, didn't he inform you he has no more interest in feuding with the Bells?"

Ebner narrowed his eyes but didn't answer. His look

grabbed Duke's throat. Did the man intend to ignore direct orders? Or only make it plain he obeyed them reluctantly?

"By the way," Duke continued, "does he know you go into his office in his absence and help yourself to his cigars?"

Ebner pulled the cigar from his mouth with no sign of guilt. His eyes narrowed to slits. "Your pappy considers me a valuable asset to his business. He counts on me to carry out his wishes."

Duke noted that Ebner hadn't said Father's "orders." That gave him hope that Father didn't know the specifics of what Ebner had been doing. Duke simply could not believe his father would stoop to approving some of the underhanded, cruel things Ebner had done to the Bells. After all, grandfather would certainly have drummed the Caldwell motto home to his son as thoroughly as he had to his grandson. Honor Above All.

He drew himself up tall. He was the Caldwell here and as such he had authority over Ebner. "I'm in charge while my father is away and I certainly don't need to explain myself to you. Now, if you'll excuse us…" He tipped his head toward the door.

Ebner didn't move, his scowl challenging Duke.

Duke refused to budge.

Ebner snorted. "You aren't near as big as you think you are." He stomped from the room and slammed the door as he left.

"What did he mean?" Billy's voice trembled.

"Nothing. It's just talk."

But a warning shuddered up his spine. Ebner was not a man to take lightly.

Chapter Thirteen

The next day Rose hitched the horse to the sleigh Pa had built. It wasn't a thing of beauty but would travel the snow-covered roads easily so she could go to town and back.

As she worked, she considered the two days of the storm. She'd been kissed twice, Duke had promised the feud was over and he said he'd deal with Ebner. But was it all just a dream—a span out of time? Duke hadn't returned to visit. Not that she'd expected it. There really hadn't been time, although the hours had passed so slowly that the past day had felt like three days. Yesterday she'd glanced out the window so often that Ma had asked if she'd expected someone to come calling.

"No, just feeling cooped in. I think I'll go for a walk." She'd had to wade through snowbanks but it had been better than being indoors wondering and waiting, regretting and wishing. The walk had been invigorating. The frozen river lay between whipped-cream drifts of snow. The tree branches wore a snowy covering, their shimmering surface reflecting the blue sky.

She'd stood on the bank overlooking the scene for a long time, her thoughts soothed by the beauty and peacefulness in front of her.

"A reminder of God's power and majesty." She'd spoken the words aloud in the silence. She needed to trust God to take care of all the petty details bothering her.

She'd returned to the house more peaceful and had spent the rest of the day working in the barn. It hadn't skipped her attention that Duke seemed closer in there.

Now, as she finished harnessing the horse, she turned to survey the hill in the direction of the Caldwell Ranch. She had no reason to expect Duke to visit and yet she wished he would.

Likely she'd see him in town. Eagerly, she loaded some vegetables into the sleigh and covered them to prevent freezing, then with a final glance to the crest of the hill, said goodbye to Ma and Pa and started toward town.

At the fork that led to the Caldwell Ranch, she paused. Nothing moved but the clouds in the sky. Realizing the irony of her longing, she laughed. For years she had glanced up the hill and down the road with dread and had released a sigh of relief when she'd seen nothing headed her way. Now here she was wishing for a rider to approach.

Her feelings toward Duke certainly had changed… but until she could be certain the Caldwell cowboys posed no further danger to the Bells, she must continue to be cautious. She would take care of business in town and hurry home to make sure the Caldwell cowboys didn't do any damage while the place was unguarded except for Ma and Pa. Pa would no doubt think he could ward off any cows or cowboys riding across the land. She didn't want him to do anything to slow his healing.

Her muscles tensed. Her chest grew tight. She urged the horse forward and the sleigh skimmed across the snow-covered trail.

It took the better part of an hour to distribute the vegetables and visit the three people Ma had asked her to take medicinals to. She went to the store for the mail and the few supplies on Ma's list. A pink and red valentine card displayed under the glass counter caught her eye. On the outside was a lacy white heart filled with red roses. What would the verse inside say? She puffed out her cheeks. Likely something syrupy sweet. Not the sort of thing she'd give to someone like Duke.

Would she give him a valentine card this year? He'd kissed her, didn't that mean something?

She half turned away, then looked again at the valentine.

She and her classmates had exchanged valentine cards at school. Ma had insisted she give everyone a card. Even Duke. Like most of her friends, she and her sisters had made their own cards.

A smile accompanied the memory. One year she'd made a card covered with roses and inside had written "Roses are red. Violets are blue. Skunks stink and so do you."

She had waited until she was at school to complete the poem knowing Ma would forbid it.

That was the year Duke had given her a huge, rose-covered card with a syrupy verse inside. What had it said? As if she could forget, especially as it came almost directly from one of Ma's favorite poems that she read every Valentine's Day.

Love is like a red, red rose that's newly sprung in June.
Love is like a melody that's sweetly played in tune.

She'd thought he meant the words to mock her hair and would have torn the valentine to shreds but Lilly had snatched it away, saying, "It's too beautiful to destroy."

"Here you go, miss."

Rose jerked her attention to the storekeeper who held out a sack full of her supplies. She gathered up the sack and returned to the sleigh. But nothing could stop her thoughts from returning to the memory of that card.

Had Duke meant the verse as a compliment?

Had she been guilty of cruelty throughout their school days, dismissing his offerings with harsh words and actions? The idea lay like a hot, accusing rock in the pit of her stomach.

She climbed onto the seat of the sleigh and looked up and down the street. No sign of Duke. She couldn't say if she was grateful or otherwise. She needed to apologize about the valentine and dreaded the idea he might hold some resentment over her bad behavior, but more urgent than that, she longed to see him. To assure herself he was okay.

Another fact hit her. In all her time in town, she'd not seen Ebner, either. She'd feel much better if she saw him. At least she'd know he wasn't up to mischief at the farm.

She turned down the street toward Lilly's house. If she didn't stop by for a minute or two, Lilly would worry that some harm had come to them at the farm. Besides, she needed to speak to her sister.

Lilly threw open the door as soon Rose drove up and rushed out to hug her.

"I can't stay but a moment. I need to get home and make sure Ma and Pa are all right."

Lilly pulled her indoors. "How did you fare during the storm?"

"Good. Duke and Billy rode out the storm with us."

Lilly stood back and stared. "And you are both still alive?"

Rose laughed. "It was actually okay." She told Lilly everything, except about the kisses in the barn.

"Do you really think he persuaded his father to end the feud?"

Rose shrugged. "He was quite certain he had."

Lilly tilted her head. "Do you trust Duke?"

Rose stared at her twin. "I do but I don't."

"What does that mean?"

"When he was there and we were face-to-face, I believed him, trusted him, but now—" She fluttered her hands. "I wonder if I'm being too easily swayed." She pushed to her feet. "I need to get home. You know what Pa would do if Ebner tried to start trouble."

They hugged and Rose left the house. Her footsteps ground to a halt when she saw Duke waiting by the sleigh. "What are you doing here? Where's Billy?" She glanced up and down the street.

"Billy's at the store and I'm here because I want to take you out for a meal."

"I can't. I need to get home." Her tone hardened. "I don't trust Ebner not to bother the farm while I'm gone."

"He won't be doing that today. He's over at the blacksmith shop getting his horse shod and then he has some other business to conduct."

Rose stood rooted to the spot. Did she want to go with him? Yes. Oh, yes. But dare she?

"At least join me for tea. They do a very nice tea at the hotel dining room."

The door to her sister's house creaked open and Lilly stepped out. "Say yes," she whispered in Rose's ear. "You know you want to. Hello, Duke," she called.

"How are you, Lilly?"

"Fine, just fine. Rose thinks tea sounds lovely." She gave Rose a little push.

Rose nodded. "It does." She finally lifted her eyes to Duke's. At the claiming look in his eyes, the way his gaze drifted to her lips, heat surged to her cheeks. She hoped anyone watching would put her heightened color down to the crisp winter air.

Somehow she made it to the sleigh without saying or doing anything to further embarrass herself.

Duke held out his hand to help her onto the sleigh. She knew she didn't imagine he squeezed her fingers before he released her hand and her cheeks warmed even more.

Duke turned to Lilly hovering in the doorway and sketched a salute. "Good day."

"Have a nice time. Will you be in church tomorrow?" she asked him.

"I plan to be."

"Perhaps you'd like to join our family afterward."

Rose flung a silent protest toward her sister. What

did she think she was doing? Inviting a Caldwell to the Bell farm for their family day? What would Cora say?

But she held her breath waiting for Duke's answer.

"That sounds like a fine idea."

Lilly grinned at Rose. "It does indeed."

Rose didn't wait for Duke to swing into his saddle before she flicked the reins and turned down the street toward the hotel…a very public place.

People would see them together. Would they assume the feud was over?

A shiver raced up and down her spine and not because she was cold.

She couldn't shake the feeling that not everyone would be happy about seeing Rose and Duke together. And the first name that sprang to mind was Ebner.

She glanced right and left as she stepped off the sleigh at the hotel. If they could escape his notice perhaps they could also escape his vengeance.

Duke's boots barely touched the ground before Rose scurried into the hotel. Why the hurry? He slowly wrapped the reins around the hitching post and followed at a sedate pace. Had she had second thoughts about being seen with him?

He waited until they were seated and tea was ordered to lean close to ask his questions of her.

She met his demanding look with one of stubborn defiance. "You said Ebner is in town and I can't help think he would object to us being together."

The muscle in his jaw clenched. Ebner had made it very clear what he thought of the Bells and of Duke saying the feud was over. But surely he wouldn't outright defy Duke's orders. "How can he harm you when you're with me? He's certainly no danger to the farm while he's in town."

"I've found him to be a vengeful man. Sometimes I wonder if he doesn't have some personal interest in getting us off the land. He certainly takes a great deal of delight in harassing us."

Duke couldn't help notice that she spoke in the present tense. Not Ebner *took* delight but Ebner *takes* delight. She'd told Duke of things Ebner had done so he understood her fears.

Honor Above All.

How did that fit with his father condoning Ebner's actions?

He couldn't believe his father knew and approved of what Ebner did. "You might have something there." Ebner must have acted on his own initiative. But what did Ebner hope to gain by driving the Bells off?

The prim waitress in a black dress with crisp white apron set a teapot in front of them and a tiered plate loaded with dainty sandwiches and a variety of sweets.

Rose grinned and, as soon as the girl moved away, leaned forward to whisper, "Isn't this meant for sweet old ladies?"

He eyed the assortment. "Certainly not for working men." Using the tiny silver tongs provided, they each selected one of everything for their own plates.

Rose poured the tea. "Duke, answer me this. Why do our few acres matter so much to your father? He has hundreds of acres. Our farm doesn't hinder his access to the river or in any way affect the cows grazing. Why does he care?"

He'd asked himself the same question many times over the years and even asked it of his father. "You remember that picture I showed you of all that's left of the Caldwell castle?"

She nodded, her eyes guarded.

He had to make her understand. "The land was slowly taken from them. Both my father and grandfather insist their forefathers should not have let it go so easily. Both vowed they would protect their land against such erosion. My father purposely hung the picture there to remind him of the importance of holding on to what is his."

"But our land isn't his."

"He always believed it was. I think he viewed it as the beginning of having his land taken from him. Every time he looked at the picture of the Caldwell castle he said it began with one person taking just a little until there is nothing left."

Rose shook her head. "Surely you know that doesn't make any sense. No one is trying to take his land."

Duke shrugged.

She ate a tiny sandwich and sipped at her tea. "You know what you should do? Take that picture down and hide it so he doesn't always see us as the beginning of a tidal wave of invaders."

He chuckled at her unexpected solution.

Her gaze came slowly to his and at the look of regret in them, his breath lodged somewhere between his lungs and his mouth. What did she have to regret?

"Do you remember Valentine's Day at school?"

He nodded slowly. Where was this conversation going?

"I mean a particular one. You gave me a big red valentine with a poem inside." She quoted the poem.

"I remember." Even then there had been something

about Rose that drew him to her. Only then he hadn't known how to express his feelings and had hoped the poem would say it.

"It was a very sweet poem but I thought you meant it to mock my hair." She brushed at her head as though she wanted to erase any trace of her red hair and lowered her eyes. "I'm afraid I was cruel. I gave you a valentine with a mean poem in it." She lifted sorrow-filled eyes to him. "Do you recall?"

He nodded; his throat too tight to allow him to speak. He'd been cut to the quick by the words. "My mother made me bathe often. I didn't think I stunk like a skunk." He tried for a laugh but it sounded strained even to him.

"You didn't stink. I was mean to you when you didn't deserve it. I think I was looking for offense when none was meant. I'm sorry. Can you forgive me?" Her eyes were awash.

He placed his hands on his knees to keep from brushing the unshed tears away. Joy and happiness poured into his heart that she had acknowledged the pain she'd caused. "I forgive you. I did the day you gave me that valentine." It was the only way he'd gotten over the pain.

He brought the words out for her to hear. "I think I envied you a little."

"Envied me? Why?"

"For so many things. You had your sisters. They were ready-made friends and allies. I always felt my friends valued me more for being the rich rancher's son than for me. Do you know how many times someone would ask me to ask my father to buy this or that for 'us'? Meaning 'them.'" He lifted one shoulder as if it didn't matter. "Of course you don't. And I envied you because your parents had chosen you. I often wondered if my parents would have chosen me or if they were stuck with me because I was born to them." He shrugged. "Silly, isn't it?" But silly or not, he still wondered if his only value was his part in building an empire. "I think I still envy you for being chosen."

"Aren't we a foolish pair? I envied you because you knew exactly who you were and who your family was."

"I'd be glad to trade you."

They considered each other for one fragile moment, perhaps seeing each other as never before.

Her eyes seemed lit from within. He leaned close to whisper, "I like being your friend but after kissing you, I hope we can be more."

He was rewarded by a rosy blush on her cheeks.

She glanced at him from beneath the curtain of her eyelashes, a sweet, half-innocent, half-coy gesture. "Seems that's a possibility."

If they hadn't been in such a public place he would be tempted to kiss her again. Certainly he would have shouted for joy. Instead he gave a deep-throated chuckle. "I like possibilities."

They finished every bite of the goodies and drained the teapot, then he held her coat as she slipped into it. He forced himself to resist the temptation to rub his hands down her arms as he released her.

They stepped out into the cold. "I'll see you tomorrow," he said.

She nodded. "Thank you for the tea." He helped her up onto the seat of her sleigh and handed her the reins, then stood watching as she drove away.

Grinning widely, he untied King and was about to

swing into the saddle when Ebner unwound from the shadow of the wall and crossed the wooden sidewalk.

"You a Caldwell or not?" His words rasped with challenge.

"I was born a Caldwell. I'll die a Caldwell." He stared at the man. He would not flinch at the hard look.

Ebner snorted. "Your father might say to end the feud but don't fool yourself. Nothing has changed. He still wants his land back." He made a rude noise. "I intend to see he gets it. Your pappy will be most grateful." He grinned crookedly.

Duke had no doubt about what he meant. He had his sights set on driving the Bells from their land and earning approval from Duke's father. Had Father promised him a generous reward in return for that success? "My father meant it when he said to stop harassing the Bells. If you want to earn his favor, you would do well to abide by his orders."

Ebner let go a scowl fit to curdle Duke's breakfast.

He shuddered. Ebner needed watching, but it was impossible to follow him around every hour of the day.

God, please guard the Bells.

His prayer brought a tiny measure of relief from his concern. God saw everything, including Ebner.

He swung into the saddle, then turned back to the foreman. "It's time to head home."

Ebner stomped away, the sound of his boots ringing in Duke's ears. He had half a mind to hang around town until Ebner left, but surely the man couldn't do anything to the Bells so long as he remained in town.

But Ebner wouldn't stay in Bar Crossing forever. Would he return directly to the ranch or go by the Bell farm? And what would he do if he did the latter? Duke pictured damaged fences, dead animals, maybe worse. Rose might be hurt in the next mischief Ebner perpetrated on the Bells.

Duke's insides twisted into a worried knot. He simply didn't trust anything about Ebner—except his vow to get the Bells to leave.

He rode slowly down the street, trying to assure himself that Rose and her parents would remain cautious while out in the yard. It was a good thing Rose had said she wouldn't believe the feud was over until she saw hard evidence.

They had good reason to be concerned about Ebner. He shared their concern and glanced over his shoulder.

But Ebner had disappeared. A fact that caused Duke's muscles to twitch. Best if he stayed in town and kept an eye on the man.

Chapter Fourteen

Rose glanced back several times as she drove toward home, expecting—hoping—Duke would join her and at least ride as far as the fork in the road. But she reached the spot where the trails diverged. She shielded her eyes and watched a rider in the distance but couldn't make out if it was Duke. And the rider made no attempt to catch up with her.

Well, it wasn't as though she needed him to accompany her.

Need had nothing to do with it, she admitted. She wanted to share more of his company.

She reached the farm and pulled up to the house to unload the few things she'd bought and to assure her folks she was home safely. Likewise, to assure herself Ma and Pa were okay.

Pa napped on the cot but his color was good and he breathed easily. He appeared to be improving.

Ma sat in her rocking chair, the book of poems Duke had brought open on her lap. She glanced up and smiled. "I'm surely enjoying these poems. It was generous of Duke to bring it. He seems like a decent person."

Did Ma's look suggest she'd noticed Rose's changing attitude toward Duke? Rose almost snorted. Ma would have to be blind not to notice. "He's changed."

"For the better?"

"Definitely." She ducked out to take care of the horse and sleigh before Ma could say anything more.

As she led the horse toward the barn her thoughts wandered to the lovely tea she and Duke had shared at the hotel. But it wasn't the fine china and linen, or even the dainty goodies she thought of. It was the pleasant company and the growing attraction she felt toward Duke.

She moved across the yard automatically, paying no heed to the familiar path, but something out of the ordinary caught her distracted attention. In an instant her full focus returned to the present and she stared at the ground. Footprints from a boot much larger than her own. Right in front of the barn door. She pressed a hand to her chest as if she could still the way her heart beat frantically at her ribs.

Sucking in a deep breath and praying for God's protection, she eased the barn door open. "Who's there?" She congratulated herself that her voice sounded firm and challenging. She felt quite the opposite.

There was no answer but a gentle moo from the nearest cow and meows from a couple of the cats.

Not allowing herself to back away in fear, she grabbed the nearby pitchfork and stepped into the shadows. "Come out. Show yourself." She tiptoed to the tack room. No one there. Down the alley she peered into each stall. No one. She glanced overhead. No way was she going up there. Not alone.

Had someone been inside the barn?

She looked around for clues. Yes, someone had piled a small stack of hay in the corner. She stared at it a moment. It seemed a harmless thing to do yet it caused her nerves to twitch.

She returned to the doorway and studied the footprints. A pair led in and another set led out. Perhaps the invader had left. Her muscles relaxed marginally. Still carrying the fork as her only means of protection, she exited the barn and followed the tracks. They led to the back of the building, where a trampled area indicated a horse had been tied. Another pile of hay had been left close to the barn. Had it been someone feeding his horse? She had no objection to anyone with need helping themselves, but this didn't feel right.

The footprints led to the sheep shelter.

Her nerves twisted until she could barely clutch the fork.

The Caldwell cowboys had made several attempts to harm the sheep in the past.

Tracks returned from the shelter, making her certain the intruder was not there. But she had to investigate, see what harm had been done, and she forced her leaden feet onward. She eased around the corner and peered into the sheep shelter. The animals huddled in the far corner and bleated at her arrival. Apart from that, they seemed unharmed. But something had caused them to bunch up. She shifted her gaze to the left and gasped. A dead chicken. She grabbed the bird, kicked straw over the blood and hurried from the shelter.

After disposing of the body, she retraced her steps and examined the footprints again. She stood where the horse had been and looked around. From here the intruder would not be visible from the house. The tracks indicated only one man and he'd left not-too-subtle warnings. It seemed like something Ebner would do, but he'd been in town with Duke.

Hadn't they been late arriving in town? At least, she hadn't seen him until she was almost ready to leave for home.

Had Ebner done this before he and Duke had gone to town? After Rose had left the farm?

She shuddered. Whether Ebner had done this or another cowboy following his orders, the message was clear.

Ebner meant to continue his efforts to get rid of the Bells.

She must tell Duke. He'd do something to stop the man.

The thought did nothing to ease the tension in her neck, which lingered throughout the rest of the day and even as she climbed into bed. She prayed most earnestly for the safety of her parents and their farm.

And, please, God, protect us and help this land feud to end in more than hopeful words. Let the harassment end.

Ma and Pa were dressed for church the next morning when she came out of her bedroom. "Are you up to the trip?" Rose asked her pa.

"I'm feeling better every day."

He'd said the same thing every morning since the stampede. Rose hoped this time it was true.

As she did the chores she glanced around, wary of any sign of things being amiss. No cowboy or cows came over the hill. Nothing had been disturbed around the yard. On her way back to the house, she gave another slow, deliberate, complete study of the surroundings.

Grub watched her.

She patted his head. "Grub, old friend, I think we might have to find a better watchdog to keep you company." Though what difference would it make? She had half a mind to stay behind with a loaded shotgun in her hands except for two things.

Pa had never allowed the Caldwell threat to prevent them from attending church. "If they're set on mischief it will happen whether we're here or not."

Second, and more importantly, she wanted to see Duke again. When he was around she found it much easier to believe he'd changed and to trust his good intentions of ending the feud.

So she hurried to her room to change for church into her dark blue woolen dress. Did it accentuate her coloring in a flattering way?

She brushed her hair and began to braid it but Duke's words filled her thoughts. He'd said her hair was beautiful. He'd made her believe it.

Instead of a braid she normally wrapped tightly around her head and covered with a bonnet, she coiled her long hair into a soft roll and pinned it in place. It would frame her bonnet.

Pa had hitched the horse to the sleigh and was waiting for her at the door. She hurried out to join her parents. She would volunteer to drive but Pa looked so hale and hearty that she sat back, pleased he was having a good day.

Upon their arrival they hurried inside. Cora, Wyatt and Lonnie were already seated. Next to them sat Caleb,

Teddy and Lilly, who patted the spot next to her. Rose slipped in, leaving her parents to follow.

"How was tea?" Lilly whispered.

"Very fancy. The sandwiches were—"

"You know I don't mean the food."

"You did say 'tea.'"

"How was the company?" Lilly nudged Rose. "There he is now."

Duke caught Rose's eye as he paused in the aisle.

She nodded and smiled politely.

Billy waved.

Duke hesitated a moment. When she didn't invite him to join them, he guided Billy across the aisle and they sat down.

"What's the matter with you?" Lilly whispered. "You should have invited him to sit with you."

"There's hardly room."

Lilly gave her a look brimming with disbelief. She sat back with a grunt but two seconds later she turned to Rose. "Did you two argue?"

"No." But someone had sent her a strong warning and she wasn't about to ignore it. Least of all in public. They rose for the singing of the first hymn and Duke turned slightly—not enough to attract notice or speculation but enough that Rose felt him watching her. She tried to keep her attention on the hymnal in her hands but she knew the words by heart and her gaze went unbidden in his direction.

His blue eyes flashed in awareness and question.

She couldn't pull herself from the power of those eyes. Couldn't remember she meant to hide her attraction for fear of making Ebner angry enough to do something dreadful to the Bells.

The song was over and Lilly tugged at her to sit down.

She plunked to the hard bench and smoothed her skirt. Somehow she managed to keep her attention focused straight ahead throughout the rest of the service. But from the periphery of her vision she glimpsed his blond hair, noted how steady he held his head, as if mesmerized by every word Pastor Rawley spoke.

To her shame, Rose could not recount a single thing the man said.

The final amen ended the service and they rose to leave.

Duke stepped into the aisle and greeted Pa.

Pa shook his hand. "Nice to see you again, son. You'll join us at the farm for dinner I hope."

Every sound sucked from the building as people stared at her pa.

So much for being discreet about the Bells and Caldwells socializing.

Rose glanced at every face. Was there anyone who seemed unhappy about this apparent reconciliation? But none gave her cause to think they would report this to Ebner. Nevertheless, he'd soon enough know. News traveled fast in a small town like Bar Crossing.

"I gratefully accept your invitation." His smile included them all, but he held Rose's gaze until Lilly jabbed her in the back.

"I'd like to move, if you don't mind," Lilly whispered.

Rose hurried after her parents and quickly climbed into the sleigh. "The others will be along right away," she said to Pa, hoping he would take the hint and hurry home.

Not until they were back and she saw the buildings still standing and the animals all safe was she able to relax.

* * *

On horseback Duke and Billy followed the entourage of sleighs headed toward the Bell farm.

"Why didn't we sit with Rose and her ma and pa at church?" Billy asked.

"Didn't appear to be room."

"Oh." Billy sounded more puzzled than satisfied. "Maybe there won't be room at the farm."

Poor Billy. Still expecting to be turned away by people. Duke slowed King so he rode directly at Billy's side. "Do you think Mr. Bell would ask us in that case?"

Billy brightened. "I guess he wouldn't. Good. I like the Bells and want to see them again." His brow furrowed. "Will Rose's sisters like me?"

"Of course they will. You just be Billy. Everybody likes Billy."

Billy's smile barely touched his lips before he sobered. "Not everybody."

"You have lots of friends here, so stop worrying about those who might not like you."

"Ebner doesn't like me."

Billy had mentioned it before. Duke knew Ebner made unkind comments but he'd not witnessed anything more harmful and Billy seldom left Duke's side. "Ebner won't hurt you." He hoped he was right in making that promise.

They arrived at the farm and while Billy went directly to the house, Duke took their horses to the barn. Wyatt and Caleb also led in their horses. The two men watched Duke with open curiosity.

Thankfully Duke didn't detect any hostility in their looks.

Caleb spoke first. "I never thought to see the day a

Caldwell would be invited to join us. Rose, especially, has had nothing good to say about you and your family."

"But especially you," Wyatt added.

Duke finished with his horse then stood in front of them. "I was an awful tease."

They grinned. "So we've heard."

"Also heard that Rose did her best to teach you better manners." To illustrate his meaning, Wyatt tossed a pretend punch at Duke's stomach.

Caleb's eyes narrowed. "And now she has two brothers-in-law who will defend her. So be warned. Don't mess with our little Rose."

Both men crossed their arms over their chests and stood facing him.

Duke caught his fingers in the pocket of his jacket and leaned back on his heels. "Good to know. But you can relax. No one is going to hurt Rose." Again he hoped he would be able to keep that vow. He would certainly do everything in his power to do so. "Things change. People change."

The pair continued to study him.

He returned their stares without blinking.

Caleb nodded first. "I'm prepared to give you a chance." He dropped his arms and stepped back.

Wyatt nodded. "Me, too. But only one." He nodded toward the door. "Let's go join the others."

The three men marched across the yard and into the house.

The table had been extended to accommodate the extra people. The house was full but somehow it didn't feel crowded. Duke tried to analyze the feeling but Billy called to him.

"Teddy is teaching me to play a marble game." Billy

and Caleb's five-year-old son sat in the corner by the cot, each with a handful of marbles.

Duke watched the game for a moment but the rules made no sense to him even though the two players seemed to understand them.

Mrs. Bell and her three daughters hustled around with last-minute meal preparations.

Lonnie, Wyatt's almost-grown brother, bent over a drawing Mr. Bell described.

Caleb and Wyatt discussed the weather.

Duke watched them all, feeling like an outsider. Then Wyatt turned to him. "How did your animals fare during the storm and after?"

Duke joined the men. He told them he'd ridden out to the pastures and found the cows sheltered safely in a lower pasture. "Some of the men had to break the snow crust so the cows could get at the grass." He didn't mention that Ebner had pointed out that they had managed without Duke's help or presence. Or that he'd suggested Duke should stay in the house where he'd be nice and warm.

Sooner or later, Ebner would have to accept that Duke meant to help his father run the ranch even though every time he rode out to help, Ebner informed him he wasn't needed. He'd wanted to move the cows to a lower pasture that had a natural pond where they could water the animals. But the cowboys had followed Ebner's instructions and moved them to one with more trees but no water. It was the sort of thing that happened over and over.

Mrs. Bell announced the meal was ready and told everyone to find a place to sit. Somehow Duke ended up directly across from Rose, who sat next to her twin sister.

Both of them smiled at him. He wondered at the way Lilly's eyes flashed but immediately forgot it as he was captured by the warmth and welcome in Rose's eyes.

He liked her hair all soft around her head like that and quirked his eyebrows to silently tell her so.

Her cheeks blossomed. Like a beautiful summer rose.

Mr. Bell reached for his hand and the family formed a circle of joined hands as the patriarch asked a blessing upon the food and those who gathered around the table to share it.

There followed a flurry of passing food—a pork roast with three different kinds of roasted vegetables, flavorful beet pickles and generous slices of Mrs. Bell's bread.

For a bit the conversation centered on comments about the food, then it gradually shifted to questions and answers about various friends and neighbors.

Duke had been aware of Cora's careful study throughout the meal and as soon as a break came in the conversation she leaned forward from down the table by Mrs. Bell.

"I have to say I'm full of curiosity. What is a Caldwell doing in the Bell house?"

"Cora!" Mrs. Bell sounded shocked. "He's a guest."

Cora, undeterred, continued. "First and foremost, he's a Caldwell."

Lilly chuckled. "Cora, you don't know the half of it. I've been dying to tell the story."

Rose jabbed her sister in the ribs. "I'll tell anything there is to tell."

"*Someone* tell me," Cora said.

Wyatt chuckled and turned to Duke. "My wife has had a little trouble letting her little sisters grow up."

"I'll always be their big sister who promised to take care of them."

Lilly and Rose looked at each other and rolled their eyes.

"I'm waiting," Cora said, as if she knew the girls pretended to be diverted.

Mr. Bell smiled adoringly at his daughters. "Rose, tell your sister before she gets agitated."

That brought a laugh from everyone, except Teddy and Billy, who watched wide-eyed.

"Duke fell and hurt his head," Rose began.

"Well, that explains it all." Cora sat back as if the conversation was over.

Lilly laughed. Mr. and Mrs. Bell made scolding noises and the others looked confused.

"He fell off his horse," Rose continued, this time waiting for the reaction that came swiftly from Duke.

"I didn't fall. I got thrown."

Rose shrugged. "Same thing."

"Not at all," Wyatt said, and Caleb agreed.

Duke grinned at them. At least they understood the difference.

"I rode as fast as I could to get Rose," Billy said. "I knew she would help him."

Cora gave Rose a look of profound surprise and disbelief. Then she laughed. "Guess Billy didn't know he might have been putting Duke in a risky situation."

Billy's face twisted. "Did I do something wrong?"

Mrs. Bell patted Billy's hand. "You did exactly the right thing."

Bit by bit the story came out, accompanied with much teasing and laughing.

Cora sat back. "I can't believe you spent the night here."

"And now they're friends." Lilly waggled her brows as she said the word as if she meant more than friends.

Cora looked down the table to her father. "What does Mr. Caldwell think of this?"

Mr. Bell seemed unconcerned. "He is away in Helena."

Cora gasped. "So Ebner is in charge? That's even worse. He'll not like Duke being here." She looked as if she meant to chase Duke from the room immediately.

His spine tingled. Was everyone afraid of Ebner? To be honest, even he was but— "I'm in charge while my father is away." His announcement did little to ease the tension around the table.

"It's time for dessert and tea," Mrs. Bell announced. She planted her hands on the table as if to push back but instead she spoke again. "And it's time to put an end to such talk. Duke is our guest and he is welcome, as is Billy and everyone seated here. I won't hear of anyone objecting to it. Do you all hear me?"

"Yes, Ma," the girls chorused.

"Good." She rose and went to slice generous portions of chocolate cake.

As soon as the meal was over, Cora started gathering the dirty dishes. She paused between Lilly and Rose and whispered, "We aren't the one who needs to hear it but I very much doubt Ebner would listen to Ma or anyone else." She shot Duke a challenging look.

He hoped their fears were unfounded but they had

plenty of reason to expect Ebner to harm them in some way. He silently vowed to make sure nothing happened.

After that the tension eased and he spent an enjoyable afternoon with the Bells. When the afternoon shadows lengthened he knew he must leave. "Billy, I'll saddle the horses and bring them to the door."

"We have to go?"

"I'm afraid so. I'd like to get back before dark." He shrugged into his coat.

Rose followed. "I'll help. I need to check on the animals anyway."

Lilly and Cora watched Rose; Lilly with a little smile, Cora with a frown.

Duke met each of their looks with a silent promise that Rose was safe with him, then he and Rose crossed toward the barn.

"I want to show you something." Rose led him around the barn. "Someone was here yesterday while I was away."

His heart kicked his ribs hard. "Did they do anything?"

She led him to the sheep shed. The animals looked content and he said so. "Yesterday they were crowded into the corner, shaking with fear. I found a dead chicken there." She pointed.

His heart kicked again. "Anything else?"

"Just some hay kicked about." She showed him the pile behind the barn.

"Odd."

"I believe it's a warning."

"By whom, to whom and about what?" His skin felt two sizes too small for his bones.

"I suspect Ebner. He's telling us he isn't done with us no matter what promises you make."

"I'll talk to him."

"Will it do any good? The man has a mean streak as wide as the ocean."

"I am the boss in my father's absence." Though Ebner certainly didn't treat him as such.

Rose led them into the barn. "This whole situation makes my nerves twitch."

He caught her arms and turned her to face him. "We'll work this out. Do you believe me?"

She clutched at the sleeves of his coat and searched his eyes.

He let her see beyond the surface to the dreams and hopes of his heart, the longings of his soul.

She nodded; her eyes so full of trust and expectation that he wanted to shout.

He pulled her close, studying every detail of her face. Her porcelain skin, her fine cheekbones, her green eyes with thick dark lashes, her hair. "I like your hair like this." He trailed a finger over the roll, careful not to pull out the hairpins.

Her hands flattened and pressed to his chest, warming his heart and soul.

His gaze drifted to her full red lips. Kissable lips.

He lowered his head.

"I'll get the sleigh ready." Wyatt's voice came from outside the barn. "I'd like to get back before dark, too."

Rose stiffened but before she pulled from his arms, he trailed his finger along the curve of her jaw. Then they went to the horses and saddled them as Wyatt and Caleb entered the barn and prepared to leave.

Duke stayed back, letting them deal with their outfits. He led King and Billy's mount from the barn as Rose's sisters and their families drove from the yard shouting goodbyes.

Lilly's last words drifted to him. "It's about time the Caldwells and Bells became friends."

Rose smiled and shook her head. "Lilly has changed since she got married."

"I hear married life does that to people. For the better if they marry wisely. For the worse if they marry foolishly."

She laughed. "Now you're getting all philosophical."

Billy left the house, bidding the Bells goodbye.

"It's time to go." Duke made no attempt to hide the regret in his voice. "Back to the lonely Caldwell house where I'll have to rustle up something from the pantry for supper."

She grinned. "I've seen your pantry so I'm having a hard time feeling sorry for you."

"You can't blame me for trying."

"You know you're more than welcome to stay and have supper with us." Her eyes begged him to accept.

"I need to get back to check on things."

Questions filled her eyes but he didn't intend to add to her worries by admitting he felt a strong urge to check on Ebner's activities.

He and Billy swung up into their saddles. He called goodbye and thanks to Mr. and Mrs. Bell, who hovered in the doorway. Then with a final, reluctant goodbye to Rose, he and Billy rode away.

As they crested the hill, he turned. Rose stood where he'd left her. He waved again.

She lifted her hand slowly as if regretting his departure.

He tucked the thought into safekeeping in his heart and stood watching her across the distance for another moment.

A movement beyond her caught his attention. A rider. Someone bent low over the saddle and riding fast toward the river. As if trying to avoid detection. He couldn't be certain but it looked a whole lot like Ebner.

A thousand alarms filled his head.

Chapter Fifteen

There weren't a lot of chores to do but Rose wasn't in a hurry to return to the house. She wanted time alone with her thoughts so she returned to the barn. The little pile of hay remained on the floor. She scowled at it fiercely enough to send every blade and leaf scrambling as if driven by a fierce wind. Then she grabbed the fork and tossed it to one of the milk cows. Whatever the culprit meant to do she would not let him cause her to live in fear.

"Face me like a man," she muttered. "Stop hiding in the corners." She swept the floor clean. As effectively swept away a twirl of emotions—anger that Ebner would so slyly threaten them, uncertainty as to whether the feud could be ended as easily as Duke seemed to think, confusion about her feelings toward Duke.

One minute she felt nothing but a sweeping wave of affection and possibility. The next— She shrugged. It was getting harder and harder to think of him as the annoying boy from the past. More and more she saw him as a strong, kind man. Not a Caldwell so much as Duke. "Duke." She whispered the name several times.

With a sound that was half derisive snort and half chuckle she looked down and realized that she stood in the spot where he had twice kissed her and almost kissed her a third time.

With a sigh full of hopes and dreams, she put away the fork and broom and stepped from the barn. She sniffed the air.

Smoke! She smelled smoke! Her heart practically jumped from her chest. She sniffed again. She wasn't imagining it. Where did it come from? She turned her head from side to side to find the direction and followed the smell around the side of the barn.

Please, God, let it be some cowboy down by the river, making himself a pot of coffee.

She rounded the corner and her lungs constricted so hard she gasped. The pile of hay she'd discovered yesterday now smoldered. She ran so fast it was as if wings carried her feet forward. If she could stomp it out before flames started—

She beat at the fire with her feet.

Flames burst from the hay and leaped upward, reaching hungry fingers for the barn.

"Fire! Fire!" she screamed as she tossed handfuls of snow toward the flames. She might as well have spit in the fire. The snow merely sizzled and disappeared.

Tools. Water. Help. She raced around the barn. "Fire! Fire!" But would Ma and Pa be sleeping and not hear her? She didn't have time to run to the house.

She skidded to her knees as she rounded the corner toward the barn door. Grabbing the wall, she righted herself, yanked the door open and grabbed the nearest thing. A broom. She flung around. Where was the shovel? There. She grabbed it, too, and fled back to the fire.

Her arms pumping as if driven by a force outside herself, she shoveled scoop after scoop of snow onto the fire. The flames licked at the wall of the barn. She tossed snow faster and faster. Her teeth clenched so hard her jaw popped a protest. She would not let the barn burn down.

Suddenly a pair of arms moved in unison with hers, only they were tossing buckets of water. She spared a glance to see who had come to help. Duke. She'd never been so glad to see anyone.

Billy trotted around the corner carrying two pails of water, grabbed the empty ones and hurried back to the pump. Duke emptied the water on the wall of the barn. "Let the hay burn itself out. Help Billy bring water."

She skidded in the slush as she spun around to obey his orders. Billy dashed past her with full pails and she raced to the pump. How had Duke had time to find the spare buckets in the barn? She filled them and returned to toss them against the smoldering wall.

She didn't slow down as she raced back for more water, again and again, until her lungs ached, her legs quivered and her arms hurt. But she would not give up until the fire was out.

Duke stopped her when she returned. "I think we've got it." He took the buckets from her hands and set them down.

The hay fire had been extinguished. It looked as if Duke had beaten it out. The barn was blackened and wet but it hadn't burned.

"Billy, go to the house and make sure the Bells are okay. No need for them to come out."

Duke turned to Rose and pulled her into his arms.

Her knees folded. She clung to him but her arms were so shaky she would have fallen if he hadn't held her, his arms steady around her. She sobbed into the front of his coat.

"Shh. You're okay now. Everything is okay." He pressed his cheek to her head. "You're safe. That's all that matters." His soothing voice calmed her, filled her with a formerly unknown source of strength.

"I…I thought the barn would burn."

"When I came around the corner and saw the fire and you fighting it alone—" His voice caught and his arms tightened around her.

They clung to each other and in moments her heartbeat returned to normal.

"Thank God you showed up." She leaned back to stare into his face. "You left a while ago. How did you happen to be here when I needed you?"

He pulled out a checkered hankie and wiped her face. "You're quite a mess."

"I suppose I am." And yet she felt no need to hide from his inspection.

He wiped both cheeks and her forehead then held her in the circle of his arms.

"You're a little dirty yourself." She needed his explanation of why he'd been available at just the right moment but her gut warned her that the answer might rob them of this special moment and she was in no hurry for that. She took the handkerchief from him and wiped his face. This wasn't the first time she'd cleaned his face. Not too many days ago she'd wiped blood from it. But this time was different. Everything between them was different.

His eyes blazed bright blue as she dabbed at the soot and spatters of dirty water.

She finished, folded the handkerchief and tucked it into his pocket. Then she met his look unblinkingly.

Somehow she managed to squeeze a thank-you from her throat.

"You're most welcome."

His words seemed to come from a distance. But his look didn't falter. Didn't release her. And although a faint fluttering came from her throat like a trapped butterfly trying to escape, she didn't want to turn away from his look.

She opened her heart and soul to him. No matter what came into their lives, she would treasure this moment forever.

He sighed. "Remember how I turned at the top of the hill to wave to you?"

She nodded. She'd experienced a pang at having to bid him goodbye and had barely been able to lift her hand to wave.

Duke continued. "I noticed someone in the distance riding away in a hurry. I was almost certain it was Ebner. If it was, I knew he'd been up to mischief so I decided to hang about until I could be certain you were safe." He pulled her to his chest and cupped his hand to her head as if to anchor her there. "Thank God I did."

She knew he meant it as a prayer.

"He's determined to get us out by fair means or foul." She spoke into his coat so her words were muffled. "But why? What does he hope to gain if your father no longer wants our land?"

Duke eased her back. "I need to look into this."

Her knees weakened again as she thought of Duke confronting Ebner. "Maybe you should wait until your father returns."

"I will handle it." His voice had grown hard, his eyes brittle. "Don't you think I'm capable?"

She touched his face. "I think you can do anything you set your mind to. But Ebner won't fight fair." She pressed her palm to his cheek, wanting to wrap her arms around him and keep him safe in her embrace. "I just want you to be careful."

He smiled. "I will." He took her hand and escorted her to the house.

Ma and Pa hovered around her. "Are you okay? Billy said you put out a fire."

Between them, she and Duke explained what had happened and assured her parents that there was no damage to anyone or anything.

"You must come in and have tea," Ma said.

"Thank you, but we have to be on our way."

Billy didn't wait for Duke to say anything else but stepped outside and caught up the horses.

Rose followed Duke out the door. "You be careful and be safe."

He nodded, his expression serious. "You, too." Then he swung into his saddle and the pair galloped away.

Rose waited for Duke to turn and wave as he reached the top of the hill. She waved back though she wanted to call to him to return.

She pressed her hands to her chest as if she could stop the painful beat of her heart. But it was futile.

She knew she would worry endlessly until she knew the outcome of Duke's intention to confront Ebner.

She'd had enough experience with the man to know Duke might as well step on a hornets' nest and not expect to get stung.

The ride home did nothing to cool Duke's anger. It coiled and twisted inside him like a trapped wildcat. If

Ebner wasn't fifty pounds heavier than him and mean as a crazed wolf, Duke would be tempted to thrash him.

But he would not resort to dealing with this physically. He was a Caldwell. He had the authority to speak his mind and expect Ebner to pay attention.

He took his horse to the barn and left Billy with instructions to care for both horses, then go to the house and wait for him. Then he went in search of Ebner.

The foreman was strangely absent. None of the cowboys could testify to his whereabouts. Duke's teeth clenched so hard his jaw hurt. Whether Ebner was away or avoiding him, it didn't matter. Duke intended to speak to him at the first opportunity.

He lounged in the barn knowing the man would have to take care of his horse when he returned.

His patience was finally rewarded as Ebner led his horse inside.

Duke waited until Ebner had unsaddled the horse and turned him into a stall before he unwound from the shadows. "Howdy!" He had the pleasure of seeing Ebner start.

The man scowled at him. "You taken to playing hide and go seek?"

"Nope. Just doing my job."

Ebner snorted. "That's an outright fib. You been hanging around with that Bell bunch again. Everyone knows it. What do you think your pappy is going to say when he finds out?"

Anger clawed at the top of Duke's head and his pulse thundered in the cut on his forehead at the way Ebner continued to call Father pappy. It sounded so mocking. So disrespectful.

"You're right. I was at the Bells'." He calmed his

voice. "Fortunate for them I was. They had a fire and I was able to help put it out."

Ebner's scowl deepened though Duke would have thought it impossible. "Yeah? Do any damage?"

"None to speak of."

The man grunted.

"It was deliberately started." Duke narrowed his eyes, making his look serve as a silent challenge.

"Now ain't that too bad."

"I saw you riding away just before the fire was discovered."

Ebner took a step toward Duke, his fists knotted at his sides. "You accusing me?"

"You deny it?"

Ebner gave a laugh that made Duke's nerves twitch. "Just doing my job." He leaned threateningly close. "Something you fail to do."

Duke held his ground and met the man's look without flinching. In fact, if Father or Grandfather could see how impassive he appeared, they would be proud. "I don't know what orders my father gave you but I'm convinced he told you to end the harassment. Furthermore, I'm guessing he has no real idea what you've been doing."

Ebner snorted.

Duke took it for derision but he wasn't about to enter into an argument. "Whether he did or not is immaterial at the moment. I am in charge here and I will not tolerate such actions from anyone on the ranch payroll. I no longer need your services here. Pack your bags and leave."

Ebner leaned back on his heels and laughed, driving what felt like spikes into Duke's brain. What kind of reaction was that to being fired?

Ebner's laughter choked off as he leaned forward, almost nose to nose with Duke. "Sonny boy, you didn't hire me and you sure as guns ain't gonna fire me. And when your pappy returns you'll find out just how in charge you are of anything." Laughing again, he strode from the barn. "Fire me? Not a chance."

Duke's lungs emptied in a whoosh. He had thought Ebner might resort to some of his dirty tricks, perhaps even physical violence. He'd never have guessed Ebner would refuse to quit.

He considered his options. He could ask the sheriff to intervene, but Ebner could argue that Father had left him in charge, not Duke. It would be his word against Ebner's. No doubt the sheriff would walk away after giving them a warning to mind their manners until Mr. Caldwell returned to settle the matter.

Duke didn't see what he could do in the meantime.

But one thing was certain. He'd be staying close to the ranch where he could keep an eye on Ebner's comings and goings.

More than that, he would stay away from the Bells rather than risk incurring any more of Ebner's vengeance.

Rose would understand the need for caution.

Already he missed her.

Chapter Sixteen

～

Rose knew she wouldn't see Duke again on Sunday. He'd been there most of the day and had returned to put out the fire. He needed to get home and deal with Ebner. But when the next three days passed without any sign of him, she grew troubled. A dozen possibilities raced through her mind.

Had Ebner hurt him?

Had the cut on his forehead gotten infected? She reasoned that it had appeared fine when she'd last seen him but that didn't calm her worries. Perhaps he'd re-opened it fighting the fire. But wouldn't he come for help if he needed it? Or send Billy?

Unless Ebner prevented it. There she was, back to her first worry. Ebner was a real danger. She could re-count any number of things he'd done to the Bells but she wouldn't. No point in bringing up any more rea-son to fret.

God, keep him safe. The prayer had been her con-stant companion the past three days.

Maybe Billy was sick or injured and Duke needed to stay and attend him. She should ride over to check but when she mentioned it to Ma and Pa they both ordered her to stay away from the ranch.

"Ebner is a dangerous man." Pa's voice was firm.

"Yes, Pa." She knew it was true and had no wish to confront him.

But she would not confess aloud her most worrisome fear. Could it be that Duke had decided he didn't care to spend time with her? Had he returned home, looked at the thirteenth-century castle and realized how important it was to have a history?

She told herself that couldn't be the case. He'd been sincere when he'd said he viewed her as Rose, nothing more, nothing less. He'd convinced her she was enough for him. He'd sealed his words with a kiss. She believed him with her whole heart.

Or was she so eager for acceptance that she saw only what she wanted to see?

Oh, for goodness' sake. Was she losing her mind? She smiled. Not a chance. She knew herself and she was discovering new strengths every day.

What she needed was something to occupy herself in a constructive manner. She went to the cupboard and looked inside. A bit of lace and some fancy red paper gave her an idea. She'd make him a valentine. One that expressed her feelings and hopefully made up for the mean-spirited one she'd given him when they were children.

She spent the next two days cutting and shaping the card just right. Then she read poem after poem in Ma's book, looking for the right one.

"Why not simply write what you want to say?" Ma asked.

"I couldn't." If she used a poem written by another

and he was cold toward her, she could more easily shrug it off than if he dismissed a poem she'd composed for him alone.

But after searching for endless hours, she still hadn't found anything that suited her.

That night she sat on her bed and started putting her thoughts to paper. Rose. A flower. Symbol of Valentine's Day. Symbol of love. But was it? And why the rose? Why not, say…a dandelion? She chuckled and began to compose a poem. Well, not quite a poem but as close as she could get.

Saturday morning she hurried through her chores, anxious to get to town. Surely she'd see Duke there.

"You go without us," Ma said. "Us old folks enjoy a lazy Saturday at home."

Rose knew the "lazy Saturday" would include preparing the Sunday meal and baking goodies of one sort or another, but she gratefully went to town on her own. Ma and Pa would keep an eye on things while she was away. She wished it gave her more comfort than it did. Part of her felt they would be safer if they were with her, but they'd made their preference known and she had to obey.

In Bar Crossing she glanced up and down the street at the numerous wagons and riders on horseback, as well as the pedestrians on the board sidewalks. But none had the familiar blond hair and confident swagger of Duke Caldwell. Her heart shrank an inch.

She delivered the goods she'd brought to town, then hurried to the store. Perhaps he'd be there. Again nothing but deadening disappointment.

She almost decided against visiting Lilly but knew

her sister would worry if she didn't stop. Besides, if she was honest with herself, she needed Lilly to comfort her.

The sleigh bounced across the uneven snow as she drove up to Lilly's house. She stopped, jumped down and hurried toward the door.

"Rose." A harsh whisper sent her heart into a gallop. She glanced around.

"Duke? What are you doing here?" He was pressed against the corner of the house, his hat pulled low. His gaze darted to the street.

"Duke?" Such strange behavior.

"Come here." He slipped out of sight and she followed. Her nerves twitched and she glanced over her shoulder, but saw nothing to cause such caution on his part.

He pulled her into a corner formed between the shed and the fence, sheltered by a bare-limbed tree.

"Duke, what on earth—"

"I can't be too careful." He quickly relayed the events of Sunday afternoon. "Ebner refuses to be fired. I have to wait until my father returns. I've sent him a message but I don't know if he'll take me seriously or not. In the meantime, I must stay away from you. I don't want to add fuel to Ebner's anger."

"Oh, Duke, I've been so worried." She wrapped her arms around his waist and pressed her face to his shoulder. "Are you going to be safe?"

Duke held her close. "I'll be okay. After all, I am the son and heir. He wouldn't dare do anything to harm me."

Rose jerked so hard he ducked his head and looked into her face with concern.

"What's wrong?"

"It hit me how what you said has a spiritual lesson."

"What? Trust God in the hard times?"

"That, too. But Jesus is God's son and heir, and what did people do to him? They murdered Him. I never before realized the full meaning of that." And the knowledge that being son and heir didn't guarantee safety made her hold him tighter.

Duke looked startled. "Nor did I. Of course it was all part of God's plan to provide salvation from our sin, but still…"

She nodded. "Still."

"I must go." He planted a quick kiss on her nose and ducked out the back gate.

Rose stared after him. If people could murder God's son, what was to stop Ebner from doing something to Duke?

With a cry, she raced inside to pour out her fears to her sister.

Lilly held her through the sad tale. "I'm sure he's safe. You're fussing needlessly."

Rose sniffed back her tears and nodded. "No doubt you're right, but you know how little regard Ebner has for anyone's property." She thought of how close Pa had come to more serious injury, even— She couldn't think the word *death*. "Thank God, Pa wasn't hurt more seriously, but it proves Ebner has no more concern for life than he does for property."

"True, but one thing comforts me." Lilly rose and went to the window to peer out. "At least with Duke watching Ebner, we know Ma and Pa will be safe."

Rose nodded. "At least we can be glad about that. I wish—"

Lilly rushed back to Rose and hugged her. "I know.

You wish you could be so certain that Duke and Billy are safe."

To Rose's shame, she'd given little thought to Billy and now she bolted to her feet. "If he hurts Billy I'll—" Her fists bunched at her sides.

Lilly stepped back and studied her with a mixture of amusement and surprise. Then her eyes narrowed. "What would you do? Please tell me you won't really do something foolhardy like confront the man."

"I won't do anything stupid, but neither will I stand back and do nothing."

"Rose, sometimes you scare me. When you decide to tackle some problem you are like a stubborn dog with a tasty bone."

Rose squinted at her sister. "You mean I enjoy it?"

"Enjoy it a little too much sometimes. But I mean you simply won't let it go. For instance, always trying to find out who our birth parents were."

With a start Rose realized she hadn't given the idea any thought for several days. She tucked a smile into her heart as she acknowledged the reason. Her thoughts had been on Duke and how much she enjoyed his company.

Now the bulk of her thoughts and prayers were for his safety.

"I haven't given up hope that someday we can find them."

Lilly shook her head. "I wish you'd let it go. You— we—might discover something we don't want to."

"You're always saying that, but what's the worst thing we could learn?" She gratefully shifted the conversation to this familiar topic. It was better than worrying about Duke.

"What if they were running from the law?" Lilly

turned back to the window. "What if our father is in jail? Or has been hanged? Maybe I don't want to know if they were outlaws."

Over the years Rose had listened to many reasons for Lilly's reluctance to discover their background, but this was the first time she'd heard this one. She went to her sister and wrapped an arm around her shoulders.

"It wouldn't change who we are."

"Maybe. Maybe not. What if there is something hereditary like madness? How could I wish to bring a baby into the world if I knew that?"

Laughter burst from Rose. "All my life I've worried about that very thing. Many suitors shared the same concern, but I'm beginning to see that with God's help and the love we've had all our lives, we are equipped to make our own future."

Lilly turned to stare at Rose. "You've changed."

"Maybe I have."

"But you still want to discover the identity of our birth parents?"

Rose considered the question carefully. Finally she answered. "Yes, but not because I think it will make people look at me differently."

The sisters studied each other, searching for understanding. A slow smile creased Lilly's face. "You've really changed." She tipped her head. "Does Duke have anything to do with it?"

Rose didn't often hide anything from her twin but she was reluctant to admit how her feelings for Duke had gone from resentment to affection. "I misjudged him."

Lilly chortled.

"He says he's always admired me."

"Well, I guess that would make you feel good about yourself."

"It does." Her insides felt warm and syrupy, but she didn't want to discuss it further, especially when it made her think of Duke dealing with Ebner. "I hope and pray he will be safe."

A few minutes later she headed for home. She looked up and down the street hoping for a glimpse of Duke, but he wasn't among those visible.

Be safe.

God, please protect him.

She rose Sunday morning with a song in her heart. Surely, Duke would come to church. She tried not to rush her folks out the door, and then refrained from suggesting Pa going a little faster on the way to town. She glanced across the churchyard before she jumped from the sleigh. King was not among the horses tied to the rail.

Nevertheless, she wasted no time entering the church on the off chance she was mistaken. But a quick glance around the sanctuary revealed Duke was not there.

She slipped in beside Lilly and tried not to be obvious in turning to watch every person who entered.

Lilly leaned close to whisper in her ear. "He won't be here. Ebner knows there is no one at the farm on Sundays so Duke will be watching him."

Rose nodded. She'd guessed as much. It was a generous and brave action on Duke's part, but oh, how she wished for just a glimpse of him.

Her sisters and their families came to the farm for dinner. Rose was sure everyone enjoyed themselves though only a portion of her mind was in attendance.

The largest part of it worried about Duke. She missed him. Wanted to see him. Most of all, she wanted assurance that he was okay.

The next few days she labored over the valentine card she made for him. She wrote and rewrote the verse she'd composed.

Valentine's Day was only a few days away. Would she be able to give him his card?

She rubbed at a spot over her heart that had developed an odd ache a day or two ago. But no amount of massaging eased the feeling. Only one thing would relieve it—seeing Duke and knowing he was safe.

Needing to escape her feelings, she grabbed her coat and headed outdoors. "I'm going to check the animals," she said by way of explanation to her parents, who looked at her with concern.

They were well aware of her restlessness and worry since Duke had last visited. They offered words of wisdom and encouragement but nothing would suffice until she could see him with her own two eyes and wrap her arms around him.

She smiled as she imagined herself tipping her face upward, inviting him to kiss her.

Her smile faded and she pressed her hand to her aching lips. Oh, to see him. Hold him.

Ebner knew Duke watched him. He did his best to make it impossible for Duke to keep track of his whereabouts. Duke had taken to spending much of his time in the barn so he'd know when Ebner saddled his horse and rode away. Then he followed. There wasn't much Ebner could do to stop him, but the man's scowl grew darker by the day.

Duke mostly left Billy in the house with Patches to amuse him. Ebner scared Billy almost to the point of tears. The man enjoyed tormenting Billy with his muttered threats of hurting him or his cat.

Spending so much time in the barn also gave Duke plenty of opportunity to notice all the things that needed repairing. He replaced broken hinges and broken boards. One stall had been so badly damaged by one of the horses that Duke knocked down the planks and started building a new one—stronger than the original.

The work occupied his time but only a fraction of his thoughts. Often he stopped and stared at the barn wall in the direction of the Bell farm. How was Rose? Did she miss him? Did she understand why he must do this? He snorted at his final question. She knew better than most why Ebner needed watching. What he really meant was that he missed her and wished he could ride over and visit.

He especially missed her on Sunday. Likely Cora and Lilly and their families joined the Bells for dinner and the afternoon. The nice weather would draw them outside. He'd imagined them walking by the river, enjoying the shapes of the snow carved by the water and wind.

If only his parents would return so this situation with Ebner could be resolved. Surely, his father would side with Duke. After all, he was a Caldwell and Ebner a hired hand. But doubt whispered in the back of his mind. Questions plagued him. Had Father really instructed the men to end the feud? Or was Ebner following direct orders from Duke's father? Did his father know and approve of Ebner's actions? He shook his head. He didn't want to believe his father had a hand in the things done to the Bells but neither did he believe his father could be uninformed as to Ebner's activities.

He prayed as never before in his life for wisdom and the words to make his father see the foolishness and cruelty of Ebner's actions. The feud must end in more than words and promises.

With a shrug that was half despair, half resignation, he turned back to building the new stall. He struggled to hold a heavy plank so he could drive the spike in to secure it. It required another set of hands. Billy could help. He set aside his tools and stepped outside. His attention was immediately drawn to the sound of an approaching buggy. He squinted against the bright sun to see who it was.

Mother and Father. His lungs tightened with a rush of emotion—welcome and uncertainty combined.

He hurried to greet them. "Welcome back." He helped Mother to the house. She kissed his cheek.

"I'm glad to be home."

Father shook hands. "I got your message. We'll discuss it later."

Duke nodded and carried in the many bags, then called one of the hands to tend the horse and buggy before he joined his parents in the sitting room.

"Mrs. Humphrey is away," he explained. "I'll send someone to tell her to return, but in the meantime, I can make tea if you wish some."

"That sounds lovely," Mother said. "Are you sure you can manage?"

He laughed. "We've been managing quite well on our own, haven't we, Billy?" He called to his friend who hovered at the kitchen door. "Come and say hello to my parents."

Billy knew them but he acted as though they were strangers as he eased into the room and murmured a greeting to both Duke's parents.

"I'll make the tea." Duke headed for the kitchen door.

"I'll help." Billy rushed after him. "Will I have to put Patches in the barn now?" The cat sat curled in a ball in front of the stove on a little mat Billy had discovered somewhere.

"I wouldn't think so as long as she stays in the kitchen."

Billy's breath whistled out. "Good. Ebner will hurt her if she's in the barn."

Duke clenched his jaw. He wished he could assure Billy nothing bad would befall his pet but he knew he couldn't as long as Ebner remained on the ranch.

"Billy, you take in the plate of cookies. I'll carry the tray with the teapot and cups." In the sitting room he presented the tray to his mother as Billy set forth the cookies.

He waited until both Mother and Father had sipped some tea and eaten half a cookie each to say, "Do you like the cookies?"

They both nodded.

"Billy and I made them." He laughed at the surprise in their faces.

"You don't know how to make cookies," Mother said.

"Turns out it's not so hard." *Especially with a teacher like Rose.* But he would save that bit of information until he could speak to his father.

They took their time about drinking tea and eating another of his cookies. He waited patiently for Father to address the concern Duke had expressed in his message to him.

"That was very good. Thank you." Father set his cup aside. He brushed a few crumbs from his lap, then turned to his wife. "Mother, Duke and I have some things to discuss, if you'll excuse us."

"By all means." She waved them away.

Duke followed his father across the hall to the office. Father sat behind the big desk and indicated Duke should take a chair on the other side.

"Now, what is this urgent matter that required I return home immediately?"

Duke had had plenty of time to consider how he would present his case. He slowed his breathing and calmed his nerves as best he could. Here he was, a man wanting a man's respect and responsibility from his father, yet sitting at the desk feeling like a little boy.

He rose to stand behind the chair. That was better.

"I need to speak to you about the Bells."

"I see." His father's words offered no indication of what he thought. "Continue."

"I thought you said the feud was over." He waited for a response.

Finally, Father nodded. "It is."

"You told the cowboys so?"

Father barely hesitated before he nodded.

Duke pressed on. "You told Ebner to stop harassing the Bells?"

"I believe he understood me." He planted his palms on the top of the desk. "Is this the reason you called me home?"

Duke sat. "I'm not sure how much you know of Ebner's activities." He waited, hoping Father would give some indication, but he merely sat with his hands clasped together on the desk and his eyes revealing nothing.

"Ebner tried to burn down the Bells' barn. He would have succeeded if I hadn't been nearby and helped put out the fire."

Still Father gave no indication of what he thought.

"I knew you wouldn't approve of such behavior. It's bullying in its worst form. So I told Ebner he was fired."

"I don't remember giving you that kind of authority. Where is Ebner now?"

The floor must have tipped, because Duke fought to restore his equilibrium. Did Father mean he supported Ebner? "He refused to leave. Said you hired him so you have to be the one to fire him."

Father and son did silent battle with their eyes. Duke refused to yield.

"If this is the way a Caldwell behaves, I wish I'd never been born into this family." With that, Duke bolted to his feet and headed for the door.

"Son." His mother caught his arm as he passed. "I couldn't help but overhear. Might this have anything to do with that pretty young Rose Bell?"

"It has everything to do with her."

She smiled. "I always suspected you were attracted to her." Her smile faded. "But you might be forced to choose sides and I don't want to see that."

"That's just it, Mother. There is no need for sides. This feud is so unnecessary. They aren't taking Caldwell land. We're trying to take theirs. The big landowner stealing the little guy's land. It's wrong. I want no part of it." His feelings had never been clearer. He would walk away from the ranch rather than be involved in such behavior. Let Father keep Ebner if that's what he wished.

His long strides ate up the distance to the barn and he stepped inside.

Ebner lounged against the nearby wall. "I see your pappy's home and from the look on your face I'm guessing he ain't none too happy with your failure to live up to the Caldwell name."

Ebner gave a triumphant little chuckle as he walked past Duke.

Duke wanted nothing to do with the Caldwell name.

The hammer and spikes were where he had left them by the new stall. He heaved the plank into place, held it with his hip and drove home the long spikes. *Bang. Bang.* The jolt along his arm hammered away at his troubling thoughts. After a bit, he stepped back and admired the pen. No half-wild animal would kick this one to pieces.

He heard Ebner pass the barn whistling. The man seemed completely sure of Father's support.

Duke put away everything he'd been using as he considered his choices. This had been his home all his life. He'd grown up riding with the cowboys. Dreamed of the time the ranch would be his and he would be able to make some changes.

But he would not be part of cruel, senseless activity.

He didn't know where he'd go or what he'd do but there were plenty of opportunities for a young man willing to work hard. And Duke was. And when he had a place of his own, he'd court Rose the way she deserved.

One thing he would be certain of. He would stay close by and make sure the Bells were safe, even if it put him and his father at odds.

Or perhaps he should remain at the ranch against his better judgment, against his conscience, simply to protect Rose and her parents.

He struggled between the two options until his insides hurt. *God, show me what to do.* Until he was certain which way was best, he'd simply bide his time.

He returned to the house, grateful his father had remained in the office and Mother had retired to her room to rest.

He'd sent someone to fetch Mrs. Humphrey, who returned in time to make the evening meal.

Billy joined the Caldwell family in the dining room though he'd said he'd sooner eat in the kitchen.

To her credit, Mother did her best to keep a conversation going, but the atmosphere was as thick as a spring fog. As soon as was polite, Duke excused himself and Billy jolted to his feet and followed him.

Outside, Duke stared across the dark plains in the direction of the Bell farm.

"When we gonna see them again?" Billy sounded hopeful.

Duke didn't need to ask who he meant. "Soon, I hope." He waited quietly and patiently for some inner guidance as to what his choice for the future should be, but by the time he and Billy went inside and retired to their rooms he still didn't know.

All he knew for certain was that whatever choice he made it would be made with Rose's safety and happiness in mind.

He tossed and turned much of the night, prayed fervently. By morning he knew he couldn't stay. He would always be a Caldwell but he'd be one that could hold his head high knowing he'd conducted himself with honor.

He made his way to the kitchen and gratefully accepted a cup of coffee and a hot breakfast.

"Billy's not up yet?"

Mrs. Humphrey shook her head. "You're the only one I've seen and you're up unusually early."

"Got things to do. It's not like him to sleep in. I'll get him up." Wherever he went, he'd take Billy with him. He climbed the steps quietly, not wanting to bring either Father or Mother from their room, and tiptoed into Billy's room, which echoed with his footsteps.

"Billy." He glanced around. The bed was mussed. But then, Billy made his own bed and the covers were never pulled perfectly flat as Mrs. Humphrey would have done.

He circled the room, looked in the wardrobe, though he couldn't say what he expected to see. Because it was obvious Billy wasn't there.

Perhaps he had risen earlier and slipped outside. Duke moved to the window. Several cowboys headed for the cookhouse. The horses penned beside the barn blew out billows of steam.

Ebner stepped from the bunkhouse, hitched his pants higher and looked toward the house.

Duke felt sick when he saw the triumphant look on the man's face. A dreadful thought jolted through his body. Had Ebner hurt Billy?

Unmindful of any noise he made, he clattered down the steps and rushed into the kitchen. He stared at the mat in front of the stove. "Have you seen Patches—Billy's cat?"

"Not this morning." Mrs. Humphrey stirred batter for something. "I assumed Billy had let her outside."

Duke's heart delivered a punch to his ribs.

Billy never left the cat unattended outside.

"He's not upstairs. I have to find him." He grabbed his coat, shrugging into it as he leaped from the steps and glanced around.

"Billy," he called softly, not wanting to alert Ebner, who had gone into the cookhouse.

Perhaps Billy had taken the cat out back. Duke circled the house, but there was no sign of cat or owner. He trotted to the barn. "Billy!" All he heard was the rustle of mice overhead and the coo of pigeons in the loft.

He checked every stall and then climbed the ladder to the loft. Billy was not there.

Duke sat on the loft floor and forced himself to breathe deeply. *Think. Think.* Where would he be?

Chapter Seventeen

Rose spent more time in the barn than her chores required but Duke's presence seemed closer there. She stood in the spot where he'd kissed her. Her insides felt hollowed out and empty with missing him. She'd never considered herself impatient before but now her entire being had stalled, unable to function until she saw him again.

She tipped her head. Did she hear approaching hoofbeats? She sighed. How many times over the past few days had she imagined a rider approaching and rushed outside to stare at the empty landscape?

Didn't the sound grow louder? She listened closer. Yes. She heard a horse. Her heart leaped with joy. Coming fast. Very fast. Someone approaching at that speed meant danger. Fear replaced joy and clawed at her throat.

Could it be Ebner bent on another attack?

Or a messenger bearing bad news?

She rushed headlong from the barn, prepared to stop any threat. Never mind that she'd failed to do so in the past.

The horse and rider raced toward her. Her breath whooshed out. It was Duke coming as fast as he could. She laughed—a sound of pure joy. He'd missed her as much as she'd missed him.

"Have you seen Billy?" he called as soon as he was within shouting distance. "Is he here?"

She blinked; tried to make sense of his questions. "Of course not. Isn't he with you?"

King skidded to a halt five feet from Rose and Duke jumped to the ground. "I can't find him." He rushed past Rose into the barn. "Billy!" His yell rang with desperation.

Rose hurried after him and caught his arm. "Tell me what's going on."

Duke shuddered. "Billy's not at the ranch. I thought he'd come here. Where else would he go?" He pulled her into his arms and held tight as if to hold him together.

"I suppose he might have gone into the house while I was in the barn."

He grabbed her hand and they raced across the yard and flung the door open.

Ma and Pa stared at them.

"What's wrong?" Ma said.

"Billy's missing. He's not here?"

Pa got to his feet with more haste than he'd showed in several weeks. "How long has he been missing?"

"I don't know. He was gone when I got up this morning." Duke rubbed the back of his neck.

"Sit down and let's reason this out," Pa said.

Duke perched on the edge of the chair.

Rose sat next to him and, not caring what anyone thought, squeezed his hand.

"Did something trigger this?" Pa's voice was calm, reassuring.

"My parents returned. I tried to convince my father to end the feud and to fire Ebner." Duke shuddered and clutched Rose's hand so hard her fingers turned white but she didn't care. It was the least she could offer him.

"It didn't go well," Duke continued. "Billy knew that. I suppose it frightened him. But where would he go?"

Pa patted Duke's shoulder. "We'll find him. Did he take a horse?"

"All the horses were present and accounted for."

"Then we know he couldn't go far. Did he have any favorite places?"

"Only here."

"Then I suggest you and Rose have a better look around. He might be hiding."

Before Pa finished speaking Duke was on his feet, still holding Rose's hand as he rushed outside. They searched every building. They explored the nearby trees. Nothing.

"I can't believe my father chose to keep Ebner on after what I told him," Duke said as they poked through Pa's workshop. "I can't stay there. I can't be part of what they are doing to you." He sounded so miserable she wrapped her arms around him.

"I'm sorry."

"But if I leave the ranch, who will make sure you are safe?"

She held him tight. "If Ma and Pa were younger I think I'd beg them to move." She shuddered and his arms tightened around her.

They clung to each other for the space of three heartbeats.

"First things first." His lips barely curved in his attempted smile. "We must find Billy. I simply can't imagine where he's gone."

"Would he go to town?" she asked. The idea was more preferable than him being lost outside with the temperature falling. And he could walk that distance, though he would have had to walk in the dark and cold. Her insides frosted at the thought.

"Where would he go if he did? He's uncomfortable around strangers."

"Lilly." She almost shouted the name. "He'd go to Lilly."

They raced for the barn. His horse stood where he'd left him. Rose saddled Hope faster than she'd ever done in her life and led him from the barn to where Duke stood.

"Someone coming." He pointed down the road at an approaching wagon.

They waited side by side, dread pitting the bottom of her stomach. No one would come calling this early in the morning unless it was an emergency. Sometimes people came with requests for Ma's medicinals, but her twisted insides warned her this would be about Billy.

The way Duke squeezed her hand, she knew he suspected the same thing.

She was the first to recognize the occupants. "It's Lilly and Caleb." The wagon drew closer and she made out Teddy peering over the back of the wagon. She squinted at another person beside him. "It's Billy." With a cry of joy they raced toward the wagon.

"Billy, you're safe." Tears washed her face.

Duke trotted beside the wagon, his hand on Billy's head. "You gave me an awful scare."

Caleb pulled the wagon to a halt. "Let's go inside and talk."

They marched into the house where Ma and Pa waited. Ma held out her arms to Billy, Patches clutched to his chest, and hugged him. "Praise God you're safe."

"Are you angry at me?" Billy's voice trembled.

"We're only grateful you're okay."

They pulled out extra chairs and gathered around the table. Rose stayed close to Duke's side. She hoped he needed the comfort of her presence as much as she needed his.

Pa looked from one to the other, his gaze resting at last on Billy. "Tell us what happened."

Billy shuddered and hung his head and soothed Patches. "I didn't want anything to happen to her. I knew Lilly likes all sorts of animals."

Duke opened his mouth to say something. Likely to ask for more explanation.

Ma signaled him to let her. "Billy, why did you think something might happen to her?"

"Ebner said it would."

Duke squeezed Rose's hand as his breath escaped in a blast.

"Nothing will happen to Patches while you're here," Pa promised.

"Can I stay here?" Billy's eyes brimmed with pleading.

Ma and Pa looked at each other and silently communicated. They both smiled.

"You're welcome to stay as long as you want," Pa said.

Billy bent over Patches.

Two tears dropped to the cat's fur. Billy brushed them away.

Pa turned to Duke. "I think it's best for Billy to stay here for now. He'll feel more at ease."

Duke nodded. "I agree." He freed his hand from Rose's grasp and rubbed his palms against his thighs.

Her heart ached for him. He felt he had to abandon his home and family.

"Duke, do you mind if I explain the situation to my family?"

All misery, he shook his head. "I could certainly use some wise advice."

So she repeated what Duke had said, how he'd asked his father to end the feud, how his father had said he had and how Duke, when he'd discovered Ebner still harassing the Bells, had tried to dismiss Ebner, but his father had chosen to keep the man, even knowing the specifics of what he'd done. How Duke didn't feel he could stay on at the ranch.

When she finished, a deep silence hung over the table.

Duke squared his shoulders as he faced her parents. "I'll understand if you want me to leave. If you feel uncomfortable offering me friendship."

Rose found his hand and held tight.

Pa squeezed his shoulder. "Nonsense. We want no such thing. But, son, you face a difficult situation for which it would appear there will not be a happy outcome." He turned to confront those gathered around the table. "We need God's wisdom in this situation. Let's pray."

The family, Duke and Billy joined hands around the table as Pa prayed. "God, grant wisdom to Duke to resolve his problems with his father. We ask you for peace, as well. Peace between neighbors that your name might be glorified. Amen."

Ma served tea and cookies. Slowly, Duke relaxed. "I served my parents cookies I'd made." He laughed. "They couldn't believe I knew how."

Ma chuckled. "It appears they are unaware of many of your abilities."

Beside him, Rose felt him stiffen.

"That's the problem in a nutshell," Duke said. "They don't see what I'm capable of."

"Son, maybe you need to make them see," Pa said. "But how?"

Pa shook his head. "I can't say. It might be they'll see you as a man if you confront the situation. Or they might see your strength if you leave the place. You'll have to trust God to guide your steps."

"I wish He'd send me a map."

Duke seemed in no hurry to leave and Rose certainly wasn't anxious to see him go. But the horses were still saddled and standing where they'd left them.

"We need to see to the horses," she said.

"And we need to get back home." Caleb and Lilly and Teddy prepared to leave.

Lilly took a moment to go to Billy and give him a sideways hug. "I'm glad you knew you could come to me for help and I'm equally grateful you'll have a safe place with my parents."

"Me, too," Billy said. He turned to Ma. "Can I keep Patches inside?"

"Yes, of course. I can't imagine how you'd manage without her."

Rose loved her mother then as never before. Ma

didn't care for cats in the house but knowing how important it was to Billy, she allowed it without second thought.

"You don't care that I'm stupid and useless?" Billy's voice quivered and he kept his head down.

Rose and Duke both sprang to his side and the rest of the family gathered 'round.

Rose spoke. "Billy, it's what's inside you that matters. Not what people might say about you. It's what you know about yourself and I think you know you are a good, kind person."

Billy nodded. "Yes, I am."

"You hold on to that thought and don't let anyone take it from you."

The others murmured further encouragement.

As soon as Lilly and her family departed, Rose and Duke went outside and led the horses to the barn to tend them.

Rose could see he struggled with a thought and waited quietly for him to reach a decision.

He sighed. "I must go home. Mother will be worried. I don't want her to think I've run away. Nor my father, either."

"I understand." It touched her that he could be so considerate of them even though his father had hurt him so badly.

He let out a gust of air. "What you said to Billy applies to me. I won't let my father make me think I'm useless. I always thought of myself as being part of the Caldwell Ranch but only if my opinions are valued."

She watched him struggle with his choice. Pain darkened his eyes and pulled his mouth back into a firm line. "I'm sure you'll do the right thing. My prayers go with you."

"Thank you." He stood at King's side but made no effort to mount.

Her insides crackled, knowing he meant to say something more to her.

His jaw muscles twitched and his eyes searched hers. But he said nothing. Instead he swung up into the saddle. As he reined around he finally spoke. "Goodbye." And then he galloped out of the yard.

She waited for him to turn at the top of the hill and wave but he raced onward without a backward look.

She cradled her arms around her. Surely she was only being fearful. He had been so focused on speaking to his father that he'd neglected to turn and wave.

It meant nothing.

Goodbye. Had he meant it as final? She reviewed everything he'd said, but could find no reason for her quaking uncertainty.

Did he mean to confront Ebner with or without his father's support? Would Ebner kill the son and heir in the hope of getting a stake in the Caldwell Ranch?

She knew what she must do and she raced to the house. "Ma, Pa, I'm going after Duke. Whatever he plans to do, I'm going to stand at his side."

"Don't do anything foolish," Pa said.

"Don't turn your back on Ebner," Ma warned.

"I'll be careful. I'll also make sure Duke is careful." She had no idea what he was riding into. She glanced at the shotgun.

Pa noticed. "Whatever happens, you'll have to settle it peaceably."

Rose nodded. She'd use a gun to protect Duke if she

had to, but there was no point in borrowing trouble by showing up with a firearm. She dashed out the door and leaped onto Hope's back.

Pa watched from the doorway. "We'll pray for you."

She breathed her own prayers as she thundered after Duke, knowing she had no chance of catching up to him and his big horse before he reached the ranch.

What if Ebner intercepted him on the way over?

What if he watched for her and tried to stop her?

Her throat choked off at the thought, but nothing would stop her from reaching Duke's side.

Duke allowed himself to cling to the memory of Rose's sweet look as he galloped toward the ranch. Her confidence in him encouraged him. She was the sort of woman who would stand by him through good times and bad. Through sickness and health. For richer or poorer.

He realized those words were part of the marriage vows.

Love is like a red, red rose.

He'd found his love and his red, red rose. But now was not the time to tell her. And after today he would not be in a position to speak of his feelings. A man had to have a home, a future…something to offer a woman besides sweet words.

She trusted him to do the right thing but there were times he didn't even know what that was. As now. He'd been taught to honor his father and mother. He'd been raised to respect his father's authority. It seemed wrong to ignore all that. But his family motto was Honor Above All and there was nothing honorable about Ebner's activities.

The ranch buildings came into sight. He rode past the barn and corrals toward the house. Ebner must have been watching for him, for he crossed the yard and followed Duke up the steps.

Duke turned. "This is family business. You can wait outside." He stepped inside and shut the door to bar the man but not before he heard Ebner mutter, "We'll see about that."

When Duke walked in, Mrs. Humphrey nodded toward the sitting room. "Your folks are in there."

He thanked her and crossed the kitchen to the room so full of pleasant memories.

Mother and Father sat in comfortable armchairs, reading.

Mother looked up.

Father's mouth tightened to a thin line before he spoke. "What do you have to say for yourself?" The words were stiff and formal.

Duke squared his shoulders. "Father, I cannot be part of this feud with the Bells. It's simply wrong to harass them, to damage their property. Mr. Bell was injured when cattle were stampeded over their farm."

Mother gasped. "Is this true?"

Father silenced her with a lift of his hand and spoke to Duke. "Am I to be held responsible for every stampede injury that occurs?"

Duke nodded. "When it's instigated by men under your authority, then yes."

The hallway door crashed open and Ebner strode into the sitting room as if he owned the place.

Duke's spine tingled. The man had gall to spare.

Mother looked him up and down. "I'm sorry. I didn't hear your knock."

Duke half snorted. Because Ebner hadn't bothered.

The man barely spared a glance at Mrs. Caldwell. Instead, ignoring the others, he turned to Mr. Caldwell.

Mother slowly, deliberately, set her teacup on the table at her elbow and slowly, deliberately, rose to her feet.

Duke sat back. He'd only seen his mother angry twice in his life and both times it had been a sight to behold.

Mother swept across the room to crowd Ebner so he had to step back. "How dare you intrude into our home as if you own it?" She kept her voice low but each word carried the weight of a dagger.

Father sighed, not wanting to make a scene with Mother. "Ebner, you better leave."

Ebner's jaw almost hit the floor before he stomped from the room.

Mother returned to her seat and told Duke, "Now let's hear the whole story."

Duke sat and began. He wished he could hope this would be resolved the way he wanted but Father's look was not encouraging.

Chapter Eighteen

Ignoring the way her heart thumped against her ribs, Rose rode up to the kitchen door of the Caldwell Ranch.

Ebner stormed past, giving her a look that turned her stomach sour. She swallowed hard and stared after him. She'd wait to see if he rode from the yard in the direction of the farm. If he did, she'd ride after him and stop whatever mischief he planned. When he stepped into the bunkhouse, she let her breath out in one harsh gust then sucked it in and faced the door.

Gathering up her courage, she knocked.

She knew the woman who opened the door. Mrs. Humphrey, who worked for the Caldwells. Her eyes widened at Rose standing in front of her, then she smiled. "About time. Come on in." She stepped aside and offered to take Rose's coat. Rose didn't need help to remove it. She hung it on the nearby hook, tugged her clothes into place and then squared her shoulders.

"I've come to see Duke." *And his father*, though she wasn't brave enough to speak those words aloud for fear the woman would chase her off the place.

"Through there." Mrs. Humphrey led her to the door

of the parlor. When she hesitated, the housekeeper gave her a little push into the room.

Mr. Caldwell stared at her, his expression forbidding. "To what do we owe this honor?"

Mrs. Caldwell turned. "Hello, Miss Bell, how are you?

"Fine, thank you."

Duke pushed to his feet and came to her side. "Rose, what's wrong?"

She smiled up at him, her lips quavering. "Nothing." She turned back to Duke's father. "Mr. Caldwell, I think a neighborly visit is long overdue."

The man scowled in a most unwelcoming way.

"I have come to remedy that."

"Do sit down," Duke's mother said, and called for Mrs. Humphrey to bring tea.

The woman hustled in with it all prepared and took her time about leaving. Rose imagined she hovered just outside the door where she could hear the conversation.

"How was your trip?" Rose asked and thanked the woman for the cup of tea handed to her.

"I enjoyed the break from the ranch."

"It must have been exciting to visit the capital of our new state of Montana. I understand the state legislature building is going to be beautiful."

"If it ever gets built." Mr. Caldwell sounded disgusted.

"Oh, is something wrong?"

"You could say that. Some underhanded work going on. People trying to scam money from the taxpayers."

Rose looked shocked. "Why, that's terrible. Where's the honor in our country?" She set aside her teacup and folded her hands in her lap. This was the opening she had prayed for. Outwardly she hoped she gave the impression of calm. Inside, her stomach filled with a hundred fluttering butterflies. "I am indeed interested in Helena and our new state, but I do have another reason for visiting besides the fact it is long overdue."

Mrs. Caldwell nodded. "It truly is."

The woman's welcome and support were an unexpected treat.

Rose spoke to both Mr. and Mrs. Caldwell and tried not to look too often at Duke for fear she'd be unable to tear her gaze away. "This is not my first visit, however."

Mr. Caldwell's eyebrows pushed at his hairline.

She rushed on. "Did Duke tell you about his accident?"

His mother jerked around. "You were hurt?"

"Nothing serious." Duke lifted his hair to reveal the red line across his forehead. "Thanks to Rose. She found me staggering around in the snow and brought me home and tended my wound."

Mrs. Caldwell reached over and squeezed Rose's clasped hands. "Thank you."

"So you've come seeking a reward, I suppose?" Mr. Caldwell said.

"Not at all. Seeing your son doing well is reward enough." She wondered whether to add the next bit but now was not the time to hold back. "Helping others is what the Bells do."

Mr. Caldwell squirmed ever so slightly at that.

"No, I've come on a more serious errand." She forced her lungs to work. "When I was here, your son showed me through the main floor of the house." They needed to be assured she and Duke had not been inappropriate in any way. "He showed me the picture at the bottom of the stairs and told me about the Caldwell land."

Mr. Caldwell leaned forward. "It reminds me that I will never let go of my land."

"Sir, what I suggest is it makes you capable of understanding how important our land is to us." She let the statement fall into the silence.

Duke's father jerked back. "I want my land back."

"Sir, it was never yours. You are doing to my father exactly what others did to your forefathers. If they were cruel opportunists, then what does that make you?"

Thunder couldn't have made her shudder any worse than his scowl but she forged on.

"Duke told me of your family motto. Honor Above All. How honorable is it to try to force an elderly man from his land? To allow—perhaps order—your cowboys to ruin our crops and garden? To harass and kill our animals? To try to burn our barn down? To stampede cows over our land and almost kill our father?"

Mr. Caldwell rose to his feet. "I've heard enough. It's time for you to go."

Mrs. Caldwell rose, too, and planted herself directly in front of her husband. "Cecil, first Duke and now this young lady make these accusations. Is what they say true?"

"This is ranch business."

Rose edged to her feet and tried to creep away. She wanted nothing to do with a family argument.

Mrs. Caldwell would not be denied. "This is my home. My family. I've always been proud of that, Cecil. But now I feel shame clear to my toes. How dare you harass these people? Of course I knew you had tried to buy them out. But they have the right to refuse your offer. However, you don't have the right to threaten them." She turned her back to her husband and reached for Rose's hands. "My dear, I am so sorry."

Mrs. Caldwell turned to Duke. "So this is what your argument was about? I mistakenly thought you and Ebner had argued about your authority. Whatever you decide to do, I will stand with you."

She turned again to her husband. "I married a man I admired for his integrity and honor. What happened to that man?"

At first Mr. Caldwell looked angry and defensive, then his expression changed. He reached for his wife's hands. "I'm still that man, though for a little while I've forgotten it. But I promise you I won't disappoint you again."

She smiled at him. "I know you won't." She patted his chest affectionately.

"I didn't know the details of what Ebner did." He hung his head. "I chose not to know. Then Duke came to me making it impossible for me to pretend I didn't know." He turned to Duke. "I tried to fire Ebner yesterday but he said he would go to the sheriff and say I'd done it all myself."

Duke held his arm out to shake his father's hand. "I'm glad to know you believed me. I wish I could say Ebner is all talk and threat, but I've seen enough of him to know he's a real danger."

"Mr. Caldwell," Rose said, "I can honestly say I never saw you doing any of those awful things but lots of times I saw Ebner."

"That should be enough to prove your innocence, Father."

Mr. Caldwell sank back to the chair. "Except I'm not

innocent. You're right, young lady. I was doing all the things I resented others for doing."

"I speak for my entire family when I say we're ready to forgive you and start over." She stood in front of him. "Let's end this feud and start being the kind of neighbors we should be." She held out her hand to Mr. Caldwell.

"Agreed." He rose and they shook hands.

Mrs. Caldwell stood at her husband's side. "I'm proud of you."

Mr. Caldwell smiled at his wife. "And now I have something to deal with. Duke, do you want to come with me?" He led his son from the house, purpose in every step.

"Goodbye to Ebner," Mrs. Caldwell said. "Or should I say 'good riddance'?" She studied Rose with the same blue-eyed intensity Duke did.

"Your son is very much like you," Rose said.

"Thank you. But I believe he's the best of both of us. And you, Rose Bell, are quite the gal." She tucked her hand around the crook of Rose's elbow. "Do you want to watch Ebner ride away?"

Taking Rose's agreement for granted, she led them to the kitchen window. Mrs. Humphrey joined them in watching the two Caldwell men confront Ebner.

Ebner waved his arms in protest but the Caldwells didn't back down. Then Ebner stomped away to the bunkhouse. Duke and his father stood side by side waiting for Ebner to reappear, saddle his horse and ride from the ranch.

Mrs. Caldwell brushed her palms together as if ridding them of something dirty. "That's the last we'll see of him. If I know my husband and son, they made it clear that it would be in the man's best interests to never again show his face. Now, my dear, let's have tea and you can tell me all about yourself."

When Rose left a short time later, she had the Caldwells' agreement to come to tea at the Bells' on Friday.

Not until Duke had escorted her almost back to the farm did she realize that would be Valentine's Day.

The end of the feud between the Bells and the Caldwells was better than any valentine card but she hoped she and Duke would get some private time so she could give him the card she'd made.

They reined to a halt at the top of the hill and slipped from their horses. He came around to stand in front of her.

"I can't believe you confronted my father." He ran his finger along her chin. "It reminded me of the time you confronted Morty back in school—all fierce and defensive."

It was on the tip of her tongue to say she was very protective of those she loved—

Was it true? Did she love him? The thought both excited and frightened her. After all, she had promised herself she would never allow herself to become vulnerable by opening her heart.

She smiled, her heart bursting with the secret of her feelings. She moved to within inches of him. "You need to know how much I admire you. How I see you as a good man with noble intentions."

His eyes darkened. "Not the nasty little tease I used to be?"

"I'm not sure you were the tease I made you out to be." She'd wait until Friday to give him the card she had prepared for him. Surely those words would convince him that her feelings had changed.

He leaned forward until their foreheads touched. "I'm very glad of your moral support." His voice deepened. She tipped her head and their gazes fused. Their lips were a breath apart. His eyes smiled and he claimed her mouth in a sweet kiss. She wished it would last forever but he eased away. "You better go let your parents know you're safe. Won't they be pleased to know the feud is truly over?"

"They certainly will." They parted ways as she rode down the hill and he waited to wave to her as she reached the barn before he rode for home.

She was glad the feud was over but the fact didn't mean near as much as her discovery of what lay in her heart.

He'd not said a word about his feelings. She might well be mistaken in thinking he felt the same as she. It wouldn't be the first time. Her lungs clenched at the idea.

But the joy of the time they'd shared would be worth whatever pain might lay in store.

She snorted. As if she believed that. But she clung to the thought because the alternative was too dreadful to contemplate.

Ma fussed with the array of cookies and the chocolate cake she'd made. Rose draped an arm across her shoulders. "Ma, I wouldn't have invited them if I'd thought it would upset you."

Ma gave a quick laugh. "I'm glad you did. It's time we became proper neighbors. But I want everything to be just right. After all, they're the Caldwells."

"Nonsense," Pa said. "They're ranchers, neighbors… people just like us."

Ma nodded, then grabbed a tea towel and wiped a cup. Again.

Rose smiled. Her parents were going to be pleasantly surprised.

Billy clutched Patches to his chest. "Are you sure Ebner left?"

"I watched him ride away with my own eyes." She understood it would take time for Billy to feel safe again.

She glanced out the window. They would come in their buggy so they would have to follow the road. Still, her glance went to the well-used trail over the hill. A horse and rider appeared. "Duke is coming." She rushed out to greet him and accompanied him to the barn as he led King inside.

He released the horse and hurried back to Rose's side. He swept her off her feet in a hug. "I have missed you so much. When was the last time we had a chance to visit? To enjoy each other's company? There has always been other things to deal with—Billy, Ebner, my parents." He set her feet on the floor but kept his arms around her.

Her heart threatened to explode with warm, sweet joy. "I missed you, too." More than she dare confess, though if he were to offer any clue as to his feelings—

Her heart did a little flip in anticipation of giving him her valentine. She'd changed the wording of the verse at the last minute and hoped she wasn't being too bold.

He lowered his head so he could search her gaze. "Why are you smiling so?"

"I'm happy."

"Because the feud is over or because I'm here?"

"Yes." She boldly tipped her head. She planted her hands on either side of his neck and thrilled to the drum of his pulse against her palms.

The blue of his eyes offered sunshine and so much more. "Rose Bell, sweetest flower of all." He caught her mouth with his own.

She pressed her hands to his head and clung to him, feeling the crisp winter air in his hair, tasting it on his lips. She wondered if her heart would ever beat normally again.

The rattle of harness and the creak of leather warned them that Duke's parents had arrived. They ended the kiss.

Their gazes refused to part. His eyes glistened as if they had stolen stars from the night sky.

She expected hers were equally bright.

He brushed a fingertip to her lips.

"I hear your folks." Her voice sounded as though it came from the most distant corner of the farm.

He nodded but didn't move.

When she heard her pa call out a greeting to the Caldwells, she caught Duke's hand and propelled him toward the door. "Come on. We have to go."

As they stepped outside, he dropped her hand and hurried toward the buggy to help his mother down.

Rose rushed forward. "Come in. So glad you could make it."

The Caldwells stopped at the door. Pa offered his hand. "We are glad you've come."

Ma squeezed Mrs. Caldwell's hand. "I've prayed for this day. Do come in."

Rose and Duke held back. Rose, too, had prayed for

the day she'd see an end to the land feud. She'd received so much more.

Or so she hoped. Her nerves twitched as she thought of the card she meant to give to Duke today. Would he receive the message in the way she hoped he would?

Duke sat quietly through the tea. Mrs. Bell served a number of goodies but for some odd reason they all tasted the same. He knew the reason. Even though he was thrilled that his parents were sitting at the Bell table, talking about ordinary things, his mind was on something else.

Since Mother had pointed out they would be going to the Bells' on Valentine's Day, and suggested Duke should keep it in mind, he'd thought of little else. He'd found the perfect valentine to give Rose and he'd added a little surprise.

He believed she would welcome this card, unlike the way she'd received the special one he'd given her when they were much younger.

But would she also accept the surprise? Or call him a skunk?

He grew so impatient he could feel every heartbeat thud inside his head. How long must he sit at the table before he could find an excuse to ask Rose to go walking with him?

"Duke?" He jerked toward Rose's ma when she called his name.

She smiled at him, her eyes full of understanding. "No need for you young folk to stay here. I'm sure Rose is as bored as you are. Why don't you take her for a walk in the nice sunshine?"

At that moment he respected Mrs. Bell more than

ever. She was astute, kind, generous—no wonder Rose had turned out so well.

He faced Rose. "Would you like to go for a walk?"

She was already on her feet. "I'll be just a moment." She disappeared inside her bedroom and emerged seconds later, her cheeks flaring pink.

Billy sat on the cot playing with Patches and showed no sign of wanting to be invited.

Good. Duke wanted to be alone with Rose.

They stepped outside and blinked in the brightness. "Where do you want to go?"

"Down to the river." She indicated a narrow trail that meant they must walk single-file.

He didn't much care for that. He wanted to hold her hand, to pull her to his side. But having asked, he must accept her answer.

In a few minutes they reached the banks of the river. The wind had swept the ground bare near some trees. He stopped there and held out his hands to her.

She hesitated just out of reach and fumbled inside her coat. "I have something for you."

If he wasn't mistaken she sounded a tiny bit nervous, which caused him to tense. He loved her and hoped she loved him, but there remained a thread of uncertainty.

She handed him an envelope.

He lifted the flap and pulled out a valentine. "It's beautiful. There's a lot of red roses."

"Read the verse." Her voice trembled.

He opened the card and read aloud.

"My love is like a red, red rose.
Delicate, fragile, sweet.
A tender flower requiring

Gentle care.
My love is also a like a dandelion
Tough, enduring, resilient
Thriving through stormy gales and desert heat
Cheerful and bright.
These two flowers portray a lasting and beautiful love."

His vision blurred as tears stung his eyes. "It's beautiful." His throat clogged and he couldn't go on.

Rose twisted her hands together. "I wanted to make up for the nasty card I once sent you."

He nodded. "You certainly did." Was the verse generic or did she mean it from her heart? He knew one way to find out.

"I've got a card for you, too." He could feel his heartbeat pound as he reached into his inside pocket and withdrew the card. He hoped she wouldn't notice how his hands trembled as he handed it to her.

She pulled the card from the envelope.

He'd chosen one showing a little boy handing a bright red heart to a sweet little girl.

Rose darted a glance at him. "No roses?"

"Only one. You."

Her cheeks blossomed pink.

"Open it."

She nodded and turned her attention to the card.

She didn't read it aloud but she didn't have to. He knew the words.

My heart belongs to you, my love.

He'd tied a ribbon bow beneath his name. "Undo the bow."

She did so and gasped as the ring he'd hidden fell into her hands. The valentine fluttered to the ground.

He caught it, then fell to one knee and took her hands. "Rose Bell, I love you. Will you marry me?"

He held his breath. He believed she loved him but until she said so, doubts would linger.

Her eyes flashed as if the sun had filled them. She leaned over to cup her hands around his face. "Yes. Yes. Yes." She kissed him soundly.

He got to his feet and pulled her into the circle of his arms. "Does that mean you love me?"

"With all my heart, tough like a dandelion, sweet like a rose."

He slipped the ring on her finger. "You are the sweetest Rose ever created." He kissed her so soundly he could barely remember his name.

Epilogue

They waited until spring to get married. Not that Rose minded. She and Duke had enjoyed getting to know each other better. She'd grown to understand even more why he'd been such a tease in school. Partly because he longed for her friendship and partly because he felt his father thought him useless.

His father had certainly come around on that notion. He'd allowed Duke to find Angus, the former foreman, and hire him again. He'd given Duke authority to make some changes. And recently, Mr. Caldwell had accepted a position in Helena working with the new state legislature. He would be in charge of overseeing land development. Because of that, he'd made Duke a full partner on the ranch. Duke's parents would be living in Helena for the time being.

Duke and Rose would have the ranch house to themselves.

Rose hugged herself with joy. She imagined many a pleasant evening in the sitting room. And she could glance out the kitchen window to watch Duke riding out to tend the cows.

Mrs. Humphrey had offered to stay on and cook for them, but Rose wanted to manage on her own. At least for the present. Mrs. Humphrey had chuckled and patted her hand.

"I don't blame you."

Rose turned around to look at the bedroom where she had spent the past nine years of her life. First Cora had married and moved on. Then Lilly. And now Rose. She would worry about leaving Ma and Pa, except Billy had asked to live with them. Billy had proved to be a faithful friend and good worker once he'd learned a job. Both Ma and Pa had the patience to teach him well.

The wedding dress both her sisters had worn lay on her bed waiting for the moment she would don it. She'd promised Cora and Lilly she'd wait for them to come and help her.

The sound of an approaching wagon said they were almost there.

"Your sisters have arrived," Ma called.

Rose rushed out to greet them. Only Wyatt was with them. "The others stayed in town taking care of last-minute things," Cora explained.

"Besides," Lilly asked. "I didn't want to have to bathe Teddy again. You know what he's like when he's out here. Running around, getting into every dirty corner."

"Come in, girls," Ma called. "We don't want to be late."

The three of them marched into the bedroom. Rose began to slip out of her garments.

"Just a minute," Cora said. "I have something for you."

"A gift? But I don't need anything."

Cora sat on the edge of the bed that had once been

hers and patted a spot on either side of her. "Both of you come here."

Rose chuckled as the twins sat beside Cora. "Just like old times." Only she didn't want to go back to the familiar ways. Duke and their future beckoned.

"This is a gift we've all wanted for a long time." She lifted her bag to her lap and pulled out a heavy black Bible. "This is our family Bible."

Lilly and Rose stared at Cora.

Rose found her voice first. "What? When? Where?" Surely Cora hadn't had it all this time and hidden it. That was impossible. She'd been a five-year-old child when they were abandoned.

"The sheriff gave it to me ten days ago. Some trappers had brought it to him." She pressed her fingers to the black cover. "They'd found the old wreckage of a wagon that had tumbled down a cliff. No one could see it from above. They'd only found it because they'd been searching for minerals. Of course everything was about gone after all this time…except a strongbox. They'd brought it to the sheriff and he opened it." She lifted the front cover. "This is a picture of our parents and us."

The girls bent over it, greedy to see their parents for the first time.

They recognized their much younger likenesses.

"Guess the sheriff would remember us when we weren't much older than this."

Cora nodded. "There was a letter from our maternal grandparents in the Bible and this." She turned the pages to where the family history was noted. "Our name was Brighton."

The news stunned Rose. "All these years I thought it

would make a difference but it doesn't. We're the Bell sisters and always will be."

Cora and Lilly agreed.

Cora continued. "See the notation on our mother. Died 1874 of a strange fever. The sheriff tried to contact our grandparents but they are deceased and he couldn't find any family. But he did find people from the group our parents joined in their trek west and learned that when our mother was ill, the others feared it was contagious and asked them to leave the wagon train. They said our father headed off in search of help. He was miles from where he'd left the wagon train. The sheriff thinks he must have suffered from the same fever. I guess more than a dozen who were in the group succumbed to it. So God spared us from that fate."

The three of them held hands.

"Girls," Ma called, "are you about ready?"

They each stroked their hands across the cover of the family Bible. Lilly and Rose spoke in unison. "Cora, you should keep it."

She nodded, tears clinging to her eyelashes. "I remember our mother looking like this picture." She tucked it back into the Bible and returned it to her bag. "Now let's get you ready."

Rose allowed her sisters to fuss over her as they pulled the dress over her head and fastened all the satin-covered buttons up her back. Then they arranged her hair around her head and fixed a gossamer veil over it.

"We'll have to tidy you when we get to the church."

They went outside and Rose was helped onto the wagon seat. In a few minutes the wagon was on its way.

At the church they slipped in the side door. Rose allowed the others to adjust her veil and smooth her dress, but all she cared about was what awaited her down the aisle.

The organ music began. She shoved her sisters to the door. "Stop wasting time."

Lilly giggled. "My, my, aren't you in a hurry?"

Cora stepped from the room. Lilly followed. Then Rose stood in the doorway, her eyes finding Duke's as if drawn by a magnet. Or rather by their love.

He was resplendent in a black suit with a black tie. His blond hair gleamed. Even from this distance she could feel the power of his blue eyes. She knew Caleb and Wyatt stood at his side, but she barely noticed them.

Duke smiled.

Pa pulled her arm through his. "Let's not keep the man waiting any longer."

She held Pa's arm and walked down the aisle at his side. The church was full. Many of Duke's family had come from Philadelphia. Rose had met the grandfather— a formidable-appearing man with white whiskers and thinning white hair, but she'd discovered the old man had a dry sense of humor and they'd enjoyed several visits.

She didn't look either to the right or the left. Couldn't have said who filled the pews. She had eyes for one face only—Duke's. His blue eyes blazed with love so strong that she was grateful her veil hid her face. She knew her cheeks would be a bright pink.

They reached the front and Pa put her hand on Duke's arm. "With my blessing," he said.

Duke pulled her to his side. "Thank you," he said to Rose's pa.

And before God and man, they exchanged their vows. *For better, for worse. For richer, for poorer, in sick-*

ness and in health, to love and to cherish; from this day forward until death do us part.

He'd told her how he'd thought words similar to their wedding vows shortly before she'd ridden to the ranch to confront her father. Thinking of that, she choked up momentarily, then swallowed and finished in a firm, steady voice.

They sealed their vows with a kiss.

"My red, red Rose," he murmured.

The way he said it made her proud and glad. She would never again hate her hair.

"My noble, handsome husband," she whispered back.

They smiled at each other, their hearts sharing the secret knowledge that once they got home they would have plenty more sweet things to say to each other.

And a lifetime to share their love.

Thanks to their love for each other they would never again feel insignificant or unimportant.

To God be the glory.

* * * * *

Dear Reader,

Isn't it amazing how much of life occurs at the kitchen table or while food is being prepared? It certainly proved to be the case in this story. I thought I'd share with you the butterscotch pudding recipe that Rose prepared for Duke while she cared for him at his house.

I've seen many variations of this recipe. In fact, it seems as if a version is found in almost all cookbooks. This one is the one I've adjusted for my use.

BUTTERSCOTCH PUDDING
1 cup flour
½ cup sugar
2 tsp. baking powder
½ cup milk
2 tbs. oil
½ cup raisins (optional)

Mix together in a bowl. Spread into a greased 8" square pan or casserole. (I use a casserole or deep pan because I like lots of sauce.)

In same bowl, mix:
1 cup brown sugar
2 tbs. flour
½ tsp. cinnamon (optional)

Sprinkle on the batter.
Pour 2 cups hot water over the contents of the pan.
Bake uncovered at 350°F about 30 min.

I hope you enjoy the dessert just as I hope you enjoy the story.

I love to hear from my readers. You can contact me at www.lindaford.org where you'll find my email address and where you can find out more about me and my books.

Blessings,

Linda Ford

COMING NEXT MONTH FROM
Love Inspired® Historical

Available March 3, 2015

WOULD-BE WILDERNESS WIFE
Frontier Bachelors
by Regina Scott
Nurse Catherine Stanway is kidnapped by Drew Wallin's brother to help their ailing mother...but she soon realizes that she's also been chosen by Drew's family to be his bride!

HILL COUNTRY COURTSHIP
Brides of Simpson Creek
by Laurie Kingery
Maude Harkey is tired of waiting for love. But then an orphan baby is suddenly put in her care, and the generosity of her handsome rancher employer offers a chance at the new beginning she's always wanted...

THE TEXAN'S INHERITED FAMILY
Bachelor List Matches
by Noelle Marchand
When four orphaned nieces and nephews arrive on his doorstep, Quinn Tucker knows they'll need a mother. Could marrying schoolteacher Helen McKenna be the most convenient solution?

THE DADDY LIST
by DeWanna Pace
Despite their rocky history, Daisy Trumbo agrees to nurse injured Bass Parker back to health. Bass hopes standing in as father figure to Daisy's daughter might put them all on a new path together...as a family.

LOOK FOR THESE AND OTHER LOVE INSPIRED BOOKS WHEREVER BOOKS ARE SOLD, INCLUDING MOST BOOKSTORES, SUPERMARKETS, DISCOUNT STORES AND DRUGSTORES.

LIHCNM0215

REQUEST YOUR FREE BOOKS!

2 FREE INSPIRATIONAL NOVELS

PLUS 2
FREE
MYSTERY GIFTS

Love Inspired

HISTORICAL
INSPIRATIONAL HISTORICAL ROMANCE

YES! Please send me 2 FREE Love Inspired® Historical novels and my 2 FREE mystery gifts (gifts are worth about $10). After receiving them, if I don't wish to receive any more books, I can return the shipping statement marked "cancel." If I don't cancel, I will receive 4 brand-new novels every month and be billed just $4.74 per book in the U.S. or $5.24 per book in Canada. That's a saving of at least 21% off the cover price. It's quite a bargain! Shipping and handling is just 50¢ per book in the U.S. and 75¢ per book in Canada.* I understand that accepting the 2 free books and gifts places me under no obligation to buy anything. I can always return a shipment and cancel at any time. Even if I never buy another book, the two free books and gifts are mine to keep forever.

102/302 IDN F5CN

Name	(PLEASE PRINT)

Address		Apt. #

City	State/Prov.	Zip/Postal Code

Signature (if under 18, a parent or guardian must sign)

Mail to the Harlequin® Reader Service:
IN U.S.A.: P.O. Box 1867, Buffalo, NY 14240-1867
IN CANADA: P.O. Box 609, Fort Erie, Ontario L2A 5X3

Want to try two free books from another series?
Call 1-800-873-8635 or visit www.ReaderService.com.

* Terms and prices subject to change without notice. Prices do not include applicable taxes. Sales tax applicable in N.Y. Canadian residents will be charged applicable taxes. Offer not valid in Quebec. This offer is limited to one order per household. Not valid for current subscribers to Love Inspired Historical books. All orders subject to credit approval. Credit or debit balances in a customer's account(s) may be offset by any other outstanding balance owed by or to the customer. Please allow 4 to 6 weeks for delivery. Offer available while quantities last.

Your Privacy—The Harlequin® Reader Service is committed to protecting your privacy. Our Privacy Policy is available online at www.ReaderService.com or upon request from the Harlequin Reader Service.

We make a portion of our mailing list available to reputable third parties that offer products we believe may interest you. If you prefer that we not exchange your name with third parties, or if you wish to clarify or modify your communication preferences, please visit us at www.ReaderService.com/consumerchoice or write to us at Harlequin Reader Service Preference Service, P.O. Box 9062, Buffalo, NY 14269. Include your complete name and address.

LIH13R

SPECIAL EXCERPT FROM

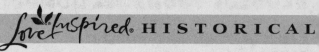

Love Inspired® HISTORICAL

*Nurse Catherine Stanway is kidnapped by Drew Wallin's
brother to help their ailing mother...but she soon
realizes that she's also been chosen
by Drew's family to be his bride!*

*Enjoy this sneak peek from
WOULD-BE WILDERNESS WIFE by Regina Scott!*

How could his brother have been so boneheaded? Drew
glanced over his shoulder at the youth. The boy had absolutely no remorse for what he'd done. Where had Drew gone
wrong?

"I'm really very sorry," Drew apologized to Catherine. "I
don't know what got into him. He was raised better."

"Out in the woods, you said," she replied.

"On the lake," he told her. "My father brought us to Seattle
about fifteen years ago from Wisconsin and chose a spot far
out. He said a man needed something to gaze out on in the
morning besides his livestock or his neighbors."

She smiled as if the idea pleased her. "And your mother?"
she asked, shifting on the wooden bench. "Is she truly ill?"

"She came down with a fever nearly a fortnight ago. I hope
you'll be able to help her before we return you to Seattle tomorrow."

"You did not seem so sure of my skills earlier, sir."

With Levi right behind him, he wasn't about to admit that
his fear had been for his future, not the lack of her skills.
"We've known Doc for years," he hedged.

"My father's patients felt the same way. There is nothing
like the trusted relationship of your family doctor. But I will do

whatever I can to help your mother."

Levi's smug voice floated up from behind. "I knew she'd come around."

Drew was more relieved than he'd expected at the thought of Catherine's help. "As you can see," he said to her, "my brother has a bad habit of acting or talking without thinking."

"My brother was the same way," she assured him. "He borrowed my father's carriage more than once, drove it all over the county. He joined the Union Army on his eighteenth birthday before he'd even received a draft notice."

"Sounds like my kind of fellow," Levi said, kneeling so that his head came between them. "Did he journey West with you?"

Though her smile didn't waver, her voice came out flat. "No. He was killed at the Battle of Five Forks in Virginia."

Levi looked stricken as he glanced between her and Drew. "I'm sorry, ma'am. I didn't know."

"Of course you didn't," she replied, but Drew saw that her hands were clasped tightly in her lap as if she were fighting with herself not to say more.

"I'm sorry for your loss," Drew said. "That must have been hard on you and your parents."

"My mother died when I was nine," she said. "My father served as a doctor in the army. He died within days of Nathan."

Drew wanted to reach out, clasp her hand, promise her the future would be brighter. But he couldn't control the future, and she was his to protect only until he returned her to Seattle. He had enough on his hands without taking on a woman new to the frontier.

Don't miss WOULD-BE WILDERNESS WIFE
by Regina Scott,
available March 2015 wherever
Love Inspired® Historical books and ebooks are sold!

Copyright © 2015 by Harlequin Books S.A.

LIHEXP0215

Love Inspired

JUST CAN'T GET ENOUGH OF INSPIRATIONAL ROMANCE?

Join our social communities
and talk to us online!
You will have access to the latest
news on upcoming titles and special
promotions, but most important,
you can talk to other fans about your
favorite Love Inspired® reads.

 www.Facebook.com/LoveInspiredBooks

www.Twitter.com/LoveInspiredBks

Harlequin.com/Community

LISOCIAL